'If only I had a brother who was even half a man,' Cassie cried angrily, venting her rage now there was a chance they might be safe.

'He's a disgrace to the human race. He—'

Ross tried to hush her. He needed to listen for their pursuers. In fact, he thought he could hear something. Closer than before.

'James Elliott should be dead and damned to all eternity,' she raged. 'He would be well served in hellfire. For he is the very devil—'

'Miss Elliott. Hush! I think I hear horses!'

She ignored him. 'And if he burns, it will—'

He had two choices. Silence her by brute force, or… He pulled her into his arms and kissed her.

Joanna Maitland was born and educated in Scotland, though she has spent most of her adult life in England or abroad. She has been a systems analyst, an accountant, a civil servant, and director of a charity. Now that her two children have left home, she and her husband have moved from Hampshire to the Welsh Marches, where she is revelling in the more rugged country and the wealth of medieval locations. When she is not writing, or climbing through ruined castles, she devotes her time to trying to tame her new house and garden, both of which are determined to resist any suggestion of order. Readers are invited to visit Joanna's website at www.joannamaitland.com

BRIDE OF THE SOLWAY features characters you will have met in MY LADY ANGEL.

Recent novels by the same author:

A PENNILESS PROSPECT
A POOR RELATION
MARRYING THE MAJOR
RAKE'S REWARD
MY LADY ANGEL
AN UNCOMMON ABIGAIL
   (in *A Regency Invitation*)

BRIDE OF
THE SOLWAY

Joanna Maitland

MILLS & BOON®
Pure reading pleasure

First published in Great Britain 2007
Large Print edition 2007
Harlequin Mills & Boon Limited,
Eton House, 18-24 Paradise Road, Richmond, Surrey TW9 1SR

© Joanna Maitland 2007

ISBN: 978 0 263 19413 5

Set in Times Roman 14¾ on 17 pt.
42-1207-87482

Printed and bound in Great Britain
by Antony Rowe Ltd, Chippenham, Wiltshire

BRIDE OF
THE SOLWAY

Prologue

London—Wednesday, 22nd June, 1815

Ross gritted his teeth and started for the door. Once through it, he might just have a chance of breathing again.

'Captain Graham.' Julie's beloved voice was full of concern.

Ross turned back to her, slowly, trying to school his features into mere friendliness.

'Pray do not leave us, sir,' she said quietly. 'There is so much still to discover. And so much to thank you for.'

He shook his head at her, forcing a smile. He found he could not speak.

'And you must have so much to say to your friends here.' She nodded in the direction of their hostess and her escort, talking together in the far corner of the room, sharing thoughts so intimate that they had brought a slight blush to the lady's cheek. There stood a man whose love was returned, Ross thought. A fortunate man.

'Most of all, my *dear* friend,' Julie continued rather earnestly, 'I should like you to know Pierre, to have him esteem you as I do.'

She was looking past Ross as she spoke, her eyes searching the room before fixing on a point beyond Ross's shoulder. He knew, without turning, that her eye had lighted on her lover. The sudden softening of her glance and the glow of her complexion betrayed the depth of her feelings for the man.

Another shaft of pain stabbed deep into Ross's gut.

Swallowing hard, he steeled himself to act the part of the gentleman and friend, the part he had been forced to play for months now. Yesterday, he had had hopes of winning her. No longer. All that was left was pride.

He bowed slightly to her. '*Mademoiselle,* I am at your service, as ever.'

Chapter One

'You harlot!'

His insult was the last straw. Cassandra Elliott launched herself at her half-brother in yet another attempt to retrieve the remains of her letters. But James was too big and too strong. He fended her off with one long arm, using the other to push the torn fragments of paper into the depths of the fire. Cassandra could do nothing but watch, while they twisted and blackened in the flames. 'You are hateful,' she spat, with a sob that was part fury, part frustration. 'You have no right—'

'I have every right! Now, you will tell me his name.'

Cassandra shook her head vehemently. 'Never! You can—'

James pushed Cassandra roughly on to the oak settle. 'I am the head of this family, and I will not have you bring disgrace upon us by your wanton behaviour.'

'*My* wanton behaviour? I have done nothing but

receive a few harmless love poems. Nothing more. But you, Jamie Elliott—'

'I am—'

'You are the one who spends every other night in the whorehouse. When you are not lifting the skirts of our own maids, that is. It is not I who bring disgrace on the Elliott name. You—'

'You forget yourself, sister. I am a man, and the laird, besides. I—'

'You are a—'

'Enough! Hold your tongue!'

He towered over her, menacing, his brows drawn together in a black frown, his fists clenched.

Cassandra tried not to cower away from him. She must not give him the satisfaction of knowing she was afraid. If only she were not so alone.

'No one but you would dare to question my actions. I will have no more of it. You are only a lassie. You will do as you are told. And if you don't…'

He bent down so that his face was within an inch of hers. She could feel his fury like the waves of heat from a roaring fire.

'You'll not be forgetting what happened to your mother, will you now?'

His voice had suddenly sunk to a snarling under-tone, far more terrifying than all his bellowing. At the mention of her mother, Cassandra's heart began to race. Now she was surely lost.

'I can put you in the Bedlam just as easily as Father did your mother. There's no man here will gainsay me. They all know what a mad, headstrong lassie you are—have always been. I have only to say that you've been playing the harlot, following in your mother's footsteps, and every man among them—aye, and the women, too—will help me carry you through the Bedlam door.'

She reached a hand out to him. 'You would not—'

'Do not put me to the test, lassie. Remember, I am my father's son.' Snatching up the single candle, James strode to the door and left the little parlour, without once looking back.

Cassandra heard the sound of the key turning in the lock. She did not need to try the door. She was imprisoned—again—and it would be a long time before James relented and permitted her release. If she were truly unlucky, he would not even allow her food and drink.

She looked around the room in the feeble glow of the dying fire. She must have some light. She could not bear the thought of being shut up alone, in the dark, in this bare and hostile chamber. She knelt before the hearth to light a spill from the embers but, as she touched the flame to the tallow dip, she noticed a scrap of paper on the floor behind the chair leg. It was the last remaining evidence that anyone in the world truly cared for Cassandra Elliott.

She pulled the fragment from under the chair and smoothed it once, then again and again, as if willing it to be whole again. At least one person did care. Just one. But he could not help her.

Impatiently, she brushed away a tear. It was anger. Only anger. She was not so weak that her half brother could make her cry. She was not!

She caressed the paper yet again. There was so little left. It was barely an inch wide and held only a few disjointed words, part of three lines of Alasdair's bad poetry. She had smiled when she first read it, recognising the evidence of the boy's calf-love. He might be only fifteen, but he idolised her. He saw himself as a knight, winning her love by deeds of great daring. But if James Elliott once discovered the lad's identity, the daring would be thrashed out of him. She would never betray his name, no matter how much James threatened.

She dropped on to the hard oak settle once more and stared at the scrap of paper. Like her Trojan namesake, she, too, could prophesy, all these centuries later. She could prophesy that the Elliott family was doomed. First her father, and now her half-brother. Drunkards and gamblers, both. Neither of them caring anything for their land, or their people. Both of them wasting their substance in the pursuit of pleasure. Both of them treating their womenfolk worse than their cattle.

If only she could get away. But where could she go?

She had no money and no friends in Galloway who would dare to take her part against the laird. Everyone hereabouts knew exactly who she was. It would be impossible to hide from James on this side of the Solway. If she did run away, James would find her and bring her back. He might even carry out his threat to lock her away in the lunatic asylum. Cassandra's own mother had died there, imprisoned on trumped-up accusations of adultery. Had she been mad? Not at first, perhaps, but certainly at the end. And her husband, Cassandra's father, had shut the door on her as if she had ceased to exist. From the day she was put in the asylum, he had never visited her, never sent to ask after her, and never once mentioned her name.

James Elliott was capable of doing exactly the same to Cassandra if she did anything more to thwart his plans to marry her off. She had to protect Alasdair. But if James really believed she was unchaste—

Cassandra shuddered and dropped her head into her hands. She would not weep. She refused to be so craven. She would—

The key grated in the lock.

Cassandra quickly wiped her face and squared her jaw. If James had returned so quickly, it boded ill. She hastily tucked the precious scrap of paper into her pocket.

'Miss Cassie?' It was Morag, Cassie's maid, who had served the family since Cassandra was a child.

'I've brought you some warm milk, dearie, and some bannocks and cheese. The laird is in a fearful temper with ye, but he's off to the whor— He's gone out. He'll not be back till the morn, ye ken.' Morag put a pewter plate and a mug on the low table. 'Eat up, Miss Cassie. I'll be back in a wee minute to take they things away.' She said nothing more. There was no need. They both knew that if James discovered what Morag had done, she would be dismissed on the spot.

Cassandra ate greedily. She had had nothing since early morning. The cheese was strong and delicious, the oatcakes newly baked. All too soon, the plate was empty. Cassandra licked her finger and ran it round the rim to pick up any stray crumbs. She was still hungry.

Ross looked up at the sky. He had become used to the longer days as he moved north, taking advantage of the extra hours of daylight to put the greatest possible distance between himself and the pain of London. Here in the Scottish border country, the light held till well-nigh midnight when the weather was fine, as it had been for most of his journey.

But now the weather was changing. And suddenly. On the western horizon, huge black clouds were rearing up like angry stallions, ready to attack with flailing iron-shod hooves. A mighty storm was coming. And there was precious little shelter available for a solitary traveller and his faithful mare.

Ross touched his heel to Hera's chestnut flank. She needed little encouragement to quicken her pace. She had probably smelt the coming storm long before Ross had noticed anything amiss. He began to regret that he had decided to travel on to Annan instead of stopping on the English side of the border, where there were good beds to be had, and good food for man and beast. Here, so close to the Solway, there was no sign at all of any habitation as far as Ross could see. Probably the ground was too treacherous.

In the distance, he spied a small copse of trees. Dangerous, of course, if there was lightning. He looked up at the sky again. The black anvil clouds were swelling even before his eyes. And they were racing towards him. He had no choice.

He turned Hera towards the copse. He dared not go in. But, in the lee of the trees, they would find some shelter from the increasingly sharp wind, even if not from the wet. He pushed Hera on, urging her to a faster pace than was truly safe in the deepening gloom. 'Not far now, my beauty,' he murmured gently, laying a gloved hand on her neck. The mare's ears twitched at the sound of his voice. She was unsettled by the coming storm. Even her master's voice was not enough to calm her. 'Not far now,' Ross said again.

The mare slowed at the edge of the copse. Its old and misshapen trees had been bent almost double by the prevailing winds. 'Better than nothing, I fancy,' Ross said half to himself, preparing to dismount.

An enormous flash of lightning split the sky, followed by seconds of eerie silence. Hera laid her ears back and rolled her eyes in fear. Then came the thunder, growling like a pack of ferocious wolves. Hera tried to rear up, but Ross held her steady, automatically reaching out his hand to calm her.

But he was not thinking about his mare at all. He was concentrating on the sound that he had picked up in that tiny silence. Galloping hooves. Someone else was out on this wild night. By the sound of it, his horse was bolting.

Ross peered into the night, trying to identify the sound against the keening wind. Yes, there! The horse was racing towards him. And its pace had not slackened one jot.

He turned Hera towards the sound, readying her to intercept the stranger. But he had reckoned without the storm. Just as the unknown galloped past him, there was another flash of lightning. Hera reared up again. This time she almost unseated Ross. He wasted precious seconds regaining control, and even more in persuading her to follow the bolting horse.

He had no choice. For in that flash of lightning, he had clearly seen a terrified bay horse and, on its back, an equally terrified girl dressed in what looked like a long white shift and with her dark hair streaming behind her. Heaven knew what she was about, fleeing alone into the night. She might be a thief. She might even be mad. But whatever she was, Ross could not leave her to the mercy of the Solway and the terrible storm.

He kicked Hera into a gallop and cursed loudly when she baulked. 'Come on,' he breathed, leaning over her neck. 'Come on, Hera. Don't let me down now.'

Obedient to his voice, the mare started bravely forward once more. Ross knew that his chances of catching the girl were slim—she was already well ahead of him and he did not dare to force Hera to match the pace of the bolting horse—but he still had to try. Somewhere in front of them lay the Solway with its quicksands and unpredictable tides. Unless the horse stopped of its own accord, it would probably kill itself and its rider. The odds were against him. But Ross knew he had to try.

Another huge lightning flash, followed immediately by thunder. This time, Hera's only reaction was a nervous twitch of the ears. Ross was almost sure that he had seen the girl, a long way ahead. There was something white up there, certainly. He urged Hera to move faster.

Now they were in the eye of the storm. The thunder was almost constant. Lightning forked to the ground. The storm seemed all around them, and very dangerous. The sudden drenching rain of high summer had started, too. Ross could feel it soaking through his clothes and running down on to his saddle. He gripped the slippery reins more tightly. He was sure, now, that he was gaining on her. Her horse must be tiring. In that last glimpse, she had seemed much nearer than before.

There was another bright flash and a huge crack of thunder, directly overhead. Ross saw the girl about fifty yards ahead of him. Her horse reared in fright, unseating her. Then it started off again, pulling the white-clad figure behind it.

Ross breathed a curse. She must be caught in the stirrups! The animal must slow now, surely, with such a weight dragging behind it? But the girl… How would she survive such an ordeal?

It seemed to take an age before Ross caught up with them. He reached out to grab the horse's bridle and force it to a steaming halt. Only then was he able to do anything about the fallen rider.

He threw himself out of the saddle and knelt by the sodden body on the ground. The girl was not moving. Perhaps she was dead? He put a hand under her shoulders to raise her inert form.

'I can shift for myself, thank you, sir,' said a sharp voice from underneath the mass of wet hair.

Ross sprang back as if stung.

The girl sat up and tried to push the hair from her face. Then she thrust an arm up in triumph. 'He thought he had the better of me,' she cried. 'Ha! As if I would ever let go.'

In her right hand, twisted round her palm, were the horse's reins.

'You could have been killed,' he said, aghast. 'Why did you not let him go?'

'Because I need him,' she said simply, looking up at Ross through her unkempt mane of hair. 'Without him, I could never escape.'

Ross shook his head. Perhaps she was mad, even though she did not sound it. 'Hold my horse,' he said sharply, thrusting Hera's reins into the girl's free hand. 'Now...' He jumped to his feet, hauling the girl up after him. Then he took off his coat and placed it round her. She was shivering with cold. And she was wet through.

'You must not, sir,' she said crossly, trying to push the coat off her shoulders. 'I am perfectly well as I am. I was only—'

'Nonsense,' he snapped. 'You will get the ague if we do not get you warm. Now...I presume you are from these parts? Is there any shelter to be had hereabouts?'

'Well...there is old Shona's cottage, I suppose. I was going there when Lucifer bolted.'

Ross laughed shortly. 'He is well named. What on earth made you try to ride such an animal? And dressed as you are, too?'

'You sound like the dominie. Why is it that every

man I meet wants to tell me what to do? I am perfectly capable of making my own decisions.'

Ross quirked an eyebrow. She was clearly a lady, but she looked anything but capable. Besides, she was probably no older than fifteen or sixteen. She was soaked to the skin, and her garb was barely decent. And she was riding an ungovernable horse. She clearly needed someone to take charge of her.

'I am not a schoolmaster, ma'am, even if I sound like one to you. My name is Ross Graham, and I am a stranger in these parts. If you will permit—' he sketched a hasty and inelegant bow in her direction, which provoked a hint of a smile '—I will escort you to safety. Perhaps you would…er…point me in the right direction?'

The girl shook her head at him. 'Any man who can remember the courtesies of the drawing room in the middle of a raging thunderstorm must be addled in the brain.'

Ross put a hand firmly on her shoulder and squeezed. He had had enough of courtesies. They were getting wetter by the second. 'Which way, ma'am?' he demanded sharply.

'Oh, very well. Help me to mount, and I will show you.'

'You don't mean to ride that animal again, do you?'

'Of course I do! It will be much quicker than walking, you know. And I shan't let him get away from me again, you may be sure of that. Besides, the storm is passing over. He will be calmer now.'

'Good grief!' said Ross to himself, but he threw her up into her saddle, none the less.

The girl set off at much too fast a pace. Unless she knew every inch of this ground, she risked her horse at every step.

'Have a care!' Ross cried to her retreating back. 'You will kill your horse at such a pace in the dark!'

'Not I!' she retorted over her shoulder. 'Follow me if you dare!'

For ten minutes, he did, wondering all the while whether he was right to risk his mare in such conditions. She had carried him through the final two years of the Peninsular War. It was no fair recompense to risk her on the links of the Solway.

'There!' cried the girl, pointing to a tiny building, almost hidden against a slight rise in the ground. It looked to be little more than a ruined wall from this distance. 'Come on!' She set her heels to Lucifer and pushed him to even greater speed.

Watching her, Ross realised that it was no longer quite so dark. The storm was indeed passing. The rain had almost stopped. He could see the girl quite clearly ahead of him. Her white skirt hung down below the borrowed coat, gleaming against her horse's dark flanks in spite of the many mud stains upon it. And her legs and feet were bare.

Reaching the tiny cottage, she threw herself from the saddle and began to pound on the door. It opened just as Ross climbed down from Hera's back and started after her.

From the doorway stepped a tall, black-browed man, grinning fiercely down at the girl. 'I thought so,' he said shortly, seizing her by the arms and pushing her roughly towards one of the three men who had followed him from the hut. Ross's coat fell from her shoulders to the ground. The speaker took no notice. 'Take care of her while I deal with this blackguard.'

'Let her go!' Ross cried. The girl's captor simply grinned and put a filthy hand across her mouth, muffling her scream of outrage. Ross reached automatically for his weapon. He had none. He had not worn a sword since he had put off his regimentals, and his pistols were snugly holstered by his saddle. He had nothing but his fists. He squared his shoulders. Even one against four, he would show them what a man could do.

The dark man must have sensed something. From nowhere, he produced a pistol and casually pointed it at Ross's heart. 'So you're the man, are ye? Y'are good for nothing but poetry, it seems. Well, we shall see how many lines you can compose among the rats. Take him and bind him, lads.'

The other two men grabbed Ross by the arms and,

in spite of all he did to resist, Ross soon found his hands tightly bound behind his back with rough hempen rope, and a dirty piece of sacking tied around his mouth for a gag.

'Put him on his horse and bring him,' ordered their leader. 'Ned, fetch the horses.'

Perhaps, in the dark, they had not noticed the pistols by Hera's saddle? If only Ross could free his hands, he might be able to—

'There are pistols here, maister,' cried one of the ruffians, pulling one from its place and brandishing it in the air.

'Give them to me. And those bags of his as well. I'll look through them when we have more light. His coat, too.'

Ross's captor pushed him onto Hera's back. With his hands tied behind his back, it would be a dangerous ride.

'And the leddy, maister?' The ruffian nodded in the direction of the girl, whose thin gown was now sticking to her limbs, making her look almost naked. She seemed oblivious to that, however, for all her efforts were bent on freeing herself from the man who held her fast.

'You and Tam, take her back to the house and lock her up,' cried the master. 'And make sure she does not escape from you this time, Tam, or it will be the worse for you.'

At that moment, the man Tam cried out in pain and pulled his hand from her mouth. 'The wench bit me!'

The girl paid not the least attention to Tam. She was glowering at the dark man. 'Curse you, Jamie Elliott,' she screamed, with loathing in her voice. 'May you rot in hell!'

'I may well, my dear,' Elliott replied coolly, mounting his horse, 'but not at your bidding. I will see to you later. For the present, I have more important work to do, in dealing with your lover.' Leaning forward, he took hold of Hera's rein and kicked his own mount into a fast trot, pulling Ross's unwilling mare after him. They were twenty yards away before Ned, standing open-mouthed, hauled himself into the saddle of the second horse and galloped after his master.

Behind them, the girl shouted something, but her words were carried off by the wind. Ross and his captors were alone.

'Oh, Miss Cassie! Ye're fair drookit! Just look at you! Did ye not think to take a cloak, at least?'

'If I'd stopped to find a cloak, I'd not have got away at all.' Cassandra forced herself to smile at the maid who was fussing around with warm towels and a dry nightgown.

'But you didna get away, dearie,' Morag said sadly. 'And after this, the laird will make sure to keep ye even closer. When he saw that you'd climbed down from your chamber, he was that fashed, he nearly threw

Tam out after you. We could hear him yelling, from down in the kitchen. Tam's to put bars on yer window, first thing in the morn.' Morag began to towel Cassandra's sodden mane of hair. 'My, but ye're soaked, lassie. 'Twas a daft thing to do. You'll be getting the ague, next.'

'That's what he said, too,' murmured Cassandra, snuggling into the thick wrapper that Morag had added over her nightdress.

'The laird said that?' Morag sounded astonished.

'Not he,' said Cassandra, on the thread of a laugh. 'Jamie Elliott cares not a whit whether I live or die, provided that I do not inconvenience him and his plans.'

'Wheesht, lassie!' Morag's finger went to her lips. Her eyes registered shock. And fear.

'It's no more than the truth,' Cassandra said, though more quietly than before. 'If I died of the ague, my brother would think himself relieved of an unwelcome burden.'

Morag looked grim, but she did not attempt to argue. The whole household knew what the laird thought of his young half-sister. And how unfairly he treated her.

'Morag,' said Cassandra urgently, 'when the laird and the men come back, you must do your best to find out what they have done with him. Please.'

'What d'ye mean?'

'The man who tried to rescue me.'

'Rescue…? I think you'd better start at the beginning, Miss Cassie. You've got my head in a whirl.'

Cassandra patted the woman's work-roughened hand and let out a long sigh. 'Aye, I suppose… Well…I thought Jamie planned to leave me locked in the little parlour downstairs. I was surprised when Tam said I was to be locked in my own chamber instead. Until I thought about it, of course. From the parlour, I might have been able to speak to someone outside, even when the shutters were barred. From my own chamber, there was no chance of that. Not without shouting and being caught. It's too high up.'

'D'ye tell me you climbed down the wall?'

'I… No, I didn't. But Jamie must think I did.'

'But if the door was locked—'

Cassandra smiled knowingly. 'There are ways of getting a key from the other side of a door, you know, Morag.'

The maid looked unconvinced.

'You'll keep my secret, Morag?'

The woman nodded.

Cassandra knew Morag was to be trusted. 'I slipped a paper under the door and then I turned the key from the inside. It took a while. It was very stiff. Then I pushed it out and it fell on the floor. I was lucky. It fell onto the paper and there was just room to pull it back under the door.'

'Oh!' said Morag in wonderment.

'It's an old trick. I'm surprised Jamie didn't work it out. Maybe he was fooled because I relocked the door and left the key there. And the window open.'

'But why did you go off in just yer thin gown? And not even a pair of shoon on yer feet?'

'It was all I had, apart from a shawl. And I lost that when Lucifer bolted. Jamie had Tam clear out my clothes press. He said I should get used to living in a shift. That's how I'd be dressed when I was taken to the Bedlam, he said.' Cassandra swallowed hard at the terrifying memory, even more terrifying now that she had tried, and failed, to escape.

'He'll not send ye there,' Morag said firmly. 'Nobody thinks ye're mad. And he canna marry you out of the asylum, can he?'

'But he says I'm a…a harlot. Like my…' her voice dropped to a strangled whisper '…like my mother. He could confine me for that. You know he could.'

'He'll not do that. He'll…he'd have yer godfather to reckon with if he did, and he'll not take the chance of that.' Morag nodded, as if to confirm the truth of her words.

And it was true, Cassandra thought. Her godfather, Sir Angus Fergusson, had once promised to stand by her, even though he had been estranged from the family for many years. And he wielded just as much clout as Jamie, perhaps more. If only she'd been able to reach him…

'Was that where you were going?' At Cassandra's answering nod, Morag burst out, 'You were going to cross the Solway in the mirk? Alone? Ye *are* mad, lassie!'

'It wasn't that dark. Not till the storm came. And I was going to get Shona to take me across. Only Lucifer bolted in the storm. It was all I could do to hang on to him.' She did not add that she had been hanging on while being dragged along the ground. Better to let Morag think that she had still been on his back.

'Ye might have ended up in the quicksands,' Morag breathed in horror.

'Well, I didn't. A man caught us. He… I couldn't see him very well in the gloom, but he spoke like a gentleman.' She smiled to herself. He had acted like a gentleman, too. Such fancy manners he had. Ross Graham. Who stopped to introduce himself in the middle of a thunderstorm.

'But the laird wouldna lay hands on a gentleman, surely?'

'I doubt he knows, Morag. They bound him and gagged him before he had a chance to say a word. And in the dark, no one would be able to tell from his clothes. Besides, they were all dripping wet.' She stopped, twisting her hands together. 'You must find out what they did with him, Morag. You must. Even if they…even if they've killed him.' She shut her eyes tightly for a second against the horrifying picture her own words had conjured up. Jamie would not stoop to murder. Would he?

Chapter Two

Ross opened his eyes. He could see absolutely nothing. It was pitch dark. But he did not need his eyes to know just what sort of place he was in. His nose told him that. It reeked of damp and decay. More muted was a clear reminder of the stench of human bodies kept imprisoned for too long. There was something else, too, that he could not quite identify.

Where was he? He stretched out a hand, touching damp straw over the stone floor where he lay. He had already felt the cold eating into his body. Clearly, this place—whatever it was—never saw the sun. He made to sit up. Too quickly. A searing pain in the back of his skull stopped him dead.

Ah, yes. Now he remembered. He had tried to escape when they reached the outskirts of Dumfries and had been struck down for his pains. He put a hand to the back of his head and gingerly felt for blood. There appeared to be none, though there was a distinct lump under his hair. Well, he had suffered worse in the wars. He would mend. At least Elliott and his dastardly companion had untied his arms.

Ross felt about in the dark. He had been thrown down near a wall and so he sat up, rather more cautiously than before, and leant his aching head against it for a few moments. Where was he? Somewhere in Dumfries, he supposed, but clearly a prisoner of the man, Elliott.

Ross's fingers began to quest around in the dank straw beneath him. His left hand met something different. Why, it was his sodden coat! He should have recognised that pervasive smell of wet wool. He pulled the coat towards him and quickly checked the pockets. Not surprisingly perhaps, his money was gone. He cursed roundly. Then, with a grim smile, he ran his fingers down the inside of the lining, where the hidden pocket lay. It remained intact. He still had his English banknotes. But it was a pity that he no longer had golden guineas with which to bribe his way out of whatever prison Elliott had thrown him into. Elliott. And that girl. He remembered her vividly, lying crumpled on the ground. Who was she? Whoever she was, Elliott certainly had some hold over her. She—

Something scuttled over Ross's foot. A rat. Of course. There were bound to be rats in a place like this. It was bad, but no worse than many a Spanish billet during the war. Ross shrugged philosophically. The gesture reminded him, painfully, that he should not make any hasty movements. His head was not up to it. He must move slowly and carefully. He should explore his prison and find out whether there was any possibility of escape. In this clammy darkness, he could not tell whether there was even a window.

He pushed himself on to his knees. Then, with a hand on the wall for support, he slowly began to get to his feet. Just at that moment, a door opened in the far wall and a lantern appeared. Ross was temporarily blinded by the sudden light and unable to see what was beyond.

A man's voice said, 'Och, so ye're no' dead then,' and broke into raucous laughter.

Ross stared towards the doorway, trying to make out the features of the man who stood there. It was neither Elliott nor his henchman, Ross decided. This man was much stouter than either.

'I've brought ye a wee bit dinner,' said the man. The lantern stooped and there was the muffled clatter of a metal plate on the straw-covered stone floor.

Ross took a step towards the door.

'Stay jist where ye are!' cried the man quickly. 'I've a pistol here and I'll shoot ye, if ye come a step nearer!'

Ross stopped in his tracks, allowing his arms to hang loosely by his sides, palms forward. 'You must know that I have no weapons,' he said calmly.

'Aye, but the laird said ye was dangerous. I am no' to take any chances with ye.'

'And you are the laird's man?' said Ross, proudly.

'Nothing o' the kind,' protested the man at the door. 'I do my duty by ye, as I would by any other prisoner.'

A cold chill ran down Ross's spine. 'Where am I?'

'Where d'ye think? Ye're in the gaol, in Dumfries.'

'And with what crime am I charged, to be held here? I have done nothing to warrant it.'

The turnkey laughed. 'That's no' the way the laird tells it. He says ye'll hang.'

'Dammit, man!' Ross took another step forward. 'I've done—'

'Stop where ye are!'

Ross stopped dead. However, the gaoler had moved smartly backwards and closed the door between them. The lantern now showed the bars in the tiny window in the door.

'Ye'll learn yer fate soon enough,' said the man with a low chuckle as he turned the key. 'Soon enough.' The lantern receded and disappeared. Ross was alone again. In the dark.

He had endured too many hardships in the Peninsula to dwell on might-have-beens. His first thought was to secure the plate and whatever food had been provided, before the rats ate it. He got down on his knees once more and then felt his way towards where the light had been, until his outstretched fingers found the plate. It contained a largish piece of hard bread and nothing else. Ross grinned into the darkness. It was quite like old times.

He broke off a chunk from the stale bread and chewed it thoughtfully. He needed to get a message to someone. Was there anyone in Dumfries who would help an unknown gentleman from England? Perhaps with one of the banknotes from his hidden store, he could bribe the gaoler to take a letter to the provost or the local magistrate? Yes, he would do that.

A thought struck him. He was surprised into a burst of hollow laughter. What if the local magistrate was the Elliott laird?

Cassandra paced the floor of her chamber. Her gaol. Her only consolation was that her clothes had been returned to her. She was decently clad, and shod. But now there were bars on her window, making the room feel even more like a prison.

She refused to dwell on that. With luck, she might be able to unlock the door using the same trick as before. But first, she must have news of the man who had tried to rescue her. What on earth was keeping Morag? Surely she should have been able to glean some news by now?

The sound of the key turning in the lock brought a halt to her pacing. Morag?

The door opened. 'Morag!' Cassandra cried as the

servant entered, bearing a tray of food. 'Have you found out what happened to the ma—?'

Morag frowned warningly and gave a tiny shake of her head.

'She has tried, sister,' said a voice from the darkness beyond the doorway. James Elliott stepped forward into the room and pushed the door behind him. 'She has tried so hard that even Tam noticed her eagerness for information. And you will agree that our Tam is not the quickest of nature's creatures. So, since you are so desperate for news of your lover, I have come to bring it myself.'

'He is not my lover!' Cassandra protested hotly. 'I never saw him before yesterday!'

James ignored her. 'Return to the kitchen,' he ordered sharply. 'And remember what I said, woman. You will not attend on my sister until I give you leave. If I find you have been alone with her, you will find yourself in the workhouse. Or the gutter.'

Morag had shrunk away from his terrible words. Without venturing even a glance at Cassandra, she hurried out. Cassandra's only ally had been defeated.

James threw himself down into the high-backed oak chair and stretched out his long legs. He had every appearance of a gentleman sitting at his ease. But James Elliott was no gentleman. He was—

'Now, sister. We have matters to discuss. First, that woman of yours. She will no longer serve you. Not alone. Tam will make sure that you have no opportunity for private speech with her. Or with anyone else who might try to help you. Understand that I am the laird, and my will is to be respected. No one will be allowed to cross me. Not even you.'

This time, Cassandra did not protest. She refused to look at him. She clenched her jaw and stared at the floor. Hot words clamoured for release, but she would not give in to them. A moment's satisfaction was not worth weeks of even greater restrictions on her person.

'Lost your tongue sister?' James's voice was now thoroughly nasty. He paused for a few seconds. Then, realising that Cassandra was not about to respond, he said, 'You wanted information about your lover. You thought I had killed him, did you not? Faith, lassie, I am not such a fool as to put myself on the wrong side of the law. Not when it stands ready to help me.'

Cassandra raised her eyes to his face. At least Ross Graham was not dead.

'Your lover, my dear sister, is in Dumfries gaol awaiting his trial. And, after it, he will hang.'

'No!' Cassandra shrieked. 'No! You cannot! He has done nothing!'

James raised his eyebrows and glared mockingly at her. 'Nothing? I think not, my dear. Abduction is a serious offence. A hanging offence. And I stand ready to swear that he abducted you. I have no doubt that the law will dispose of your lover to my complete satisfaction.'

'You would perjure yourself? Before God?' whispered Cassandra in horror.

'It is no perjury. I found ye both, remember? And I have three witnesses to the fact, besides old Shona.'

'James…please.' For herself, she would not plead. But she could not allow an innocent man to be hanged. 'He is not my lover. I will swear it, on a stack of bibles if you wish. I had never seen him before. I was alone.' At the look of disbelief on her half-brother's face, she became even more desperate. 'I was alone, I swear it. I was going to cross the Solway. I thought if I could get to my godfather's—'

James's head jerked up. He scowled blackly at the reminder that he had one enemy who was powerful enough to take his sister's part.

Cassandra rushed on. 'The storm caught me. Lucifer bolted. If that man had not appeared from nowhere and stopped us, Lucifer would have bolted straight into the firth. 'Twere better if he had, perhaps. Then you would have been rid of an unwelcome burden.'

James looked unconvinced. But he ignored most of what Cassandra had said, merely replying, 'You are a burden, indeed. You and your lovers. I warn you. You are likely to seal your own fate. An unmarried sister has a degree of value. But only if she is known to be chaste.' He rose. Ignoring Cassandra's gasp of outrage, he bent forward, seizing her chin and forcing her head up so that he could assess her features. 'You are not so bad looking when you lose that mulish expression. I might be able to get a good price for you.'

'You would sell me? Like a...a horse?' Until that moment, Cassandra had dared to hope that she might have at least some say in the choice of a husband. She should have known better. She knew James.

'Why, sister, what else did you think I would do? I had no intention of keeping ye here much longer in any case. I can easily find another—cheaper—house-keeper. A sister costs too much. But, after this escapade, I must get you safely leg-shackled before the rumours start. Like mother, like daughter, they'll say, and then you'll have no value at all.'

Cassandra gasped, then bit her lip. Hard.

'What? Nothing to say, girl? Don't you wish to plead with me to find you a handsome young buck for a husband?'

Cassandra said nothing.

'Well, no. Perhaps you are right to hold your tongue. You know as well as I do that handsome young bucks rarely have the blunt that old men do. So, I fear that your husband is unlikely to be young. Or handsome. Indeed, the man I have in mind is—' He stopped short, waiting for her question. When she remained stub-bornly silent, he strolled to the door. 'One thing I will promise you, though,' he drawled, as he opened it.

'Your husband may be old and cross-eyed, but he *will* be a gentleman. I *do* have my position to consider. Good morrow to ye, sister.'

Then he was gone. The door was locked behind him. Cassandra was alone again. And now she was desperately afraid. She must do something to save Ross Graham. She must! She could consider her own predicament later. It was much less important than a man's life. James intended to use the law to kill Ross Graham. And he was ready to perjure his soul to do it. She must do something. She must! But what?

Cassandra resumed her pacing. The tray of food remained untouched on the table. If she swallowed a bite, it would choke her.

It was still dark. But it must be morning by now, surely? Ross knew he had not been asleep for more than a few hours, at most. Even with his coat wrapped around him, the cold had penetrated his bones. He had woken, shivering. So now he paced the floor of his tiny cell, trying to get some warmth back into his limbs. Three paces, turn about, three paces, turn about, three paces…

He had too much time to think here. That was the real problem of his confinement. He could do nothing more now until the gaoler reappeared. Nothing except pace. And remember. He tried to focus instead on Elliott and that girl. By Jove, she was a handful!

Ross tried to picture what she looked like, but failed. He could see only a mass of dark hair, tangled and dripping, and a white gown that clung to her limbs. He recalled his shock at discovering that her feet and legs were bare. But he could not recall her features. Had he actually seen her face in the darkness? He had had a vague impression of huge dark eyes in a pale face. Nothing more. He was not at all sure he would recognise her if he saw her again.

Still pacing, he grinned into the darkness. See her? How could he? He could not even see his own hand in front of his face!

His decision was already made. When the gaoler returned, he would offer him a bribe in return for pen and ink, and the promise to take a letter to the provost. Ross fingered the hidden pocket and the riches concealed there. It had served him well in France and Spain, and had saved his beloved Julie from many a hardship.

Julie… The memories came flooding in, like the rush of water when the sluice is released. He remembered every detail of her beautiful face, her peach-bloom complexion, her golden hair. The sinuous curves that moved beneath the plain cheap gown she wore, causing his breath to catch in his throat and his body to heat. Her low husky voice, her brilliant smile, the way she worried at her full lower lip when her thoughts were far away—

Enough! He knew now what she had been daydreaming about. Certainly not about Ross Graham, much though she had tried to cozen him into believing that her regard for him might soon turn into love. She had played him for a fool.

A part of him—the gallant, honourable part—attempted to defend her still. Perhaps he had misunderstood her behaviour? Was it not possible that she had intended to show him only gratitude, and friendship? That he had simply seen what he longed to see?

He paused to think back over the months of their escape together, the hundreds of miles they had tramped from Julie's humble cottage along the French Mediterranean coast and across the north of Spain to find a ship to England. She had been so brave and determined throughout their ordeal, in spite of all the dangers, even when they had so nearly been captured by Bonaparte's soldiers. Was that what had blinded him to her wiles? For they were just that—wiles. She was a lady, of course, but that had not stopped her from flirting with Ross: those frequent little touches of her fingers, how she insisted he take her hand to help her over uneven ground, the way she looked up at him with those wide trusting eyes, running her tongue over her lips as if inviting him to kiss her. Damn it, she had known he could not. Not while he alone was responsible for bringing her out from under the nose of the enemy and delivering her safely to her relatives in London. She knew he was a man of honour. That was surely why she had agreed to escape with him? Was it necessary to make him love her, too?

He shuddered. Whatever her motives, she had succeeded. Twice—at Perpignan and at Santander—he had tried to declare himself. Twice she had silenced him with a soft finger across his lips. 'Say nothing now, my dear friend,' she had said, that last time. 'We shall be in London soon, and free. There we may both say everything that is in our hearts.' And then she had smiled her blinding white smile and moistened her lips with the tip of her tongue. Almost as if she were tasting him.

Ross's body began to harden at the very thought. He cursed aloud at his own weakness. For a woman he had never even kissed!

Fool that he was, he had believed that Julie, the granddaughter of a marquis, would stoop to consider a man with little wealth and no family. He had persuaded himself that once she was free, and safe in London, she would admit that Ross had captured her heart.

It had not happened. They had arrived in London on that strangest of days, when the whole city was rejoicing at the news of the victory at Waterloo. Julie had almost been run down by one of the mail coaches, all hung with oak leaves, racing out of the city to carry the tidings to the furthest corners of the land. Ross had pulled her into his arms to save her, feeling the rapid beating of her heart against his chest, filling his lungs with the scent of her skin and her hair, holding her close as he had been longing to do… For seconds only. And then it was over. She had drawn away from him. With the utmost propriety, they had made their way to Berkeley Square to be welcomed into her noble English family.

There, for one more second—just one—he had smiled, knowing that on the morrow he would finally tell her everything that was in his heart.

And then he had seen it. Julie's eyes were fixed on that other man. Her face was lighting up with love. As hers blazed brighter, Ross's hidden flame of love and hope had flickered and sunk to a dull ember. And then to cold and twisted dross.

She had never loved him. Never. She could have been in no doubt that Ross was losing his heart to her. Did she care? Certainly not enough to tell him the truth, that her heart was already given. She had prevented him from declaring himself, no doubt to save her own blushes, not his heartbreak. For, if he had once spoken, she would have had to refuse him. And to tell him why. Oh, it was so much easier to play him like a fish on a hook, a little slack here, a little tug there. Keep the stupid fish thinking that it is not being duped, that it has free choice. Never let it see that it is about to be served up on a plate.

Incensed at himself, and at Julie, Ross slammed his

clenched fist into the wall. For a moment, the pain stopped him from thinking. Then bleak sanity returned.

Was I bewitched? he wondered. One beautiful woman, helpless, dependent on me for her safety, relying on my honour to preserve her virtue? Is that all it takes? Aye. One beautiful woman gazing up into my eyes and my wits go a-begging. After all those years in the wars, I should have learnt to deal better with women. God knows there were enough of them asking for our help, for our 'protection'. And beautiful women, too. But not one of them wormed her way into my heart.

Until Julie. Beautiful, desirable, bewitching Julie. With a heart encased in cold stone.

Ross felt as if a powerful fist had grasped his own heart and was squeezing fit to crush the life out of him. The pain was immense. Unbearable.

'No!' he cried the single word aloud. No! I will not let one scheming woman ruin my life. I will forget her, as she deserves. She is not worth one instant's suffering. And I will never again allow a beautiful woman to bewitch me as Julie did. If ever I take a wife, let her be dark and ugly and…and mute. I will not be beguiled again, not by beauty, or honeyed words, or gentle touches on my skin. If ever I find another woman in distress, pleading for my help, I shall turn my back on her, and laugh as I ride away.

A sudden spasm of pain in his injured hand caused him to gasp aloud. And then he began to laugh, a great gale of cleansing laughter welling up from deep inside his soul, sweeping away the bitterness and the anger. When at last it subsided, he felt totally drained. But now, finally, he was free.

He had loved Julie. He would willingly have died for her. But the love was gone, extinguished like a single candle flame doused by a torrent of water. He was whole again. He could go forward. Like an adder, he had sloughed off his old damaged skin. In its place was a new whole one, strong and supple, with a clear warning pattern.

He forced his shoulders to straighten into something resembling his normal upright carriage. He must look to the future, however threatening it now seemed. He had come to Scotland to solve the mystery surrounding his family and if...when he managed to escape from this prison, that was exactly what he would do. No one, however noble, would be able to look down on him in the future. He would still be an officer and a gentleman, but he would find a family to be proud of. It would be a new life.

In that new life, he would keep his heart well-armoured against tender feelings. For any woman.

Chapter Three

Stooping, Cassandra muttered darkly under her breath. There was light coming through the keyhole. James had clearly taken the precaution of removing the key. Perhaps he suspected that Morag had helped her to escape?

She crossed to the single chair and dropped heavily into it. She must protect Morag from James. The maid would be prepared to take risks for Cassandra—out of love and devotion—but she must not be permitted to do so. For James was a cruel and vindictive man. He would take pleasure in dismissing Morag and in doing everything in his power to ensure she starved.

There must be another way.

Ross Graham was in Dumfries gaol. He was to be brought to trial. That meant an appearance before the provost, perhaps even before the Sheriff himself. The provost would believe Jamie's accusations of abduction. He would authorise a trial. He had no reason to doubt the Elliott laird's word.

Unless the Elliott daughter herself disputed it.

She had to find a way of persuading the provost to call her as a witness. She had to tell him what had really happened. Perhaps Morag…? No. Too dangerous. Not Morag. Besides, the maid would have no plausible reason for going to Dumfries, and no means of travelling there, either.

Cassandra leant her elbows on the table, picked up her pen and began to chew the end of the quill. She must do it herself. Somehow.

She could write a letter, of course, but there was no one to whom she dared entrust it. Morag was the only one who would take her part. And using Morag for such a hazardous task was out of the question.

She raised her hand to wipe her damp brow. She must have caught a chill from being out in that thunderstorm. She felt a little hot. But what did that matter? It was but a minor indisposition when a man's life was at stake. She felt in her pocket for a handkerchief.

Her fingers found, not fine linen, but a tiny scrap of paper.

Alasdair! The fifteen-year-old youth from the nearby estate who fancied himself in love with Cassandra. The lad who wrote her bad poetry in which he swore to serve her unto death. Would he dare to serve her now, in spite of the risk of crossing her fearsome half-brother?

She must try. If Alasdair were caught, James would give him a thrashing, but nothing more. Even James would not dare to do real harm to a gentleman's son, especially when they were such near neighbours. James could not afford to make even more enemies in Galloway.

Cassandra swallowed hard. If only she could escape! She had absolutely no wish to put Alasdair in danger, but what choice did she have? None. She was about to wager a beating for Alasdair against a hanging for Ross Graham. She could not allow her rescuer to die.

She rose and began to pace, planning what she must do. She must write a careful note to the provost. But not now. Not yet. There was always the chance that James would have her chamber searched, or walk in on her, as he had done when he found her with Alasdair's poems. No. The note must be written just before it was despatched.

But how to despatch it? She could drop it out of the window, perhaps, but only if Alasdair were already there. And the lad knew better than to be found on Elliott land. What if—?

A tiny knock on the door interrupted her ravelled thoughts.

'Miss Cassie!' The strident whisper could be clearly heard. Morag must be at the keyhole.

Cassandra ran to the door. 'Morag!' she whispered urgently. 'Be careful! If my brother hears you—'

'Dinna fret, Miss Cassie. The master's at his meat. And Tam is waiting on him. I've told Tam that ye need feeding too, but—'

'Never mind that, Morag. Listen. I need you to get a message to Alasdair. Tell him to come here as soon as it's dark. I'll drop him a note. He's to take it to Provost Scobie. Tell him it's urgent. Can you do that? Please, Morag? I know that—'

'Wheesht, lassie. Of course I can do it. I'll tell Tam I'm away to see the cook at Alasdair's house, that I need to borrow—'

Even through the barrier of the heavy bedroom door, Cassandra heard the sound of footsteps on the stairs. Oh, God! Morag would be caught! And it was Cassandra's fault. She held her breath, waiting for an outburst from Tam, or from her brother.

None came. Instead, she heard weary footsteps toiling to the top of the stairs and then plodding along the corridor to her door. It could only be Tam. Her brother was younger, and much lighter on his feet. Slightly relieved that Morag seemed to have escaped detection, Cassandra moved quietly back to her chair and sat down, resting her head on her hand and breathing deeply in an attempt to calm her nerves. She must not let Tam see how frightened she had been that Morag might be caught. She must appear to be totally downhearted at the turn of events, and at her brother's victory over her. She must appear to be cowed.

Tam did not knock. He simply unlocked the door and walked in.

That changed Cassandra's mind completely, for she knew better than to permit such behaviour from her brother's servant. She rose from her place and glared at the man. 'You did not knock,' she said coldly.

'I thought I heard somethin'. I had to see that ye—'

'Nothing of the kind. I'll warrant you marched into my chamber in hopes of finding me in a state of undress. Do you know what happens to such men, Tam? Peeping Tom was struck blind, remember?'

Tam began to bluster.

'Enough of your lies! I shall tell the laird of your unseemly behaviour as soon as I see him. He will not believe your excuses, either. He knows full well there is no escape from this room, now that the windows have been barred.'

Tam's colour had fled at the mention of the laird. 'There's no need to say anything t' the laird, mistress. He— I was coming up to see ye anyway, to find out what ye was wanting for yer dinner. There's fresh-baked bannocks. And Morag's made a great kettle o' venison stew, if ye'd like. And—'

'That will do me very well, Tam, for I have not eaten today. Perhaps tomorrow you will be more mindful of your duties towards me. It falls to you, after all, to ensure that I am well enough fed that I have no grounds

for complaining to my brother.' She stared him out
until he looked away.

'I'll fetch yer food right away, mistress,' he said,
slinking out of the room.

Cassandra listened. Tam was not so intimidated that
he failed to lock the door. A pity. But at least he would
not dare to walk in again unannounced. She could
write her letter to the provost, knowing that she would
have time to hide it if he came upstairs again.

She sat down at the table and picked up the chewed
quill. She dipped the pen in the standish and began to
compose one of the most important missives of her life.

'I've brought yer coat, sir.'

Ross pushed himself to his feet and strode forward
to take the coat from the gaoler. Under his shirt, the
comforting wad of banknotes moved against his skin.
He would keep it there from now on.

'My missus did her best, sir, but it's no' what it was.
It's dry enough, and she brushed it, but—'

'No matter,' Ross said, beginning to shrug his arms
into the sleeves. It struck him, absurdly in the circumstances, that it was as well that he had never indulged
in the form-fitting coats made by Weston, for this one
had shrunk a fraction. It felt distinctly tight across the
shoulders. A Weston coat would have split.

'The provost wants to see ye, sir. I'm to bring ye to
his house.'

'Excellent,' said Ross. 'I take it that the provost has the power to get me out of this pestilential hole?'

'Aye…that is…I don't rightly know if… Thing is, sir, I have to take ye through the streets an'…an' ye'll have to be in shackles.'

'What?' Ross barked.

'It's more than my place is worth, sir, to take ye wi'out. If ye was to escape—'

'I have no intention of trying to escape, gaoler. Where would I go? I have no horse, no clothes… I am a gentleman. I will give you my word that I shall not try to escape on the way to or from the provost's house. Will that content you?'

'If 'twere only me, sir, I'd take yer word like a shot, but it's the provost, ye see, sir, and—'

Ross calmly fastened the buttons on his coat. 'You have received a certain degree of…er…compensation from me in the matter of the letter you delivered to the provost, gaoler. It is possible that you may be able to render me similar services in the future. But only if you are prepared to treat me as a gentleman.'

'Weel…'

'And then, of course, there would be no need for me to mention our…understandings to the provost.'

'Aye. Ye're right, sir. There'll be no need for they shackles if I have yer word on it.'

Ross nodded solemnly.

'And anyways, I'll still have my pistol. If ye was to

run, I'd have to shoot ye.' He grinned slyly, raising the huge old-fashioned pistol that had been hidden by the skirts of his coat.

Ross raised his eyebrows. 'I was rather hoping it was my hat you had there.' He ran the fingers of both hands through his unkempt hair. 'I am in no fit state to meet the provost, or any other gentleman. I don't suppose your wife has saved my hat as well as my coat?'

'Ye didn't have no hat when ye arrived, sir. Nor gloves, neither. Jist the coat, and what ye stood up in.'

Ross shrugged his shoulders. His hat was probably somewhere out by the Solway, half trampled into the mud. He ran his fingers through his hair one last time. 'Very well. That is the best I can do. Will you lead the way, gaoler?'

With a grin, the turnkey shook his head and stood aside to allow Ross to pass out of the tiny cell. 'We'll jist walk along thegither, sir.' He lifted his pistol a fraction. 'Jist so as I can see ye.'

Ross grinned back and walked out towards the daylight that he had not seen for more than two whole days.

'Why is the prisoner not shackled?' Provost Scobie was a small round man, but he had drawn himself up to his full height to berate the gaoler.

'I have given my parole that I will not attempt to

escape, sir,' said Ross calmly, before the gaoler could say a word.

The provost looked Ross up and down. His lip curled a fraction.

Ross took a deep breath. 'Allow me to introduce myself, sir. I am Captain Ross Graham, late of his Majesty's Fifty-second Regiment. A holder of the King's commission does not break his word.'

The provost recoiled half a step in the face of Ross's implacable stare. 'Ah, indeed, sir. Indeed. As you say. But the charges against ye, they are serious, very serious. I have read yer letter but…well, I can't see my way to… With James Elliott a witness against ye, there's nothing to be done until you come to trial.'

'And when will that be?'

'Well, that's difficult to say. It depends on the witnesses and—'

'This is a civilised country, Provost. You cannot just throw a man into gaol and leave him to rot. *Habeas corpus* demands that you bring me to trial or set me free.'

The provost cocked his head on one side and raised an eyebrow. 'Well, now, sir, that's just where ye are wrong. *Habeas corpus* is English law. The writ does not run on this side of the border. Even a fine gentleman like yerself may have to stay in the gaol until it should be convenient to bring him to trial.' He looked straight at the turnkey, who shuffled his feet a little, but said nothing. 'And on such a serious charge, the sheriff himself would need to preside…and he's not due to be in Dumfries for quite a wee while.' He stroked his jaw thoughtfully.

Provost Scobie was going out of his way to be un-helpful. Probably in Elliott's pocket. So Ross would have to find a way of helping himself.

'On such a serious charge, as you put it, Provost, a gentleman must be allowed to call on the services of his friends.' Ross glanced round the small bookroom and lighted on a kneehole desk piled high with files and papers. The provost was not a tidy worker, it seemed. 'You will permit me to write a letter, I take it?' Without giving the man time to reply, Ross sat down at the desk, pushed the papers into a precarious heap, and began to write on a sheet of the provost's expensive paper.

'I…well, I… Sir, you have no—' The provost paused to collect himself.

Ignoring him, Ross continued to write swiftly.

'Sir, prisoners are not permitted private correspon-dence. This is most irregular. I—'

'You are welcome to read my letter before I seal it, sir,' Ross said equably, without lifting his head. He needed to send only a very short note. His friend, Max, as a member of the House of Lords, was bound to be acquainted with some of Scotland's nobility. Provost Scobie was the kind of man who would take heed of an earl or a duke before any mere laird.

Ross sanded and folded his letter but did not seal it. Then he addressed it to Max's London home. He would still be there. Probably.

Provost Scobie came to stand by Ross's chair. 'The letter, if you please.' He held out his hand.

Ross calmly unfolded the sheet and gave it to him. The provost read it through quickly, glanced suspiciously at Ross, and then read the letter again. He frowned. And he was beginning to look a little worried, too. Good.

'It is a very straightforward letter, as you see, sir. I have asked my friend to find some persons of standing—Scotsmen—who may intercede on my behalf. You cannot object to that, I dare say?'

'Er…no. No, I suppose not. But who is to say that your friend, er—' he looked again at the letter '—your friend, Max, can persuade a Scottish gentleman of standing to perform such a service for you?' He was looking down his nose at Ross as he spoke.

Ross twitched the sheet out of the provost's hand and rose to his feet so that the little man had to look up at him instead. 'I can rely on my friend,' he said with a smile, turning the sheet over and putting it almost under the provost's nose. There, in Ross's firm hand, was the address: The Rt. Hon. the Earl of Penrose.

The provost goggled and began to stammer something unintelligible.

'Provost Scobie.' The door had opened at the provost's back to admit an ancient manservant. 'The colonel has arrived, sir. Shall I show him into the parlour, or—?'

The provost turned to the door with obvious relief. 'No, indeed. I'll come myself this minute.' Without sparing even a glance for Ross, the provost scuttled out into the hallway. The servant closed the door behind him.

'Sorry, sir,' said the gaoler with a hint of an apologetic smile. 'Looks like I'll be taking ye back.'

Ross swallowed an oath. He was not beaten yet. The provost had clearly thought his prisoner was a nobody. Now that he'd discovered Ross had high-ranking connections, the little man would be racking his brains for a way of placating both Ross and the Elliott laird. He was playing for time. But he would not be given it.

Ross strode across to the door and flung it open.

The provost was bowing to a tall, dignified man who was just on the point of handing his hat and cane to the servant. Grimly, Ross clenched his jaw and waited for the right moment to intervene. The visitor was clearly a gentleman.

'My apologies, Colonel, for keeping you waiting.' The provost bowed again to his visitor. 'Legal business, you understand, with this…er…this prisoner.' He indicated Ross with a vague hand gesture. The look that accompanied it held more than a hint of uncertainty. 'If you would like to come into the parlour, I have a very fine Madeira that I should—'

'A moment, Provost,' said the colonel sharply. 'Perhaps you would be good enough to explain what the devil is going on here? This is Captain Graham, is it not? I must ask you to explain why you have this gentleman in custody.'

Ross frowned in surprise. This colonel knew him. But how? Ross scrutinised the unknown officer carefully, but could not place him. There was something vaguely familiar about the man, but that was all. And yet—

Seeing Ross's uncertainty, the colonel stepped forward and offered his hand. 'You won't remember me, Captain Graham. I'm Colonel Anstruther. I was invalided home after Badajoz. We did not run across each other much in the Peninsula. But I remember you well enough. General Picton spoke very highly of you.'

The two men shook hands, totally ignoring the provost and the hovering gaoler. 'Thank you, sir,' Ross said. 'It was an honour to serve with him. You know, I suppose, that he fell at Waterloo?'

'Aye. I heard. A sad loss.' He shook his head regretfully.

The silence was broken by the provost. 'Colonel,' he began, stepping forward, 'if you—'

'You have not told me why this officer is being held, Provost.'

'I…er…' The provost had turned very red. 'Well, Colonel, he is facing a very serious charge. Abduction. Brought by James Elliott, the victim's brother. I would not have confined the captain, you understand, but Elliott insisted. Said he was bound to try to escape. And that he was dangerous, too. Much as I'd be minded to—' he smiled weakly at Ross '—I cannot just release him.'

Ross ignored the provost completely. 'Colonel,' he said warmly, 'I cannot tell you how grateful I am to have someone to speak on my behalf. In a country with no *habeas corpus,* it seems I can simply be left to rot and—'

'Nonsense. Who told you that?'

'I—'

'I told the Captain we have no *habeas corpus,* Colonel,' interrupted the provost. 'And it's true enough, as you know. I was just about to tell him about the Scots law equivalent when you arrived, so he may have misunderstood the situation. Scotland is a civilised country, Captain. Prisoners are not left to rot here, any more than in England.'

'And now that I am prepared to vouch for Captain Graham, there need be no delay about releasing him, Provost. The Captain will give you his parole and you will release him into my custody.'

The provost hesitated. He was shuffling his feet nervously. 'James Elliott insisted—'

'James Elliott may be assured that Captain Graham will make no attempt to escape. Unless you doubt my word in this, Provost?'

The provost almost cowered before the colonel's ferocious frown. Rubbing his hands together in his agitation, the little man looked from the colonel to Ross and back again. There was no hint of weakness in either of them. 'I must know where the prisoner is to be found, sir,' he said lamely.

'I shall be in residence here in Dumfries for some weeks now. Captain Graham will be my guest. You may rest assured that I shall not take him out of your jurisdiction.' The colonel turned to Ross and smiled. 'If you are ready, sir, I will take you to my house now. My business with the provost can wait. It was not really important.' He ignored the provost's sharp intake of breath and turned for the door.

'A moment, Colonel, if you please,' Ross said quickly. 'While I will certainly give my parole to the provost, I cannot possibly accept your generous offer of hospitality when I am in such a dreadful state. I am not fit to enter a gentleman's house. And I do not even have a change of clothes.' He looked down at his filthy breeches and boots, and his shrunken coat. He had not been able to wash for the best part of three days and he had been lying on rotting straw in a stinking gaol. He must smell like something dredged from the quicksands of the Solway.

'Provost, what has become of my mare and my travelling baggage?'

The provost would not meet Ross's eye. 'Your horse is stabled at the George. There'll be livery to pay. There was no baggage as I'm aware of. Just a horse and a greatcoat. And ye've found that, I see,' he added sarcastically.

The colonel paid no heed at all. He himself opened the street door, without waiting for the servant. 'Don't worry, Graham. Your baggage will turn up, I'm sure. And in the meantime, I imagine you would welcome a hot bath and a good meal.'

'Well, yes, sir, but—'

'Good. Then come along. It's but a step to my house. My wife will be delighted to meet you.'

Ross grimaced at the embarrassing prospect, but stepped forward to join the colonel on the threshold.

'On second thoughts,' said the colonel with a small, wry smile, 'I might delay the introductions until after you've had a chance to make yourself a little more… er…presentable.'

In the circumstances, Ross found himself grinning at the older man's gentle jibe. The poor colonel had obviously just had a lungful of gaol odours.

'I'll send a man to see Elliott, to find out what happened to your baggage,' the colonel went on, as soon as they reached the street. 'I imagine there must have been a mistake of some kind.'

Ross nodded automatically, as politeness demanded. But he knew very well that there had been no mistake. The Elliott laird had meant him to be left to rot.

Colonel Anstruther looked his guest slowly up and down. 'It's something of an improvement, Graham,' he said at last, 'though the fit of that coat is…er…'

Ross grinned at his host. 'Your coat may not fit me very well, sir, but since my own is filthy, I make no complaint. Believe me, it is a blessing to be clean again. I owe you a debt for rescuing me from that stinking gaol.'

'Nonsense, nonsense. Any gentleman would have done the same. And if we can't find your own baggage, I'm sure we'll be able to find some better-fitting clothes in Dumfries. We can do that tomorrow morning. It's too late to do anything today, I fear.'

Ross nodded. At least he would not be beholden to the colonel for new clothes. He had money enough to buy his own.

'One thing I…I must say to you, Graham, before I introduce you to my wife.' The colonel pursed his lips and put his hand to his chin. 'I must tell you that she is not in good health. She has a…a wasting disease. When you meet her, you will see. I must warn you that she will not speak of it, not to anyone. I ask you to treat her as if she were a normal healthy woman, and to ignore the fact that she can no longer walk.'

Ross took a step forward and reached out a hand, helplessly. 'Sir, I should not be here. You—'

The colonel smiled rather tightly. 'My wife would not have it otherwise, Captain. She is very much looking forward to making your acquaintance. No doubt she will quiz you about our adventures in the Peninsula.'

'I shall be of little help to Mrs Anstruther, I fear,' Ross admitted. 'To be frank, sir, I barely remember meeting you there. As for adventures…there is very little fit for a lady's ears.'

'Very true,' smiled the colonel. 'I would not have my wife learn of some of the things we had to do. On the other hand, while I would not encourage you to make things up, Graham, you might—'

'I shall do my best to keep Mrs Anstruther entertained, sir. It is the least I can do.'

'Thank you.' The colonel was silent for a moment, as if considering. Then he said quietly, 'When I left for the Peninsula, there was no sign that anything was amiss. Her disease began while I was away, and she never said a word in any of her letters. Even when I had recovered from my wounds and was back at Horse Guards, she managed to conceal it from me. When I finally came home for good last year, I could barely recognise her. The bonnie lass I'd married was almost a wraith. Then, she could still walk. Since the spring, she cannot. She must keep her chair and be carried everywhere. You will see that she weighs no more than a feather now. Each night, when I carry her upstairs, I can feel that she is wasting away before my eyes.'

Ross could find no words to convey his sympathy.

The colonel shook his head, as if trying to shake off his moment of melancholy. 'I tell you this so that you will not be shocked when you meet my wife, Graham. That is all. But she is all good humour. She never complains. You will soon discover that she is fully absorbed in her latest project, to finish our new house and garden in the country. And if you don't take care, she will no doubt be enlisting your help for some part of her plans. It can be difficult to deny her, I warn you.'

'If I can repay your kindness by serving Mrs Anstruther, I should be delighted to do it. Pray tell her that I am quite at her service.'

'Now that,' said a female voice behind Ross, 'is a very rash promise for a gentleman to make. Just think what I might require you to do!'

The colonel laughed down at his wife in her wheeled chair. 'Allow me to present Captain Graham, my dear. I did try to warn him of the risks he was running,' he added, 'but he would have none of it. So it appears you have acquired another willing cavalier.'

Ross stepped forward and bowed over Mrs Anstruther's outstretched hand, feeling how tiny it was, and how thin. The colonel's wife must have been very beautiful once. Now she was indeed like a wraith. A shadow of what she had been.

The following morning, James Elliott presented himself at Colonel Anstruther's door. Carrying Ross's bags.

Standing black-browed in the library doorway, Elliott bowed in the colonel's direction and said, 'I have come to return Captain Graham's baggage and pistols, and to apologise for bringing the charge against him. It has been withdrawn, as the provost will confirm. I jumped to an unwarranted conclusion, I admit, but if you had known the circumstances, and my sister's— Well, no point in going into that.' He bowed slightly to Ross. 'My sister has explained what took place, Captain Graham, and I have come to beg your pardon. My sister also begs to send you her thanks for rescuing her. She hopes that you have suffered no lasting hurt from your ordeal in…in Dumfries.'

Clever, Ross thought. By introducing his sister, he seeks to divert my righteous anger. And, as a gentleman, I have no choice but to acquiesce, especially here in Colonel Anstruther's home. 'Pray thank Miss Elliott for her kind enquiry. You may assure her that I am quite well, thanks to the Colonel's intervention. I see you have managed to discover my missing bags. How remarkably fortunate. The provost assured me that there was no trace of them.'

'A misunderstanding, I assure you, sir. Your luggage was conveyed to the stable, along with your mare. Both were well taken care of. And of course there is no livery to pay. I have seen to that.'

'You are all generosity, Elliott,' the colonel said, with some asperity.

'Sir, I hope it will be possible to forget this unfortunate episode. My sister joins her prayers to mine. She wishes me to invite you both—and Mrs Anstruther, too, of course—to visit us so that she may offer her apologies in person.'

Clearly the Elliott sister was not to be permitted to visit them in Dumfries. It seemed that, if Ross wanted to see the girl again, and to unravel the mystery surrounding her, he would have to go to her. But it was the height of ill manners to expect the invalid Mrs Anstruther to wait on a mere child. Ross waited to see how the colonel would respond.

'We are grateful for Miss Elliott's invitation. Of course.' The colonel's pause before those last words held a wealth of meaning. Ross fancied that Elliott was beginning to look a trifle embarrassed. However good his birth, Elliott was no gentleman, but even he must realise that it was for him, and his sister, to wait on the Anstruthers. The Elliotts, after all, were the ones who needed to apologise.

'You will understand, Elliott, that my wife is not able to travel easily. And my recollection is that the roads around your manor are remarkably bad. Is that not so?' The colonel waited for Elliott's reluctant nod before continuing. 'However, you and Miss Elliott would be more than welcome to call on us here in Dumfries. Miss Elliott would be able to make her apologies then, would she not?'

Chapter Four

'You sent a letter to the provost,' James thundered, shaking his fist at Cassie, 'and I know only too well how it was arranged. You have gone too far this time, sister. That woman, Morag, shall leave my lands this very day. No woman defies me in my own house.'

Cassandra had known he would be furious, but also that it had been right to take the risk. She owed it to the man to save him. And now she must try to pay what she owed to poor Morag, too.

'Morag had nothing to do with it,' she said quietly, knowing that she must not provoke him further. She willed herself to be calm, to swallow her boiling anger against his continuing injustice and cruelty. If she appeared submissive enough, he might listen to what she had to say.

James said nothing. But it was clear from his expression that he was far from convinced. She must try harder.

'Come, brother, you know she could not have taken a letter to Dumfries. For how would she have travelled? And secretly, too? Since I have been...er... keeping to my room, Morag has taken charge of the household in my place. If she had gone to Dumfries, her absence would have been noticed. *You* would have noticed. You are always fly to the time of day.'

Her heavy-handed flattery seemed to be working. His fists had unclenched a fraction. And he did not seem to be wanting to shout at her again. Yet.

Cassandra hurried on. 'No one in this household was involved.' His head came up sharply. 'So there is no one to be dismissed on that account.'

'Tell me who it was.' He was trying to control his anger, for once. In some ways, that made him more frightening.

She ignored his question. But she would try not to antagonise him further. 'In the end, it was as well that I did send the letter. For both of us,' she added. 'We both know we cannot afford to make an enemy of Colonel Anstruther, for he has too many powerful friends in Dumfries and Edinburgh.' She could see that her arguments were finally making an impression on James. And she spoke only the truth. James might have thought he was taking vengeance on a friendless traveller with no standing in the world. But it had transpired that the traveller was a gentleman, and one who might have the power to ruin the Elliotts. She waited for her brother to respond. She had said enough for the moment.

'It is true that Graham is a gentleman,' he conceded at last, with an angry shake of his head. 'One look at his fine linen told me that. But even a gentleman can be hanged, Cassie, if the crime is heinous enough.' The venom in his words was unmistakable.

You might be speaking your own epitaph. The thought flashed through Cassie's mind, unbidden. She was instantly ashamed. She might hate her half-brother, and with just cause, but she did not will his death. Never that. She only wished…she only wished to be free of him, and to find some degree of happiness in her life. A very little would suffice.

'There was no crime,' she said simply. 'I had never met him before.'

'Aye, so you say.'

'Jamie—'

'Enough of your wheedling, girl. You will tell me who carried the letter.'

Cassie set her mouth in a firm line and said nothing.

'So that is to be the way of it? Very well. Since I cannot punish the real culprit, I shall have to find someone else to take the blame.' His voice sank to a soft hiss. 'Yes. I think Morag will suffice. She leaves this day.'

'No. You cannot. Morag has done nothing. Please, Jamie, I promise you, she was not the one.'

'I do not doubt it. But I should make an example of someone.' He brought his face down to hers. 'You do see that, don't you, sister?'

'Make an example of me, then. For it was I who wrote the letter.'

'Oh, I intend to do that also. I have plans for you, Miss Cassandra Elliott.'

Cassie tried to suppress a shudder. She did not quite succeed.

'It frightens you, does it? Good. And so it should. Your first task is simple. You are to find out about Captain Graham. We know he has powerful friends, but we know precious little of the man himself. No doubt he will happily enlighten you about his estate and prospects. After all, you were very friendly out there together, were you not?'

'I will do no such thing. I am not a spy.'

'You will do exactly as I say, or Morag will be dismissed.' He glared at her. 'Well?'

She was firmly caught. He had left her with no choice. She nodded.

'Understand this, sister. I will be watching your every move. If you put a foot wrong, Morag will feel the weight of my retribution. Fiendish subtle, is it not?'

It was certainly fiendish, Cassie decided. He knew she would do whatever he wanted, while Morag was hostage for her obedience. She lifted her chin. 'I cannot spy on Captain Graham unless I can talk to him. And I do not expect he would wish to have anything to do with the man who threw him in gaol. Or that man's sister.'

He laughed harshly. 'You credit me with precious little wit, Cassie. The arrangements have already been made. Do not look so surprised. Did you think me incapable of making an apology, as a gentleman should? Why, Cassie, you underestimate your brother. No sooner thought than done. We are invited to call on Colonel and Mrs Anstruther, and Captain Graham, at our convenience. To give you an opportunity to apologise for all the trouble you have caused.'

'I—? Apol—?'

'In fact, I doubt an apology will be expected,' he continued smoothly, enjoying his triumph. 'The gentlemen will not wish you to divulge the details of your disgrace in front of Mrs Anstruther, I imagine. It will be…it will appear to be a courtesy visit, to allow you to enquire after Mrs Anstruther and to make the acquaintance of Captain Graham. Nothing could be simpler, surely? *Surely?*'

She nodded weakly.

'Let us be clear that your object, during this visit, is to show the gentlemen—*both* the gentlemen—that you are a fine lady with all the accomplishments necessary in a wife.'

'*Both* the gentlemen? But Colonel Anstruther already has a wife!'

'Not for much longer. He'll be a widower soon. And he's very rich.'

So that had been James's plan. Cassandra was horrified. The colonel was devoted to his wife. Everyone knew that. How could James be so callous?

Easily.

'As for Captain Graham, I have yet to discover his circumstances. He may be married already. Or worse—poor. You will do your utmost to draw him out on both counts.'

'A *lady* would not do anything so vulgar.'

For once, James did not shout. He even smiled. 'A lady has ways of extracting such information, as you very well know. Did you learn nothing at all in that fine Edinburgh seminary that Father paid so much for?'

Cassandra said nothing. There was no point.

'Now remember. You have been unwell. A slight chill has confined you to your room.' He smiled mockingly as he stressed the word 'confined'. 'You are not quite fully recovered, but you have actually made a great effort for this special visit. Have I made myself clear?'

James Elliott took the chair indicated by the colonel and then turned towards Mrs Anstruther. 'Your footman is just helping my sister down from the carriage. I have come in ahead of her to warn you that she finds herself a little frail just at present and does not think she will be able to remain more than a few minutes.'

'I am truly sorry to learn that your sister is unwell, Mr Elliott.' Mrs Anstruther looked concerned.

Elliott cast a glance over his shoulder to the half-open doorway before replying, in a low voice that reeked of false concern, 'My sister, ma'am, chanced to be out riding some days ago when a storm broke. She caught a slight chill and has since kept to her room. This is the first time she has been able to venture abroad.'

Ross and the colonel exchanged glances. How glibly Elliott lied!

'But she should not have come such a way!' Mrs Anstruther exclaimed. 'The poor child! She cannot be expected to make calls when she is ill. This visit should have been put off until another day.'

'Believe me, ma'am, it is but trifling. You know what young girls are.' He smirked then. 'They fancy themselves ailing at the slightest sniffle. And—' There was a noise of footsteps in the hallway. Elliott rose from his place. 'Ah, here she is. You shall judge for yourself whether she is well enough for visiting. Come in, Cassandra, come in. Our host and hostess are waiting.'

The colonel stood up. Ross, too, rose politely. She might be little more than a child, and a hoyden besides, but she would not find Ross Graham's manners wanting.

'Good afternoon, Mrs Anstruther,' she said quietly, dropping an elegant curtsy.

Ross caught his breath. How on earth could he have made such a mistake? He had believed Miss Elliott to be fifteen, or sixteen at most; a mere child, and an unruly one at that. But this dark-haired, dark-eyed beauty was much older—and a full-grown woman, the kind of woman that men would fight to possess.

In that split second, Ross began to understand much that had puzzled him before. About Miss Elliott and her desire to escape. And about her brother's ruthless determination to keep her close, and safe.

Cassandra had had to steel herself for this meeting. James had made his fell purposes crystal clear. And now, standing on the threshold of the drawing room, she knew that all eyes were upon her. She took a deep breath and stepped forward, trying not to look at either of the gentlemen, James's intended quarry.

'Good afternoon, Mrs Anstruther,' she said politely, dropping a curtsy to the beautiful but frail lady sitting in one of the wing chairs by the unseasonable roaring fire. James had been right about the colonel's wife. Much had changed since their last meeting. She was now clearly marked for death. She had an ethereal, translucent quality about her. Half-angel already?

'Come in, child, do. You must not allow yourself to become chilled.' Mrs Anstruther's body might be failing, but her mind seemed perfectly alert. 'There is a sharp breeze coming off the river today. Indeed, it feels more like autumn than high summer. Come and sit by me so that we may enjoy this fine fire together.' She smiled up at her husband, standing with his back to the hearth. 'The gentlemen shall make way for the needs of a recovering invalid.'

Colonel Anstruther bowed slightly and removed himself a little from the fire. To Ross's mind, the room was uncomfortably hot, but that was only to be expected; Ross had learned that the colonel permitted nothing and no one to divert him from anything that might ease Mrs Anstruther's sufferings. Theirs was real love between a man and a woman. The kind of love that any right-thinking man would envy, even though few of them would ever attain it.

Pushing that unwelcome thought to the back of his mind, Ross stepped forward to greet Miss Elliott, as a gentleman should. How would she react to him, now that she appeared in her proper guise? Did she know how to behave as a lady? With such a brother, she had had a pretty dismal example to follow. Ross bowed politely and offered her his arm. 'May I help you to a seat by the fire, Miss Elliott?'

She curtsied a second time. It was an elegant move. She had clearly been well taught, in that matter at least, for she had given Ross just the degree of respect required by their positions in society. He was an officer and a gentleman; she was a gentleman's sister. Nominally, at least.

* * *

The two women had been talking amiably for some time when the tea tray was brought in. The need to curtail the visit seemed to have been forgotten. Mrs Anstruther smiled across to where her husband stood by the window, carrying on a rather strained conversation with Elliott and Ross. 'Will you take a dish of tea with us, Mr Elliott? Or do you, like my husband, object to maudling your insides with such a beverage?'

Elliott strolled across to the fire and replied politely that he would be delighted to drink tea with his hostess. Too politely, Ross decided. The man was definitely trying to make a good impression on Mrs Anstruther, probably in order to curry favour with the colonel. But why? What was Elliott after? What could the colonel possibly have that Elliott needed?

Miss Elliott rose from her chair to help hand round the cups, first to her brother and then to the colonel. She moved with the grace of a gazelle. And she had beautiful white hands, almost as delicate and translucent as the fine porcelain she carried. 'Cream and sugar, Captain Graham?' For the first time, she smiled directly at him. He realised, with something of a surprise, that her dark eyes were not brown, but blue, the rich blue of a summer twilight sky. So very unlike her brother's shifty brown eyes. But then, they had not had the same mother. That would account for the differences between them. Ross was suddenly glad of it. He found he could not stomach the thought that Miss Elliott was in any way like her blackguard of a brother.

'Captain Graham?'

'I beg your pardon, Miss Elliott. No sugar, thank you.'

She nodded and brought his cup to him. 'It is unusual for a man to drink tea without sugar.'

'We did have tea in the Peninsula, ma'am, and sugar. But they were not always easy to come by. One learns to adapt.'

'I am surprised to learn that officers in the army were drinking tea,' she said, on the thread of a laugh. Her eyes were dancing. They were really very beautiful eyes.

'We were not all lost to the ways of polite society, ma'am. One or two of the officers were accompanied by their wives, so we single men did not become complete barbarians.' He willingly returned her smile. Her brother might be scheming, but Miss Elliott seemed to be everything a lady should be. How was it possible that she had been fleeing for the Solway, dressed only in a sodden shift? Ross determined to solve the mystery surrounding her. It was clear that she needed protection from her brother. But why?

'I find I have a picture of you in my mind, sitting on the ground around a camp fire, weapons in one hand and a bowl of tea in the other. Absurd, is it not?'

He laughed and was delighted that she did, too. She

had very even white teeth and a wide, kissable mouth. Lord, where had that thought come from? For a moment he was stunned by his own reaction.

'I can see that I must not pursue that avenue of conversation any further, Captain Graham, lest you find yourself confiding what else the single officers were doing. Tell me, what brings you north? Your accent suggests that you are originally from Scotland, but I was wondering why you chose to visit Dumfries rather than, say, Edinburgh. Does your family come from here?'

'I am not exactly sure.' He cursed silently. What on earth had possessed him to let that slip? Miss Elliott's surprise was clear and absolutely predictable. Everyone disdained a man without a family. Now he would have to explain something of his Scottish origins—not that he knew much—and to try to parry the inevitable questions.

She did not display the vulgar curiosity he had expected, however, saying merely, 'How…er… unusual. Do you plan to make a long stay in this part of the country?'

Ross was becoming more and more impressed. This was a true lady. She had seen his dawning embarrassment and had skilfully helped him through it. What had happened to the hoyden? Was this really the same woman? It seemed impossible. Yet it was true.

He must do his best to respond in kind.

'I find it strangely beautiful, I must admit. As I have no pressing reasons to return to London, I fancy I may spend some time in these parts, exploring the area. There are some fine houses to visit, I believe?'

'Yes, indeed. Many. And even finer gardens. The climate here is most clement, particularly towards the west. Some of the local gentry have created beautiful gardens and are bringing in all sorts of new plants from distant parts. I find myself envying them greatly.' She smiled up at him. 'Yes, I know it is a sin, but I cannot help myself. Whenever I visit such a garden, I cannot help but covet the glories I see there.'

'Then you have much in common with Mrs Anstruther. Oh, not the sins, I am sure,' he added hastily, 'but the love of plants and gardens. The colonel and his wife are creating a new garden at their manor near Castle Douglas, I believe.'

'The colonel's property is rather more than a manor, sir,' she replied with a twinkle. 'It is an ancient castle, built as a bulwark against the invading English. As you travel around you will see that there are many such, mostly in ruins. The colonel's family spent many years restoring it, I believe. Most other families preferred to build anew. A modern house can be more comfortable, I suppose, though it lacks the magic of the old places.'

'Ah, do I detect a lover of gothic romances?'

She blushed. Delightfully.

'Forgive me, ma'am,' he said quickly. 'That was

impertinent of me. Tell me, if you will, what places of interest I should visit while I am staying in Dumfries.'

She named several, ending with Sweetheart Abbey. 'It was built by the Lady Devorguilla in memory of her beloved husband. His heart is buried there. It is a strange, haunting place, but very beautiful. You will find it an easy journey, in the day, though better on horseback than by carriage. Are you travelling alone?'

'For the present, yes. Though my man, Fraser, will be joining me in the next few days.' He dropped his voice to be sure that Mrs Anstruther would not hear. 'He will be quite horrified, of course, about what happened. He'll maintain, loud and long, that if I had allowed him to accompany me in the first place, as he'd tried to insist, I wouldn't have been thrown into gaol at all.'

She drew herself up slightly. Ross could not decide whether it was because she wished to distance herself from her own outrageous behaviour, or whether she disapproved of his obviously close relationship with his valet. 'You will tell him what happened?' Her voice definitely held a hint of *hauteur.* So, she didn't think a gentleman should confide in his valet. How little she knew. Having shared the privations of the Peninsular War with Fraser, Ross trusted his man implicitly. With his life, if necessary.

'It matters not a whit whether I tell him or not.' Ross

grinned suddenly, remembering many instances when he had tried to keep information from Fraser. 'Fraser is the best gatherer of information I have ever known. He'd find out somehow. He'd have made a very successful spy.' Now that was not quite true. For, on occasion, Fraser had already made a very successful spy. And the British army, though unaware of the details of the man's dangerous service, had reason to be eternally grateful for Fraser's abilities.

'How very…interesting.'

He had lost her. The sparkling look was now veiled as she took his empty cup and returned to speak to Mrs Anstruther. Her brother had risen from his place and was bowing to his hostess. The pair clearly meant to leave.

'It was a great pleasure to meet you again, Miss Elliott,' Mrs Anstruther said. 'And you, too, Mr Elliott. I do hope you will come again soon, so that Miss Elliott and I can continue our discussions. I have rarely met anyone so young yet with such enthusiasm for plants and gardens. We share a common passion, I think.'

Miss Elliott smiled warmly. 'I cannot hope to match your knowledge, ma'am, but I should very much like to learn more from you. What you tell me of your new garden is fascinating.'

'I long to visit it again. But situated as I am—' she gestured impatiently at her useless legs '—it may be some time before I can do so. However, if you wish to visit the house and garden, please feel free to do so. My gardeners would be delighted to learn that there are other ladies in the world just as passionate as I am.' She looked sideways at Ross. 'Perhaps Captain Graham would like to accompany you? And your brother, of course.'

James Elliott cleared his throat and directed a swift warning look towards his sister. 'Cassandra is most grateful for the invitation, ma'am. Very generous of you, I am sure. However, we must not think of making any excursions until Cassandra is quite well again. It does not do to risk a lady's frail health.'

Ross hoped his reactions did not show on his face. The man was a lying cur. Had he not poured scorn on the assumed frailty of young ladies not half an hour ago? Why was he now declining Mrs Anstruther's invitation when he had gone to such lengths to ingratiate himself before? There was something very strange going on in the Elliott family. Very strange indeed.

Mrs Anstruther stretched up her hand to Miss Elliott. 'Forgive me, my dear,' she said. 'I hope you will be fully recovered very soon. It will not be possible for me to return your call, alas, but perhaps you will overlook my discourtesy and come to me again? I did so enjoy our talk. The colonel does his best, and he has become very knowledgeable about plants of late, but he does not share my passion. Not as you do.'

Miss Elliott blushed. 'You do me too much honour, ma'am. And I should be delighted to call on you again.' She glanced towards her brother, who was frowning. 'As soon as I am able.'

'You will understand if we take our leave now, ma'am,' her brother said. 'We must get home while it is still light. It would not do for Cassandra to become chilled.'

The normal courtesies were soon exchanged. Elliott could almost have been a real gentleman. Certainly, his assumed manners could not be faulted. Ross felt his gorge rising as he watched. The man was the very devil.

Ross insisted on escorting Miss Elliott to her carriage, offering his hand to help her to mount. With one foot on the step, she turned to look into his face. Their eyes met, and held. He felt a slight pressure of her fingers in his. 'Thank you, Captain Graham,' she said softly. 'I am truly most grateful to you.'

'Your servant, ma'am,' he said, returning the pressure for just a fraction of a second. A silent message was sent and received. Ross had no doubt that Miss Elliott—Cassandra—understood what he intended. He had risked his life to save her once. And he stood ready to do so again.

Chapter Five

Cassie shrank back into the corner of the carriage, where James could not see her if he chose to ride alongside rather than out in front. She had only the length of the journey home to order her thoughts and to decide how she would respond to his demands. For they would certainly come.

Jamie would go to any lengths to get what he wanted. And what he wanted now was to marry Cassie off to a rich man as soon as he possibly could. His debts must be even more pressing than before, she decided, for until now, he had been planning to wait until Colonel Anstruther was free to remarry. No doubt James expected to borrow money from his future brother-in-law at every opportunity. But surely that meant finding a man who was both rich and weak? Colonel Anstruther was certainly not weak. He would never be an easy mark.

And nor would Captain Graham. He, too, was every

inch the soldier—strong, determined, resourceful, and a knight in shining armour to a damsel in distress. She was sorry now that she had snubbed him when he mentioned having been thrown into gaol. But she had been mortally embarrassed at the thought that he was about to tell his valet about her outrageous behaviour. Once one servant knew of her attempted flight, it was bound to become the talk of Dumfries. What little standing she had in the community would be gone. She would not even be able to call on Mrs Anstruther again.

That meant she would not be able to meet Captain Graham again.

She felt a sinking in her stomach at the thought. She was grateful to him. Of course, she was. But it was more than that. She had not met many single gentlemen since she had left her Edinburgh seminary, and almost all of them had been old, or lecherous, or both. Captain Graham was neither. He was young and vigorous, and handsome enough if one overlooked his red hair. He had very pleasing blue eyes, too, that twinkled with good humour. And he was kind to hoydens on the banks of the Solway. Altogether the kind of gentleman that any young lady would wish to know.

But was he rich? Oh, dear, she did not know. She had discovered—quite cleverly, she thought—that he was a single man, but she knew little of his circumstances. Perhaps if she had not snubbed him, he would have been more forthcoming? But no. He had not wished to speak of his family. He had inadvertently let slip that he knew little about them. And he had been embarrassed at having said even that. There was no way she could have successfully quizzed him.

James would not accept such an excuse. What was she to tell him? Perhaps she could draw inferences from what the captain had said without actually telling a lie. *Think, Cassie, think!* She knew he had served in the Fifty-second Foot and she imagined he would have had to purchase his commission in such a good regiment. That meant he had some money, at least. Good, that was a start. His family came from Scotland, and fairly recently, too, judging by his accent, yet he knew nothing of them. So he must have been brought up in a home in England. Somewhere in England. And a gentleman's home in England, however small, would require money to maintain it. She would tell James that the captain was Scottish-born but English-bred, and that he appeared to be comfortably off.

And she would say that, if James wanted her to find out more details about the captain's finances, he would have to allow her to meet him again, in easier circumstances. She had done the best she could in the space of a few minutes' polite conversation.

Yes. She would suggest that they take up Mrs Anstruther's invitation to visit her new garden and that Captain Graham be invited to accompany them. On such a visit, there would be many opportunities to draw him out. Surely even James would see the sense in such a plan?

'Never seen yer linen in such a state, Captain. Not even when we was in the Peninsula.'

Ross sighed and set about smoothing Fraser's ruffled feathers. 'The colonel's man has done his best, Fraser, but it's been precious little use after the mauling Elliott and his men gave to my belongings. Do your best to restore what you can. For the rest, we'll have to buy new.'

Fraser was not mollified. 'And yer boots, too, sir. Surely the colonel's man knows how to black boots?'

'Indeed he does, but not boots that have been squelching through Solway mud and then spent days in a sodden and stinking gaol. I'm surprised they haven't rotted through. I doubt even you would be able to rescue them, Fraser.' Ross quirked an eyebrow at his batman and long-time companion.

'Aye, well, they may not be a total loss, sir. I'll see what I can do.'

Ross smiled. The challenge had provoked exactly the response he had expected.

'And in the meantime, you won't go barefoot. There's another pair in the bags I brought with me, and a supply of linen, too. I must have you respectable to dine with Mrs Anstruther. I can't imagine how you looked when you were wearing the colonel's coat. Disgraceful, no doubt.'

'Perhaps, but it was a great deal better than how I looked when the colonel first found me, I can tell you, Fraser. I had neither hat nor gloves, my coat and breeches were damp and filthy, and everything about me reeked of the gaol. It was a wonder the poor colonel did not put a handkerchief to his nose.' He laughed softly at the memory. 'To his credit, he did not, though he did soon learn not to stand downwind of me.'

Fraser tried in vain to hide his smile.

'So be grateful that this is the worst you see of me. Or smell!'

Fraser gathered up Ross's scattered clothing and made for the door. 'If you won't be needing anything else this evening, sir, I'd best get on with salvaging what I can.'

'Thank you, Fraser. I know you'll do your best.' He waited until the valet was halfway through the door before adding softly, 'And when you have a moment free, I have a special task for you. One that you will enjoy, I fancy.'

Fraser turned. One look at Ross's face was enough to tell him what was in store for him. He grinned widely. 'That's more like it, Captain. Sounds just like old times. What was it you was wanting me to find out for you?'

Ross beckoned him back into the room. Once the door was safely closed, he said, 'I need you to discover some information for me, Fraser, about a young lady and her family. She—'

'That would be the young lady you rescued down by the Solway, would it, sir?'

Ross groaned and struck his forehead in mock despair. 'By Jove, Fraser, is there anything you don't find out? The colonel and I have gone to considerable lengths *not* to have that tale bandied about, and yet you know about it before you have been here five minutes. I suppose there's no point in asking *how* you know, is there?'

'No, sir,' Fraser said flatly.

Ross knew there was nothing to be gained by pressing the man any further. He sighed theatrically, shaking his head. 'Very well. I shall not ask. Now, just in case you do not already know, the lady in question is Miss Cassandra Elliott and she lives with her half-brother, James, at Langrigg House, between Dumfries and Annan. I want to know what James Elliott is about and what was so terrible that his sister was prepared to take the risk of fleeing across the Solway. I need to—'

'You need to know everything there is to know about the Elliott family. Very good, sir. Leave it to me.'

Ross wondered how Fraser, a stranger newly arrived in Dumfries, could possibly hope to get the information Ross needed. But he knew better than to ask. 'Thank you, Fraser. I know I can rely on you,' he said simply, and meant it. 'Oh, and forget about the ruined boots. Better use your time for the Elliotts.'

Fraser drew himself up to his full height, which was considerably shorter than Ross. 'I shall do my duty, sir,' he said formally, 'and that, *sir,* includes your boots.'

'Make sure you take your most becoming gowns. God knows I've paid enough for them, over the years, just to make sure you look the part of a fine lady. I want my investment to be repaid, Cassie. Mark that. You must ensure that the gentlemen are suitably impressed.'

'You have changed your mind all of a sudden, have you not, James? When we visited the Anstruthers, you made quite sure that I would not accept the invitation.'

'That was before Colonel Anstruther himself became involved. Now that he is to act as our host, it is a splendid opportunity for you to display your... er...womanly attributes.'

Cassie felt herself blushing. Again! Why did her brother have to be so crass? And why was it that she always showed her embarrassment?

'Be ready to leave first thing tomorrow morning. The carriage will be at the door by nine. Do not be late. Morag will accompany you in the carriage and I shall ride alongside. We should arrive well before noon.'

'But I had intended to ride there myself. I hate being cooped up in the carriage. In summer weather like this, there is no reason why I should not ride.'

'There is every reason. I do not wish you to ride.'

Cassie bit back the angry 'Why not?' that rose to her lips. Instead, she said, 'Colonel Anstruther is a military man. He would expect his wife to ride. And ride well. Would this not be an opportunity to demonstrate my attributes in that area of a lady's accomplishments?' Good tactics, Cassie thought to herself. That had stopped James in his tracks. Captain Graham would be proud of her.

James started to speak, but Cassie heard barely a word. Why on earth was she thinking it mattered what Captain Graham thought of her?

'Cassie! Pay attention! This is no time for your eternal daydreaming. It is your marriage we are planning here.'

Cassie swallowed hard, but said nothing.

'Remember, the aim of your visit is to impress the gentlemen. Your first object must be Colonel Anstruther. He is by far the better catch. Captain Graham may not be a catch at all. So far we know nothing more of him than that he is an officer, and a gentleman, and brought up in England. For all we know, he may be simply subsisting on half-pay. That most certainly would not do.'

'Have your spies uncovered no more information, then?' Cassie said sweetly.

'No. The captain's man is remarkably close-mouthed. Even when he has been well plied with ale. At my expense.'

'Oh. Who did you send?'

'Not Tam or Ned, if that's what you were thinking. The captain's man would be bound to have learned that they were the ones who threw his master into gaol. No, I sent Malcolm.'

'Ah,' Cassie nodded. Malcolm was James's man through and through, part valet, part steward, and utterly devoted to James's interests. 'Well, if Malcolm could discover nothing, I imagine there is nothing to be learned by that route.'

'No. That leaves only one avenue. The direct one. You, Cassie, must find out the truth about Captain Graham, either from the man himself or from Colonel Anstruther. You will have the whole of our visit to do that.'

'But it is only two days and one night! Such questions require a degree of intimacy which could never be achieved in so short a time.'

James smiled nastily. 'I'm sure you will find a way, Cassie. And to give you every opportunity, I shall have your horse tied on to the back of the carriage. Make sure you take your most becoming riding habit. Riding out with the gentlemen does give plenty of opportunity for intimate conversation. Make the most of it.'

* * *

It was a beautiful, sunny summer's day as Cassie's carriage slowed for the approach to the great door to the Anstruther castle. Cassie had been gazing in awe as they drove up the long avenue. It was a huge—monstrous—edifice. She wondered that the Anstruther family had invested so much money in restoring it, for it surely belonged to a bygone age. The walls were of massive stone. There were only the merest slits of windows at ground level. And one of the towers had still not been repaired. It looked as though it had suffered from cannon fire in some battle, centuries before.

'I'm glad I packed they heavy petticoats,' Morag said. 'We are all like to freeze t' death in there.'

'I'm sure the colonel will make us more than comfortable,' Cassie said, though she was not at all sure she spoke the truth.

'Aye, well, I'll judge that after I see for myself. He'd have done much better to build a fine new house, where a body could be warm and dry. There's bound to be draughts everywhere. And the lums will reek.'

'Oh, Morag, don't be such a misery. We are here to see Colonel Anstruther's new garden, not his house. We shall be spending most of our time out of doors, where there are no draughts and no smoking chimneys. Besides, the weather is delightful. Why should we be cold?'

'Because this is Galloway, Miss Cassie, and ye ken well enough that the weather can change in two shakes of a lamb's tail. How else was it that you was caught in that awful storm?'

Oh, dear. She had left herself open to that jibe. And she was probably blushing again. 'That's enough, Morag,' she snapped, more angry with herself than with her maid. 'You are not to mention that incident again. Never. Do you understand me?'

'Aye.'

'Now, as soon as we are in the house, I need you to bring me some hot water and to lay out a fresh gown. I cannot sit down to luncheon with the gentlemen if I am still dressed in my travelling clothes.'

Ross had already spent a day and a night in Colonel Anstruther's company while they rode down to Castle Douglas and settled in on the Anstruther country estate. He had been surprised to discover that such an ancient edifice could be made so very comfortable inside. His bedchamber was large, with a splendid view out over the developing garden. It was also surprisingly warm, considering the enormous thickness of the castle walls. True, the house did not rely on Scottish sunshine. There was always a fire burning in the cavernous grate, with heat radiating out from the chimney breast.

Fraser appeared content as well, and he was by far

the more difficult to please. He reported that the colonel believed in looking after his servants, feeding and housing them well. Moreover, he had installed the most modern conveniences in the ancient kitchen in the basement, so that his cooks could produce the excellent fare he demanded. Ross had found himself in agreement there. They had been only two at dinner on the previous day, but the selection of dishes had been as good as he could have expected in any nobleman's house in England.

'Miss Elliott and her party have this minute arrived, sir,' Fraser announced as he entered the room. 'She came in her carriage, with her maid, but there was a magnificent bay stallion tied on behind. Would that be the one you spoke of?'

'It certainly sounds like Lucifer.' Ross found himself warming to the thought of riding out with Miss Elliott. Their previous ride together had been unusual, to say the least, but even in those circumstances, he had seen that she was an excellent horsewoman. He imagined that, properly attired, she would look remarkably fetching on top of that amazing animal.

'The colonel asks that you come down for luncheon now, sir. He expects Miss Elliott and her brother to join you both very shortly.'

Ross started for the door.

'A moment, sir. You cannot greet a lady dressed like that. Your cravat is a disgrace.'

Ross burst out laughing. Fraser was incorrigible, as ever.

'Let me find you a fresh one, sir.' Fraser was already rummaging in the drawer of the clothes press.

It took Ross almost ten minutes to make himself presentable enough to pass muster with Fraser. Yet, when he looked in the glass, he saw that his man had had reason. He looked very much better now. As a gentleman should.

'Now you'll do, sir,' said Fraser, opening the door for him.

'Thank you, sir. That was most pleasant,' Ross said, looking round at the remains of the cold meat and fruit, of which they had all partaken. Miss Elliott, he had noticed, had a very hearty appetite.

'Is all this splendid produce from your own estate, sir?'

'Why, yes, Miss Elliott. My wife had succession houses constructed in the walled garden, not long after we were married. Perhaps you would like to see them this afternoon? The peaches and grapes are not quite ready, of course, but we are very proud of them. Even here in Scotland, it is possible to grow such things. With care.'

'With care, I am sure. And also with all the knowledge and passion that your wife brings to it. I am so sorry that Mrs Anstruther is not well enough to join us here today.'

'As am I,' said the colonel, sadly. 'But she was determined that you should not be denied your treat, Miss Elliott, and so, untutored as I am, I am here to act as your host and to do my poor best to explain everything we have done. And everything my wife is planning to do.'

'I am truly grateful to you, sir, and sorry to learn that Mrs Anstruther is now alone in Dumfries.'

'Oh, she is not alone, my dear. She has very many friends, both in Dumfries and in Castle Douglas. Whenever I am away, they flock to her side, to indulge in the most reprehensible gossiping. When I spent all those months in Horse Guards, my house was the centre of the worst gossip in Scotland, I do believe.' He smiled broadly.

Cassie thought there was still a hint of sadness in that smile. She knew, from that same gossip, relayed by Morag, that Mrs Anstruther's condition had worsened very suddenly during the colonel's duty in London. He must feel it very much. Just as he must know that his wife's days were numbered.

'So, what would you wish to do, ma'am? I can offer you a tour of the garden and the succession houses this afternoon. Or, if you prefer, we could ride out to view the estate. I see that you have brought a magnificent horse with you. I should not have said he was a lady's mount, however.'

Cassie tried not to smile. 'Lucifer can be a bit mischievous when he is fresh, but I promise you, sir, that he has no vice in him.'

'Lucifer?' gasped the colonel.

'Yes, well…it seemed an appropriate name when he first came to me. He was rather more difficult then than he is now.'

'I see.' The colonel exchanged glances with Ross, but did not pursue the subject. 'So, what is it to be, ma'am?'

'It is such a beautiful day. I think, if I may, I should prefer to ride this afternoon for, who knows, tomorrow the weather may have changed. I can always view the gardens in the rain.'

'You are probably wise, ma'am.'

'And perhaps you could tell me of the garden plans as we go, Colonel? Then I should be prepared for tomorrow's treat.'

'Certainly, ma'am, I will do my best to oblige.'

'I am sure your knowledge of the estate and the garden is very considerable, Colonel. It would be most interesting to learn from you.' Oh, dear, Cassie thought, the moment those words were out. Surely that was doing it too brown? Still, the colonel did not seem to have taken offence. He was beaming at her, but in rather a fatherly way. James would not be pleased to see that.

'You will accompany us, Captain Graham?'

'Certainly, sir, I should be delighted. Since we saw only a small part of the estate when we rode in yesterday, I am all agog to see the improvements you have been making elsewhere. I understand you have been trying some radical new ideas?'

'Not so radical. But Coke in Norfolk has some good notions for the improvement of stock. Whether they will translate from Norfolk to Galloway remains to be seen, but anything that might alleviate the poverty of the people here must be tried.'

'Is it so very bad?' Ross asked.

'I am afraid so. Oh, better now than, say, fifty years ago, but still bad. Would you not agree, Elliott?'

James Elliott had sat totally dumb throughout the meal. Now he said only, 'They have no one but themselves to blame. If they worked harder, they would eat better.'

His sister blushed bright red with embarrassment. 'Do you have both sheep and cattle, Colonel?' she enquired hastily.

'Yes, ma'am, I do. I find the local black cattle best adapted to the climate here. They are small, but they thrive. And they do make very good eating.' He gestured in the direction of the half-eaten sirloin on the sideboard. 'The black-faced sheep do well on the hills, where there is not enough grazing for cattle.'

Miss Elliott nodded. She was obviously knowledgeable about such things, perhaps more so than her callous brother.

An awkward silence now reigned. Eventually, Miss

Elliott broke it by rising gracefully to her feet. 'If you will excuse me, gentlemen, I shall go and change. I shall be but twenty minutes. James, would you be so kind as to order Lucifer to be brought round? Tam took him to the stable.'

Elliott, who had risen to his feet along with the others, grunted an incomprehensible response.

Ross moved quickly to open the door for her. 'Twenty minutes, do you say, Miss Elliott?' he said quietly, raising his eyebrows at her. 'It sounds as though you are a more remarkable woman than I had imagined.'

She smiled serenely back at him. 'Prepare to be astounded, Captain Graham.'

And he was.

Precisely seventeen minutes later, a vision in a dark blue riding habit swept down the grand staircase and into the great hall. Ross had the sudden impression that the suits of armour along the walls were standing to attention to salute the arrival of a great lady.

It seemed all the more appropriate since Miss Elliott's habit was of a very severe military cut, with black frogging down the front. It looked, Ross thought suddenly, as if she had been sewn into it, for it showed off the contours of her delectable figure more clearly than the lowest-cut evening gown could have done. Miss Elliott certainly spent a great deal on her wardrobe, to judge by this habit, and the matching shako-style hat she wore. Ross had been out of the country for too long to know whether it was quite the latest mode, but that mattered not a whit. In that dark blue garb, which served only to highlight the intense colour of her eyes, she would be the envy of any woman. And the delight of any man.

She was certainly a delight to Ross's eye. No doubt about that.

A sudden qualm hit him in the pit of the stomach. He couldn't be attracted to Miss Elliott, could he? No, he wouldn't permit that to happen, no matter how beautiful she was. He had forsworn all entanglements with females. Julie had deceived him. He would not permit himself to be betrayed again. And certainly not by someone of Cassandra Elliott's stamp. By all accounts, her family were little better than thieves and scoundrels.

Perhaps his own family had been the same? After all, there had been plenty of reivers in this part of Scotland. And smugglers, too. Until he discovered who and what his father had been, there would always be a nagging doubt that Ross was not truly entitled to call himself a gentleman. He would have to—

'Well, Captain Graham?' Her triumphant voice recalled him to the present.

'I concede, ma'am. As you predicted, I am astounded. And now, if you are ready, the horses are waiting outside. May I help you to mount?'

Chapter Six

It was utterly delightful to be riding again, out in the open air. Cassie had not been on Lucifer's back since the night she was caught trying to escape across the Solway. The groom must have been exercising him in the meantime, for he was rather better behaved than she had expected.

She patted his glossy brown neck as she rode. 'Good boy. Good boy,' she cooed in his ear. 'You would show us just how well behaved you can be, wouldn't you? Good boy.'

'You and your horse seem to be in remarkable sympathy, Miss Elliott.' The colonel matched his horse's pace to Lucifer's walk.

'I think he is determined to prove all the gentlemen wrong. That he can be a lady's mount, even though he may not look it.'

'I am more than happy to admit that I was wrong in that, Miss Elliott. He does seem to have very easy manners.'

Cassie said nothing. She just smiled and stroked Lucifer's neck once more.

The colonel began to point out some of the interesting aspects of the estate. Over the following twenty minutes or so, Cassie learned a great deal about cattle, and sheep, and the liming of fields using shell marl. She also saw for herself something that the colonel did not mention. The workers' cottages were clean and neat, and very clearly well maintained. If there was dire poverty in Galloway, it was not to be found on Colonel Anstruther's estate. And the workers they met were always ready with a smile and a bright 'Good afternoon'. There was none of the sullen silence that so often greeted James Elliott when he chanced upon his tenants. Not that such meetings happened often, for James Elliott rarely did the rounds of his own lands.

They had come, at last, to a broad hillside dotted with fat sheep, sweeping down to a glistening loch on the valley floor. 'Oh, how lovely it is,' Cassie exclaimed. 'Your estate is truly splendid, Colonel, and you are to be congratulated on the way you have managed it.'

'Not I alone. My dear wife deserves as much of the credit as I.'

'I have no doubt of it. And if she were here, I should be the first to say so. I hope you will tell her of my delight in what I have seen this afternoon.'

The colonel bowed his agreement.

'Colonel, might I tempt you to a gallop across this

hillside? It is wonderfully alluring, and I am sure Lucifer is not the only one who is longing to stretch his legs.' Galloping might not be a very ladylike thing to do, but here there was no one to witness her transgressions, except James and Captain Graham who were dawdling a long way behind. She glanced quickly over her shoulder at them. The two men appeared to be riding in stony silence.

Cassie turned her attention back to the colonel and smiled up at him.

'I think that galloping across open country with a beautiful lady is a young man's prerogative,' he said, with a slightly sad smile. Without waiting for Cassie's reply, he turned in his saddle and called to Captain Graham, who spurred his horse forward to join them. 'Captain Graham, Miss Elliott has expressed a desire to gallop down to the loch. Perhaps you would be so good as to accompany her?'

Oh, dear. James would be furious. He would assume that this was Cassie's doing, rather than the colonel's. 'I…I…had hoped that— Will you not accompany us also, Colonel?' she said in desperation.

'I am afraid not, Miss Elliott. This old horse of mine—' he stroked his horse's neck '—is long past doing more than a gentle amble. If I had thought you might wish to race, I should have brought out one of my younger horses. But this old fellow has served me well and deserves an outing now and then.'

Cassie nodded in sympathy. 'Ah, yes. When one has a favourite mount, it is difficult to give him up, even when he is getting old.'

'You have put your finger on my weakness, Miss Elliott. It is exactly so. Now, I suggest that you and Captain Graham make the most of the sunshine. I shall sit here and talk to your brother, ma'am, while you show me exactly what this Lucifer of yours can do.'

'Are you ready, ma'am?' the captain said. 'Are you for a gallop, or for a race?'

It was so tempting, but Cassie was in enough trouble already. 'A gallop, sir,' she said quickly, trying to frown at him. 'Surely you do not expect a lady to indulge in anything so vulgar as a horse race?' Behind her, Colonel Anstruther swallowed a laugh.

The captain, however, maintained his composure. 'Lead the way, ma'am, if you will.'

Cassie resolved to forget all about James and simply enjoy the moment. Gathering her reins, she touched Lucifer's flanks with her heel and her whip. In seconds, he was flying across the hillside.

Lucifer started off so swiftly that he had a twenty-yard start before Ross had even asked Hera to move a step. It might not be a race—though he doubted that—but Miss Elliott was certainly determined to show that her horse was capable of an amazing turn of speed. If he did not start soon, he would have no chance of catching them. Hera, too, was impatient to be off. She raced down the slope after Lucifer, the moment Ross gave her her head. 'Good girl. Let's show that devil ahead what a goddess can do, shall we?'

When they were about three-quarters of the way down the slope, Hera began to overhaul Lucifer. Ross could not believe it. It should not be happening. Something must be wrong. Lucifer was at least as fast as Hera, if not faster. Miss Elliott must be deliberately allowing Ross to catch her.

He was starting to come up with his quarry. Something was very wrong indeed. Miss Elliott, though the finest of horsewomen, was slipping in her saddle. The girth must be loose! She had managed to check the horse a little from his headlong gallop, but not enough for safety. Ross must stop them, or she would take a heavy fall. This time, she might really be hurt.

Ross urged Hera to a faster pace. In moments, she came fully alongside Lucifer. Then, dropping his reins and riding only with knees and heels, he stretched across the gap, grabbed Miss Elliott around the waist and pulled her roughly out of her saddle. 'Let go the stirrup,' he ordered sharply as he took her weight. But she had already done so. She must have known what he was about to do before he touched her. He lifted her into his lap with a sigh of relief. He had saved her.

He had reckoned without her stubbornness. Damn the woman! She was still holding Lucifer's reins. 'Let him go!' he cried. But she did not.

Hera could not possibly keep pace with Lucifer, now that she carried a double burden and he carried none. If Miss Elliott clung on to the reins, Lucifer would pull her out of Ross's grasp.

'Are you mad? Let go the reins!'

This time, she did. Ross slowed Hera's pace, but Lucifer galloped on down the hill. As he did so, the saddle slipped even more, until eventually it was almost hanging on the horse's side. That soon stopped his flight. No wonder. It must have felt very strange to him.

Ross settled Miss Elliot more comfortably in his lap and, reining Hera back to a walk, let her amble down to where Lucifer now stood, quietly cropping the grass at the edge of the loch, as if nothing untoward had happened. 'My dear Miss Elliott,' he said softly into her ear, suddenly conscious of how his breath fanned a tiny curl lying against her skin, 'you seem to have remarkably ill luck when you gallop Lucifer. I should have expected a horsewoman of your stamp to be more careful in the matter of girths.'

She was already white, but now became quite ashen. 'My brother—' She bit her lip and said nothing more.

So her brother had been responsible for the saddling of her horse. He would not have slackened the girths deliberately, would he? There could have been no way of knowing what would happen. She might have broken a leg. Or her neck.

Ross put that thought out of his mind, for it made him shudder. It was too wicked to contemplate. He forced himself, instead, to focus on how rewarding it was to be holding Miss Elliott so close. She was a most delicious armful. The skin on her cheeks was as fine as the finest peaches the colonel's succession houses might produce. Perhaps finer. And her subtle scent aroused all his senses. Lavender, was it? And perhaps a hint of citrus? He could not be sure, but he knew that, in the right circumstances, it would be intoxicating. He would love to hold her in his arms—in somewhere much less public than this open hillside— and explore just which parts of her beautiful body were responsible for that fragrance.

Her next words brought him back to earth. 'Sir, I think you should set me down.'

'Why? Would you rather walk than ride the two hundred yards to your mount?'

'It is most improper for me to be riding like this with a gentleman I barely know.'

He settled his arm more comfortably around her. He had absolutely no intention of letting her go. Not while he had the slightest excuse for continuing to hold her. 'Miss Elliott, there is no impropriety. Colonel Anstruther and your brother have been witnesses to everything that has happened. They will know, just as you do, that if I had not pulled you off Lucifer's back, you would have taken a nasty fall. You knew yourself that it was the only solution. You had your boot out of the stirrup already, had you not?'

'That was not in readiness for you, sir. I was simply making sure that Lucifer would not drag me along the ground once I had fallen off.'

Ross laughed, deep in his throat. 'But you still would not give up the reins, would you?'

'I would have. Eventually. I thought my weight would have stopped him quite quickly. It did before.'

Ross raised an eyebrow.

'And if he had not stopped, I *would* have let him go.'

'Glad to hear it, ma'am. It is good to see that you have learned some sense where that animal is concerned.'

'It was not his fault!' she protested hotly. 'You could see perfectly well that it was not. The saddle was slipping and, because we were galloping downhill, it was impossible for him to stop.'

Ross was silent for a moment. In fact, there was some truth in what she said. The circumstances had been very difficult. He doubted he would have been able to do any better, in her place. 'Miss Elliott, did you say your brother checked your horse's girths?'

'I...' She was blushing again. 'I thought he did, but perhaps it was Tam. My brother is a good horseman. He would not have made such a mistake.

Tam will be lucky to escape with just harsh words over this.'

She had avoided Ross's eyes as she spoke. He was sure—almost sure—that she did not believe a word of it. Did she really think he would be so easily fooled?

Cassie was very glad to be back in her own saddle on her own horse. She was safe enough now. Captain Graham had adjusted the saddle and checked the girths most carefully before throwing her up once more.

At least he had not touched her body again. Those few hundred yards they had ridden together had been most unsettling. The subtle scent of him—soap and leather and a hint of cologne—teased at her senses still. She had felt all sorts of tingles and urges that she was sure no lady should feel—or at least, should admit to feeling. His warm breath tickling her ear had sent shivers down her spine. His strong right arm, settled around the front of her waist as if it belonged there, had made her insides glow like rippling quicksilver. And after he had dismounted, there had been an unmistakeable glint in his eyes when he put his hands to her waist to lift her down. She was no lightweight, but to him she had seemed to weigh no more than a feather. And when she slid down into his arms, she had felt almost…caressed. For a second or two, she had been unable to breathe.

Yes, she was much safer on her own horse. Safer from herself.

'Do you feel well enough to ride back now, ma'am?'

'Of course, sir. Did you expect that I would not be?' Cassie was annoyed to hear a tiny hint of a quiver in her voice. If she had been alone, she would have cursed aloud. Instead, she just hoped that Captain Graham would blame it on her near disaster. Better for him to think her a weak woman than to suspect the real cause of that catch in her voice. Her precarious composure had been much too strongly affected by that short ride in his arms. Whereas he—obviously just as insensitive as most men she knew—seemed to have noticed nothing at all out of the ordinary.

At that moment, James Elliott reached them at the gallop. Colonel Anstruther was trailing some way behind, on his old, slow horse.

'Cassie! Are you hurt? What happened? It looked as if—'

'My saddle girths were loose,' she said flatly, trying to conceal her anger from Captain Graham. She would confront James, but not until they were alone.

'Tam!' James said, with venom. 'I'll have his hide. He could have killed you.'

'Well, he did not. Thanks to Captain Graham's quick thinking.' She smiled at her rescuer. 'I am truly grateful to you, sir.' She then turned to James, throwing him a meaningful look. She was determined that her brother would swallow his spite and behave properly. 'James?'

'Ah, yes, of course. Thank you, sir, for saving my sister. If you had not been close by, she would certainly have taken a bad fall. We are both most grateful.'

'I am only glad I was near enough to save you, ma'am. Now, had we not best be returning? Look, here is the colonel at last. He will wish to be reassured that you have come to no harm.'

The captain had not responded to James, Cassie noted. His words had been clearly directed to her. But she had no opportunity to ponder the reason for that snub, for the colonel was upon them and she had to explain her misadventure all over again.

'Did you deliberately loosen my girth?'

'Of course not. Why would I do such a dangerous thing? Tam must have—'

'Tam was nowhere near my horse and we both know it. I saw you by him, James. I thought you were tightening the girths. Now I see that it was nothing of the sort. I know you detest me, but why try to kill me?'

'I was not trying to kill you, you stupid wench. I was only—'

Cassie tried to control the anger that boiled up into her throat. She had suspected him, but she had never believed he would admit it. Now, she knew for certain. 'You must have had some other reason, then. Perhaps you would care to share it with me?' She kept her tone low and measured. It was not easy.

James ran his hand through his hair and started to pace about the colonel's library. 'It was a perfectly sensible thing to try. I knew you would feel the saddle slipping and take action to save yourself from real harm. You are too good a rider to do otherwise. I thought you might have a few bruises, be winded, that sort of thing.'

'But why?'

'Good God, Cassie, have you no brains between those pretty ears of yours? To extend this visit, of course. If you were injured, however slightly, Colonel Anstruther would have had to offer you hospitality until you were recovered. He would have had to stay here with you. And he would have been concerned about your injuries. It would have brought you closer to him.'

Cassie groaned. She could not help herself, for she was beginning to wonder whether James was totally sane. She had thought his previous cruelties were the result of his hatred of her, and of his desperate need for money to pay his mounting debts, but now she was no longer sure. He was obsessed with this mad idea of marrying her off to Colonel Anstruther. Did obsession lead to lunacy?

James was no longer paying any attention to Cassie. He seemed not to have noticed her distress. He continued to pace, muttering under his breath.

For the first time, Cassie was really frightened. Before, she had been afraid that he might force her to marry some terrible drunken crony of his, if he could find one who was wealthy enough. She had tried to flee, but she had always known that, even if she were dragged to the altar, there was still a chance that she might be able to persuade the minister that she was being married against her will.

But from this madness, there might be no escape. Not alive.

She must get away. Her only hope was to reach her godfather on the other side of the Solway. This time she must plan carefully. She must wait until James was away from Langrigg House. Preferably lying drunk in some whorehouse.

This time there must be no risk that she would be caught.

It was still very light when they sat down to dinner, for the colonel liked to keep country hours. 'It would make no difference in any case,' he said, in response to Cassie's comment. 'We could sit down at eight o'clock, or even nine, and it would still be light at this time of the year. I must admit it was something I missed, when we were in Spain. Darkness seemed to fall so early and so quickly. I missed the twilight. Did you find the same, Graham?'

'The contrast with my home in southern England is

not so great, sir. So I have to admit that I barely noticed the difference.'

'Perhaps you were too busy looking for somewhere to drink tea, sir?' Cassie asked mischievously.

Ross was surprised into a burst of laughter. 'Forgive me, Colonel. Something of a private joke. When Miss Elliott called on your wife in Dumfries, she created a fantastic image in her mind of young officers, sitting around the camp fire, sedately drinking bowls of tea. I told her, of course,' he continued with a half-smile, 'that we suffered nothing but the cruellest hardships and that polite tea-drinking played no part in army ma-noeuvres. But she would have none of it.'

The colonel smiled indulgently. 'I see. You would be wise not to believe the half of what young officers tell you, Miss Elliott. Notoriously unreliable, particu-larly when their aim is to bring wonder to a pair of pretty blue eyes.'

Was the colonel flirting with her? Cassie looked across the table to where James sat, alongside Captain Graham. James was looking particularly pleased. He must think his plans were making real progress. Could he not see the difference between fatherly concern and a lover's admiration? Captain Graham, sitting on the colonel's immediate left, was showing neither. For the moment, he seemed to be giving all his attention to the dishes set before them and to the colonel's exception-ally fine wine.

Cassie wondered again, for perhaps the hundredth time, whether she could and should confide in Captain Graham about her plans. He had saved her once—twice, if she included this afternoon's accident—and he knew just how evil James could be. But, if he helped her again, in something so serious, he might truly fall foul of the law. It was so very difficult. The truth was that, if she was to have any chance of success, Cassie needed some money. There was none to be had at Langrigg House, so her only option was to borrow. And the only possible sources of a loan were Colonel Anstruther and Captain Graham. There was no one else.

Cassie's stomach churned yet again at the prospect of asking either of those gentlemen for money, even as a loan. How could she possibly explain it? And what would they think of her? A lady must never take anything from a gentleman, unless he were related to her. A posy of flowers, perhaps, but nothing more. No jewels, or dresses, or other fripperies, and certainly no money. If she had had jewels of her own, it might have been possible to sell them, or pawn them. But she had nothing.

'A little more wine, Miss Elliott?'

'Er…just a little. Thank you, Colonel.' She told herself sternly to pay more attention. Daydreaming at the colonel's dinner table, even on so important a subject, would merely bring more of James's wrath upon her head. She *must* appear to be doing everything possible to ensnare her host. Then James might relax his vigilance a little. It needed only a little.

The second course had just been set out on the long table. 'May I help you to a little of this Rhenish cream, ma'am?'

'Thank you, colonel. Only a spoonful, if you would, for I see a dish of your beautiful strawberries at my brother's elbow and I should very much like to taste them again.'

The colonel nodded and beamed.

So did James.

Cassie forced herself to give all her attention to the conversation around the table. She would have plenty of opportunity to make her plans when she was in the drawing room, while the gentlemen sat at their port. She might be alone for quite a time.

She was just about to rise when Captain Graham said, 'I do hope you are fully recovered from this afternoon's unfortunate episode, Miss Elliott.'

He was looking straight into her eyes as he spoke. Was there something more there?

'A good night's sleep is bound to restore you, ma'am. Perhaps, Colonel, we should not sit too long over our port, this evening?'

'Quite so. Quite so. I was on the point of saying the very same thing. Besides, it would be the height of bad manners to abandon Miss Elliott when I have purposely invited her here to enjoy the house and garden. If you are not too fatigued, ma'am, we might perhaps take a stroll round the garden a little later? It seems to be a remarkably balmy evening.'

'That would be delightful, sir. I am sure the garden will be particularly beautiful in the gathering twilight. And, as it seems to mean a great deal to you, I should very much like to see its effects. I have been sadly untutored in the past.' Out of the corner of her eye, Cassie could see that James was beaming again. It was bad enough that he had concocted his wicked plans, but did he have to be quite so obvious about it?

Taking a final sip of her wine—she needed a little courage—Cassie rose in her place. The colonel moved quickly to pull back her chair. 'If you will excuse me, gentlemen, I will leave you to your port and retire to the drawing room.' She smiled round at them all.

Captain Graham moved to open the door for her. He was still looking at her in that peculiar way. What was he trying to tell her? But he said only, 'We will join you shortly, ma'am. I am very much looking forward to a stroll in the garden.'

Goodness! Now, what was the reason for that? Was he planning to cut out his host with the only female guest? Cassie felt a little fluttering in the pit of her stomach, at the thought that two gentlemen might be vying for her attention. Then her practical side reasserted itself. She must be imagining it.

* * *

James Elliott had taken his sister's empty place and was pouring himself yet another bumper of port. Any normal man would have had to be carried out after the amount Elliott had drunk, but he was clearly used to it. He was slurring his words a little, but that was all. So far.

Ross was giving half his mind to his conversation with the colonel, but part of his brain continued to puzzle over Miss Elliott, her brother, and all the extraordinary things Ross had learned about that family. Fraser, of course, had been as good as his word. Ross now knew that Cassandra Elliott was the daughter of a tyrant father and a lunatic mother.

No. That was not fair. Her mother had been confined to an asylum by her husband and had died there. But Fraser had not been able to state with certainty that the woman was actually mad. Ross knew of too many families who confined relatives in asylums for reasons other than madness. Given the powers that men had over wives and children, the Bedlam provided all too easy a prison for the difficult, the imperfect, or the simply unwanted.

Ross had set Fraser on to discover what the true reasons were. With luck, he would soon have something worthwhile to report. What he had discovered about the brother had merely confirmed Ross's own conclusions. The man was bad, through and through. He was a drinker and a gambler. He was a regular customer in all the local whorehouses. And he was said to be involved in smuggling. Considering the extent of his debts—which Fraser had also reported—Elliott seemed to be a singularly unsuccessful smuggler.

Miss Elliott, in contrast, was apparently none of these things, possibly because she had spent so many years in a fashionable Edinburgh seminary, well away from the influences of her father and brother. She was believed to be well educated and well read; and she had been in charge of running the household at Langrigg for several years, since just before the death of her father. According to Fraser, the gentry in Dumfries viewed Miss Elliott as something of a recluse. She was rarely seen in the town and did not make calls. Moreover, the ladies of Dumfries were not made welcome if they visited Langrigg House. Miss Elliott herself was a perfect hostess, but her brother was always in attendance and he made callers feel uneasy. Fraser had been able to learn of no one who had visited twice.

It was a truly strange household. Ross's curiosity was piqued. If he could persuade Miss Elliott to walk with him, tête-à-tête, he might be able to discover the answers to some of his many questions.

Ross's conscience smote him then. Aye, he knew well enough that it was more than idle curiosity. He must admit that he was sorry for the girl. And that he

would help her if he could. Her life must be intol-
erable. It was only right that a gentleman should feel
compassion.

That was all it was. Nothing more. Just compassion.

Cassie sat alone by the fire, stitching methodically.
In, out. In, out. The colonel, the captain; the colonel,
the captain. In, out; in out. She could not decide.
Which of them would she dare to confide in?

The colonel was older, fatherly. He might deal with
a father's care. Then again, he might react with a
father's horror at what she was doing.

The captain was younger. Cassie recognised at that
moment that she knew practically nothing about
Captain Graham. The colonel had spoken for him—
that was in his favour—but he might be a gambler and
a drunkard, just like James. How would she ever
know?

Who to trust? In, out; in, out. She might as well
leave it to chance.

If the opportunity offered in conversation with either
of them, she must seize it. For, by tomorrow evening,
she would be back in her prison at Langrigg House.

Chapter Seven

Colonel Anstruther brought his teacup back himself. 'It is still a beautiful evening, Miss Elliott. Would you care for a stroll in the garden? I can send a servant for your shawl, if you wish.'

Cassie rose, smiling up at him. 'I came prepared, sir.' She indicated a fine Norwich shawl lying across the back of a chair by the fireplace. 'I was admiring the garden from my bedroom window and imagining just how it would be in the twilight. I am glad that the weather has remained so mild.'

The colonel beamed. Then he fetched Cassie's shawl and draped it carefully round her shoulders. 'If you are ready, ma'am?' he said, offering his arm.

'May I join you, sir?'

'Why, yes, of course, Graham. And you, too, Elliott, if you wish.'

James shook his head, muttering something about his lack of interest in gardens. As the little party made its way out through the door to the garden, James slumped back into his chair, reaching for his glass. Cassie found herself wishing that the colonel's hospitality was rather less generous. By the time she returned, her brother was likely to be very drunk indeed. She resolved to escape to her bedchamber as soon as she could. If James was going to become belligerent, as he often did when in his cups, she did not want to witness it. She had too often been the butt of his crude and cruel jokes. To suffer such humiliation in front of the colonel—or Captain Graham—would be more than she could bear.

The garden paths were not wide enough for three persons to walk abreast. Colonel Anstruther led the way, with Cassie on his arm. Captain Graham followed a pace or two behind, just close enough to take part in the conversation.

Cassie tried to swallow her frustrations. She had resolved to confide in whichever of the gentleman provided the first opportunity. But with both of them at her side, there was likely to be no opportunity at all.

Ross was listening with half an ear to the colonel's description of the plants in his garden. The names meant little to him, but he had to admit that the effect was very pleasing, even though some of the shrubs and flowers were newly planted and still small.

'In a few years' time, the jasmine will have completely covered this arch,' the colonel said, indicating a climbing plant with very dark leaves and tiny white trumpet-shaped flowers.

Miss Elliott bent down to sniff at them. 'Mmm. Such a wonderful fragrance. I would not have expected it to flower so young, sir. It must be because of the sheltered aspect of this garden, do you think?'

'Possibly. It seems to be growing away strongly. My wife tells me that, in its native habitat, it is something of a weed, romping through everything.'

'Where is its native habitat, sir?' Ross was trying to sound more interested than he really was. He had rarely given a thought to plants and gardens before.

The colonel grimaced, and then grinned a little sheepishly. 'I'm afraid, Graham, that I don't know the answer to that. I have a vague idea it might be Madeira, but… No, I think I am confusing this plant with another one. Something my wife mentioned. Perhaps Miss Elliott knows for sure?'

The lady shook her head. 'I'm afraid I'm not certain, sir. I think Mrs Anstruther did speak of a jasmine from Madeira, a very highly scented one, that she hoped one day to possess. But it is a plant for the conservatory only, I think. I must confess I have forgotten the name.'

'I shall consult my wife. If it's from Madeira, she shall have it, when my expedition returns.'

'You have sent out a plant-hunting expedition, sir?

Why that is most wonderful. To see all those amazing plants in their native abundance… Oh, what a delight that must be.'

'Forgive me, Miss Elliott. I did not mean to mislead you. I do intend to send out an expedition, but it has not yet left these shores. It had been my intention to lead it myself, but that is no longer possible, because…' He cleared his throat. 'I am now looking for someone trustworthy to take my place as leader. Once I have found him, I will be able to make the final arrangements.'

'An expedition leader would have to be a remarkable man, I would imagine,' Miss Elliott said thoughtfully. 'For he must combine so many qualities—a profound knowledge of plants, of course, and the ability to lead a band of men in often difficult and dangerous circumstances. I assume it would also help if he had some knowledge of seafaring as well. Do you think you will find this paragon you are seeking, sir?'

'I do not believe it is essential for the leader to be knowledgeable in seamanship or in horticulture, ma'am, provided there are sufficient among the expedition members who do have that knowledge. I was planning to lead it myself, after all, and I am far from skilled in such matters. As my ignorance demonstrated just a moment ago.'

Miss Elliott smiled. It was a smile full of understanding. 'You are too hard on yourself, I think, sir.

But I do understand your reasoning. The leader would need to be awake on all suits and to be ready to deal with any emergency. He would be unlikely to be doing that if his eyes were fixed on the ground, searching for rare specimens. Better that he keep his eyes on the horizon, perhaps, watching for pirates?'

'Would the necessary qualities not depend, sir, on the precise destination of the expedition?' Ross asked, trying to ignore the mischief in Miss Elliott's voice.

'Yes, of course. An expedition to Madeira alone would present no real dangers. Why, I have heard that invalids go there, nowadays, to take advantage of the climate. I believe it is very mild. And very good for the health.' He stopped abruptly. 'I wonder whether… But no. She would never stand the journey.' His voice had sunk to a whisper. He was talking to himself, rather than to his companions.

Ross felt a pang of sympathy for the man. As usual, he was thinking about his poor wife and looking for something—anything—to ease her suffering. But surely she would be unable to stand a voyage lasting for weeks? And what if the ship met bad weather?

'What is the destination of your proposed expedition, Colonel?'

'I had hoped to fund a ship for southern Africa, ma'am. That was why I mentioned Madeira. The ship would call there on its outward and return journeys. I intended to collect some plants from there on the way home.'

'Oh, I do envy you, sir. I should so love to go on such an expedition. But it would be impossible, I suppose?'

The colonel smiled indulgently. 'I have not heard that any lady has ever taken part in such an expedition, ma'am. And if you have read of the hardships experienced by Sir Joseph Banks and his companions, you will not wonder at it.'

'I have read of Sir Joseph's adventures with Captain Cook. But surely that was much different? They were venturing into lands where white men had never been seen before. Whereas your expedition—'

'My expedition is quite likely to encounter hostile natives in Africa, ma'am. It would be no place for any woman, and certainly not for a lady.'

'As far as Madeira only, perhaps?'

He patted her hand in a fatherly way. 'That might be possible. For a married lady, with her husband. But I doubt your brother would agree to accompany you on such a trip, ma'am.'

'No, he would not,' she said bleakly.

Cassie said nothing more. There was no point. The colonel, like so many gentlemen, was convinced that ladies were much too frail to undertake any journey beyond a few miles. And certainly not one where there was the least possibility of meeting danger. If she said anything more, it might allow her frustration to show.

That would be extremely unwise, besides being impolite to her kind host.

Colonel Anstruther seemed to have noticed nothing. He was in full flow about the plans for the garden. As he talked, Cassie's cross mood receded. He might not be terribly knowledgeable, but he had caught something of his wife's passion, and he spoke with real dedication. Cassie was sure that, whether or not Mrs Anstruther lived to see it, the garden would be finished.

'This part of the garden, Miss Elliott, is barely touched, so far. But we have interesting plans. I can show you a drawing, if you should like.'

Cassie nodded.

'Over there—' Colonel Anstruther pointed to where the ground rose to form a small hillock '—we plan to— Yes, Gordon, what is it?'

One of the footmen had appeared, quite suddenly. 'Begging your pardon, Colonel, but I...but Mr Elliott...' He stopped, self-consciously. The sideways glance he stole at Cassie made her shudder. What on earth had James done now?

'Well, what is it? Spit it out, man!'

'Er...Mr Elliott is...has had rather too much...' He cleared his throat. 'One of the maids says that he...'

'Ah, yes,' the colonel said before the man could finish. 'I shall come at once.'

Cassie turned to accompany him.

'No, no, Miss Elliott. There is no need for you to come.'

'But he is my brother, sir. I am well used to dealing with these…er… unfortunate starts.'

The colonel shook his head sympathetically. 'No doubt you are, ma'am, but on this occasion I fancy it would be better if a man dealt with this slight…difficulty. Your brother will be more likely to take heed of what his host has to say than his sister.'

Goodness, the colonel was being extremely blunt, Cassie thought.

'Captain Graham, perhaps you would be so kind as to allow Miss Elliott to take your arm. There is much more of the garden to see and we will not have another such evening in which to enjoy it.'

Cassie knew she had no choice. And the colonel was probably right. James had paid precious little heed to her pleas in the past. Why should he start now? But he would not be able to ignore a complaint from his host. She nodded. 'Thank you, Colonel. Captain Graham and I will miss being able to ask questions about the garden, but we shall enjoy it, none the less. And please accept my apologies for my brother's behav—'

'Nothing more to be said, ma'am. Nothing at all. I promise you it will be resolved in a trice. Enjoy the rest of your stroll.' With that, he hurried up to the house in the wake of the liveried footman.

Captain Graham offered his arm. 'Shall we walk, Miss Elliott?'

Cassie could not look at him. She knew her embarrassment was clearly written on her features. What woman would not feel stricken at the appalling behaviour of such a brother? Drunk, certainly, and no doubt pestering his host's maids before he had been in the house for half a day. It was scandalous.

Captain Graham tucked Cassie's hand comfortably under his arm. There was a smile in his voice as he said, 'I beg you, Miss Elliott, do not concern yourself. You cannot be your brother's keeper. If he behaves in a way that is…ah…ungentlemanly, it is none of your doing. If he were to take his example from you, no one would have anything to reproach him with.'

Cassie swallowed very hard. 'That is the kindest thing you could possibly have said to me, sir,' she whispered, still not daring to look up at him.

He must have sensed her continuing embarrassment, for he put his free hand over hers, where it rested on his sleeve, and squeezed gently. 'Miss Elliott, pray do not concern yourself. Colonel Anstruther does not blame you in the least. And neither does anyone else.' He squeezed again. 'Neither do I.'

A shiver of awareness rippled through the flesh of her hand and tingled up her arm. It was as if she had been touched by a hot wire, and yet it did not burn. It was more a sensation of melting and glowing, like the embers in a banked fire. What did it mean? Why was she responding in this way to a man who was almost a stranger to her? An inner voice reminded Cassie that he was a stranger who had saved her more than once. Although she had known him for such a short time, it seemed as if she understood him, almost as well as she understood herself.

She shook her head a little to clear the strange sensation. She must dismiss such fanciful notions and find a way to ask for the captain's help. At any moment the colonel might return and her opportunity to confide would be lost.

'I wonder what the colonel's plans are for this odd-shaped hummock?' Captain Graham said companionably. 'Shall we take a look? Ah, take care, ma'am.' He pulled her sharply towards him. 'The ground is muddy just here.'

'Thank you, sir.' She stepped carefully to the side. The mud had made the path so narrow that they were almost touching with every stride. Captain Graham had drawn her very close. It was only to protect her from the wet but it felt…it felt… Oh, she could not tell how it felt, except that she had spent so many years of her life avoiding men whose aim was certainly not to protect her. With Captain Graham she had no doubt that his intentions were both kind and generous.

She smiled up at him, allowing him to guide her

steps. 'You seem to have forgot, sir, that when you first saw me, I was mud-spattered from head to toe. You must know that I am not used to such courtesy.'

Was that another slight squeeze of her fingers? It was so fleeting she could not be sure.

'I have no doubt you had your reasons for what you did that day, ma'am. And at your request, I have forgotten it. In any case, it would be no justification for me to treat you as less than a lady.'

The glint in his blue eyes was not humour. Not now. It was more than kindness. There was an intensity of feeling there that Cassie did not dare to put a name to.

Now was the moment. She would never have a better opportunity. 'Captain Graham, may I ask a favour of you?'

He looked surprised, but merely said, 'Why, of course, ma'am. Please do. If I can help you in any way, it would be my pleasure.'

Cassie felt herself blushing. Just wait until he heard what she was going to ask. 'Captain Graham, I…I… Oh dear, this is going to sound so strange. And so very improper. Sir…I am desperately in need of some ready money. I…I wondered if it might be possible to ask you for a small loan?'

Now, he was clearly quite astonished. 'A loan, ma'am? But surely, your brother—'

'No, sir, my brother— I cannot apply to my brother for this. Forgive me. I cannot explain why.'

'Nor is it my place to ask,' he added quickly, smiling at her.

Cassie fancied it was supposed to be a reassuring smile. But, in truth, it contained more puzzlement than reassurance. She waited.

After a moment, he said, 'Miss Elliott, I…I find it difficult to know how to respond to such a request.'

Oh, dear. She would have to say something now. She decided to stick as closely as possible to the truth. 'I need to pay a visit to my godfather, on the English side of the Solway. It is…er…most urgent that I do so, but he has been estranged from my family for many years. My brother would prevent the visit if he knew.'

'Was that where you were going when I first—'

'Hush!' Cassie whispered, glancing round to see if they were overheard. 'Better to speak no more of that. But, yes. You are right.'

'Miss Elliott, I would willingly help you, if I could. But it does seem an extraordinary request for a lady to make. You could perhaps write to your godfather?'

There was nothing for it but to tell him at least part of the rest. 'My…er…my brother checks all the letters leaving Langrigg. He would not permit such a letter to be sent.'

'Ah, there I *can* help you, ma'am. If you were to give your letter to me, I could ensure that it was despatched without your brother's knowledge.'

Cassie grimaced a little. 'I doubt that, sir. My

brother has many spies in Dumfries and beyond. A
letter addressed to my godfather would almost certainly find its way back to James.'

'Good God, ma'am! Does the law hold no sway in
this part of the country?'

'Not when the devil is in James Elliott, I fear. Not
when he has the ability to grease palms. He may
ensure that his sister never touches a golden guinea,
but he has plenty when he needs them.' As soon as
those bitter words were out, Cassie knew she should
not have spoken so frankly. Especially to a compara-
tive stranger. But Captain Graham's face was full of
sympathy. And if she asked him to preserve her confidence, he would surely do it. He was an officer and
a gentleman, after all.

'Sir…what I said just now. I should not have— It
was not a proper thing to—'

'Think no more of it, Miss Elliott. I have forgotten
it already.'

His bright blue eyes were smiling confidingly into
Cassie's. She knew, without the trace of a doubt, that
she could trust this man. She would tell him the whole
truth. All of it, no matter how degrading.

She opened her mouth to begin, but he was before
her.

'I have another proposal to make, Miss Elliott. Give
your letter to me and I will deliver it to your godfather
personally. No one will be able to intercept it on behalf

of your brother, because no one—except us two—will know that it exists.' He grinned at her. 'Surely that is the best solution?'

No, it was not. Little did he know what he risked. 'Captain Graham, I— Might we walk a little further from the house? And away from this shrubbery? If we are to talk frankly—and I fear we must—I would prefer there to be no possibility of eavesdroppers.'

He said nothing, but a shadow of concern crossed his face. He tucked her hand more closely under his arm and walked her, in silence, into the open area of the garden where there was no cover at all. No one would be able to overhear their discussion. When they reached the low lily pond, he paused and turned to face her. He still said nothing. He just stood, waiting.

Cassie took a deep breath, pulled her hand from his arm and clasped her fingers tightly together in front of her. She must not be embarrassed by this. It was too important. If she trusted the captain—and she knew, instinctively, that she could—she must tell him everything and rely on him to help her.

'Captain Graham, you are all kindness, and I do appreciate your offer. Very much. But I dare not accept it. Allow me to speak frankly. I am very much afraid of my brother's violence. To me, and to others. If he were to discover that you were carrying my letter to my godfather, he would do almost anything to stop you. He has no scruples in such matters. On your first encounter, he merely threw you into gaol. He was relying on the law to do the vile business for him. I have to tell you that he admitted as much to me. I fear that, if he caught you, he would not involve the law again. There are many drowning accidents in the Solway, you know. One more would not be unusual. And it would not be investigated, either.'

'Come, Miss Elliott, surely you exaggerate? I cannot believe that any gentleman would behave so. Your brother clearly has a violent temper, but murder? No, it must be impossible.'

He was looking at her so very strangely. What was he thinking? And then it came to her. That quizzical look betrayed him. He thought she was mad. He thought she was imagining all sorts of plots that did not exist. He probably thought she should be consigned to the Bedlam forthwith. Oh, it would be amusing, if her situation were not so dire. How ironic that James had threatened her with the asylum and now Captain Graham had concluded the same. There was no point in pursuing this discussion any further. His mind was closed to all her entreaties.

'I can see that you find it difficult—impossible—to believe me, sir.' She shook her head firmly, with more than a hint of exasperation. She did not care if he knew it. 'So let us speak of other things. You said you live in London, I believe?'

'If I did, I misled you, ma'am.' She fancied he was

relieved that she had changed the subject. 'I do not have a house in London. Before I came north, I was certainly there, visiting…er…an old army friend of mine. He has property in London and is always happy to give me house room when I go up to town. My own house is down in Wiltshire.'

So he *did* have an estate of his own. James would crow with delight at that news. Yet, there was something in the way he had described what he had been doing in London. That uncharacteristic hesitation. Cassie could almost have sworn that he had something to hide. What on earth could it be?'

'Wiltshire. I know where it is on a map, of course. We had interminable lessons on such things in Edinburgh. But I have no idea what it is like. Is it a flat county, sir? Is it beautiful?'

'By comparison with the landscape here, it is somewhat tame, I would say. But it is beautiful in its own way. The rolling downs are very pleasant. And there are many fine old estates.'

'Yours is also an old family holding, I presume?'

'Er…no. My agent found it for me when I came of age. It was conveniently enough located. And, to tell the truth, I have spent very little time there. You must understand that I have been serving in the army for many years.'

'Of course. I had forgot. After our discussions on the availability of tea in the Peninsula, I should have remembered.' She started to walk back towards the main path, knowing that he would follow. After a few steps, she turned and smiled innocently up at him. 'I think you mentioned, when we last met, that your family came from this part of Scotland?'

'Did I? That would surprise me, for—to be frank, as you have been, ma'am—I do not know quite where my family comes from.'

This time, it was he who had been touched on the raw. His tone was surprisingly sharp. For a moment, Cassie thought she was treading on Solway quicksand, but the captain's brow cleared in seconds. He spoke again in quite a normal voice. 'Forgive me, ma'am. I did not intend to be rude. Yours was a perfectly normal question and should have received a normal answer. The truth is that I believe my family comes from the area around Dumfries, but as yet I cannot say for sure. Both my parents are dead and I have no living relatives to consult.'

'Oh!' Cassie's mind was suddenly full of questions that pushed aside her own troubles. Poor Captain Graham. It must be sad to have no roots. She determined to be helpful. 'Well, sir, Graham is not a particularly common name around Dumfries. Apart from the Graham Arms at Longtown. I should have thought it would not be too difficult to discover your ancestors.'

'I thought the same, ma'am. And the truth is that I

have been trying since I arrived in Scotland. But there is no trace of any relation of mine in these parts. Perhaps I was mistaken. I was relying on something I remembered from my boyhood. Childish memories can be notoriously fickle.'

Cassie nodded, stricken. Her own childhood memories, especially memories of her mother, had faded so much that there was precious little left. And she was no longer sure that what she did remember was true. It might only be wishful thinking that her mother had been beautiful. And had loved her.

She felt a lump rise in her throat. Now was not the time to think of such distressing things. Now she needed to ensure that Captain Graham had reason to reconsider her plea for help. Perhaps there was some way she could discuss it further with him?

'I do not recall the Graham Arms,' he said thoughtfully. 'But then I avoided Longtown on my way north. It is near Carlisle, is it not?'

'Yes, sir. At least, I believe so. I have never been there myself. Apart from my journeys to Edinburgh, when I was at the seminary, I have travelled very little. And Longtown is not on the road to Edinburgh.'

He grinned at her. 'Quite so, ma'am. But I was wondering whether there might be something to discover in Longtown. After all, such inn names usually relate to a local family of note. Perhaps there is information to be had there.'

She nodded. Perhaps there was. Her heart seemed to miss a beat. It was as if she had been startled in the midst of a reverie. She had not thought until now that he might leave Dumfries. Yet it was bound to happen. Of course it was. He had no ties here and a home in the south of England. Of course he would leave. But somehow she had come to feel that he was here to help her—to save her—and that he would always be beside her, providing a strong arm to lean on.

Cassie berated herself. Oh, foolish woman! Have you not learned, by now, that no man can be depended upon? If you are to be saved from the fate James has in store for you, you will have to save yourself.

Chapter Eight

Ross took the brandy glass from the colonel's outstretched hand and sank into one of the chairs by the fire. The colonel's library was a most pleasant room. Unlike the rest of the house, which was furnished in the latest style and with no expense spared, this room was designed for comfort and relaxation. The furniture was old fashioned and, in places, a little threadbare, but a man could easily doze against the well-filled cushions and, if snuff or cigar ash fell upon the chairs, it would be of no concern. Indeed, the colonel's favourite chair, on the other side of the fire, showed distinct signs of having been singed.

The colonel had clearly noticed Ross's inspection of the room. 'Not exactly all the crack, is it, Graham?' he said with a low chuckle. 'My wife chose the furnishings for the rest of the house, but not here. She says she would not dream of wasting my money on changing a room where I am so happy to burn the furniture and the carpets.' He indicated the Turkey rug in front of the fire.

Ross realised that the marks he had assumed to be part of the pattern were actually black burns. He smiled, conspiratorially.

Colonel Anstruther reached into his inside pocket and produced his cigar case. 'Would you care to smoke, Captain? I assume that, like me, you got into the habit in Spain.'

'Perhaps outside on the terrace, sir?'

'Certainly, if you wish, but there is no need. In this room, I do allow myself to indulge in that particular vice.'

Ross accepted one of the long thin cigars and allowed the colonel to light it for him. He slowly drew the smoke deep into his lungs and leaned back in his chair. The colonel did the same, enjoying the moment. There was no need for words. Brandy and cigars, a seasonal fire, and a comfortable room, were sufficient by themselves. Ross blew a cloud of smoke towards the ceiling and took another sip from his glass.

What a very strange day it had been, to be sure. Until today, he would not have thought of calling Miss Elliott hysterical. Even on the links of the Solway, she had seemed admirably sure of what she was about. Yet she must be wrong about her brother. No doubt James Elliott was a rakehell of the worst stamp—a drunkard, a womaniser, a gambler—but murder? Murder was something completely different. Ross could not bring himself to believe that a gentleman born would stoop to that. What's more, Cassandra Elliott seemed to be in fear for her own safety. Yet she was of the man's own blood. Surely even the lowest dregs of humanity would not injure a woman of his own blood? Did she really believe her brother might kill her?

And then there had been that hint that Elliott was not of sound mind. *When the devil was in him...* Now that, perhaps... Maybe there was something in that? Drink had unpredictable effects on a man. As did womanising. A thought struck Ross like a thunderbolt. What if Elliott were poxed? The pox was known to lead to madness. And death. Ross shook his head, trying to clear his thoughts. It *was* possible. He should have thought of it before. If James Elliott had the pox, it was most definitely possible that he was going insane. And an insane man, on the verge of penury, might do anything to save his own skin.

Ross's tangled thoughts were interrupted by the colonel, who rose from his chair and said, 'I think I shall take a stroll around the garden before I turn in. I missed the best of it when I had to come in to deal with that...unfortunate episode with Elliott. Damned blackguard, interfering with innocent maids. If it weren't for his sister, I'd have shown him the door, I tell you frankly.' He started to leave, but paused when Ross rose to accompany him. 'No need to bother,

Graham. You've already seen most of the garden. Stay and relax over your cigar. I shall enjoy a solitary stroll.' Polite though he was, the colonel was making it perfectly clear that he wanted to be alone.

Ross nodded and sank back into his chair, still wondering about James Elliott. Did he deserve the name of a gentleman? He had been born to inherit as laird, but even the grandest families had the occasional changeling. After all, this was a man who had spent his first night in the colonel's house getting drunk and then trying to rape one of the maids. If he was capable of that, was he also capable of murder? And of laying violent hands upon his own sister? Correction—half-sister. That might make a difference.

He drained his glass, took a last draw on his cigar and threw the stub into the fire. It was a very strange business, he thought, shaking his head. The question was, what was he to do about it? Miss Elliott had asked for his help—had steeled herself to ask him for money—and he had spurned her. He had more or less told her she was letting her imagination get the better of her. Good God, he had as good as told her she was mad! She had been angry at him, and no wonder. To a lady whose mother had died in the asylum, there could be few worse insults.

And what if her fears were justified?

No. No, it must be impossible. He would try to draw her out a little more, discover exactly why she believed she needed to flee across the Solway, perhaps even lend her the money she needed. But he could not bring himself to believe that the laird of Langrigg was a murderer.

'Ah, there ye are, Graham. I've been wanting a word wi' ye.' Elliott stood in the open doorway, swaying a little. He was clearly still much the worse for drink.

Ross rose from his chair and put his brandy glass down on the small piecrust table. He stood with his legs slightly apart, the weight on the balls of his feet, his hands hanging loosely at his sides. There was no knowing what Elliott might do, so it was best to be ready for anything, including a physical attack. At least, if it happened this time, it would be one against one. With those odds, Ross would not expect to lose again.

'You seemed to be enjoying your little tryst with m'sister.'

It was useless to chop logic with a drunk. 'Miss Elliott and I had a very pleasant stroll around the garden. Together with the colonel.'

'Aye. For a wee bit. Until he came back here to hassle me.'

Ross said nothing. If the man had a point to make, he would get to it eventually. Ross casually picked up his glass and drank the final few drops of his brandy, before setting it down again. He needed his hands free.

Elliott walked rather unsteadily into the room. 'Any more of that brandy? I could do with a wee reviver. I'm fair parched.' He picked up the colonel's used glass and filled it from the decanter. He drained the liquor in a single swallow and then filled the glass again.

James Elliott was certainly no gentleman.

Ross tried to keep his expression from betraying his distaste. 'You wanted a word?' he said neutrally.

Elliott slumped into the colonel's chair, his brandy balloon in one hand and the decanter in the other. 'Aye. 'Bout m'sister. Ye've caught her up twice now, so I thought ye might like to make an honest woman of her.'

'Sir, you go too far! Miss Elliott's reputation is—'

'Dinna fash yersel', man! I'm no' accusing ye of anything.' The man's cultured accent seemed to have disappeared along with the colonel's brandy. He had begun to sound like one of his own servants.

'Glad to hear it. A lady's reputation is a precious thing, and—'

'Let's cut t' the chase, Graham. Thing is, m'sister needs a husband and I'm thinking that ye might be the very man. Ye're a gentleman, wi' a guid income and yer own estate. What mair could she want?'

'Your sister and I are barely acquainted.'

'I can tell ye all ye need to know. She's a guid manager, ye ken. Been running Langrigg fer years. And ye'll admit she's bonnie.'

He was waiting for an answer, so Ross nodded. It was true enough.

'And she's still untouched. I can vouch fer that.'

Ross's flesh was beginning to crawl. The man was describing a lady as if she were a horse at auction.

'Now, the real question is, how much?'

'How much?' Ross repeated, startled into speech.

'Aye. How much will ye give me fer the lass?'

'Are you telling me, Elliott,' Ross said slowly, pronouncing each word with great care as if he were talking to a very small child, 'that you are prepared to sell your sister to me?'

Elliott drained his brandy and slumped back in the chair, laughing. 'What else can a man do wi' her? I canna take her to wife mysel', can I? If I can get her leg-shackled, I can get me a wife to run the house instead. That'd be cheaper than Cassie.' He refilled his glass. 'Aye, that'd be a fair bit cheaper.'

Ross felt the anger growing in his gut, like metal boiling in the furnace, just waiting to burst out into fiery wrath. He mastered it. With difficulty. 'How much did you have in mind?' The words came out softly, through gritted teeth, but Elliott was too far gone to notice.

'Twenty thousand.'

That was a fortune. Ross could not lay his hands on such a sum unless he sold almost everything he possessed. 'That is…a good price, certainly. And, in return, the bridegroom would get?'

'Why, Miss Cassandra Elliott of Langrigg. Whit else?'

'I was thinking of your sister's dowry, as a matter of fact,' Ross said carefully.

In spite of his drunken state, Elliott had begun to look a little sheepish. 'Ain't no dowry.'

'She has nothing from her mother? You surprise me.' Ross knew that his measured tones were getting under Elliott's skin. Good. He needed to find out as much as possible about the man's intentions.

'Nothing. It was all used up in paying for— Never you mind. It's gone. She comes with what she stands up in. An' that bluidy horse, too, since I canna ride him.'

'I have to say, Elliott, that you are making a singularly poor fist of the business of selling your sister.'

Elliott hauled himself to his feet and glared at Ross. 'Enough o' yer jaw-me-dead talk. D'ye want her, or no'?'

Ross walked quietly across to the door. 'I fear she is above my touch. You will have to look elsewhere for your rich mark. Good night to you.'

Ross drove his clenched fist into his open palm. What a fool he had been! Everything Miss Elliott had said, everything she had hinted, it was all true. And that was probably not the half of it. Hanging was too good for James Elliott. What he needed was something much slower, and much, much more painful.

Ross resisted the urge to slam the door of his bed-chamber. It would achieve nothing. And if anyone else heard, it would lead to questions. Questions which he was in no position to answer.

He had questions of his own, now. Miss Elliott could be in real danger. She had asked him for help—had breached a lady's code of behaviour to do so—and he had refused her. He had allowed his own concept of honour to colour his response, even while he knew that she was not the sort of hysterical woman to make serious allegations without reason.

It was not only Elliott who deserved to be shot. It was Ross himself. How could he have been so stupid, so prejudiced—?

Enough of that! He could indulge his guilty conscience later. For now, he had to decide on a course of action. The visit would be over in little more than twelve hours. Miss Elliott, and her appalling brother, would leave for Langrigg and for the danger that awaited her there. Ross might well have no further chance of private conversation with her. She had given him the chance, there in the garden, and he had spurned it.

'Are you for bed now, sir?' Fraser asked, appearing silently from the dressing room.

'No.' Ross took a candle to the small writing desk by the window and drew out paper and ink. He scrawled a few words, folded the sheet and sealed it with a wafer from the drawer. 'Fraser, I need you to convey this note to Miss Elliott.'

'Aye, sir.' Fraser did not move. His face was a blank mask.

'Now, Fraser.'

'Aye, sir. I take it you won't be wanting her brother to know about it?' He spoke as if it was the most normal thing in the world to be conveying notes to un-married ladies in the middle of the night.

'Correct, Fraser. Do it now, and ensure that no one apart from Miss Elliott herself is aware of it.'

'Am I to wait for a reply, sir?'

Ross could not prevent himself from grinning at his imperturbable manservant. The situation was more than ridiculous. 'No, Fraser. No reply. Just get it done as fast as you can. Then come back here. I may need you again.'

Fraser nodded and left as quietly as he had come.

Ross began to pace the room, trying to come up with some kind of a plan. The question of money was easily resolved. He would give—no, lend—Miss Elliott whatever she required. But should he tell her what her brother was about? Should he hint at his suspicion about Elliott's sanity? Surely not. How could he do that, without also speaking of the foul illness that was the likely cause? Miss Elliott was a woman of decided character, but even she would be mortified by talk of brothels and the pox.

He was still undecided when Fraser returned.

In response to Ross's raised eyebrow, Fraser said simply, 'It's done, sir. I gave it into her own hand. Her woman saw me, of course, but you need have no worries on that score. Morag would never betray her mistress.'

Yet more of Fraser's information gathering, it seemed. Ross nodded, reassured. What he was planning to do could put Miss Elliott in danger. He needed to take every possible precaution to protect her.

'I have asked Miss Elliott to meet me in the garden, Fraser. As soon as she is able. I will do my best to ensure we are not seen, of course, but I need you to guard my back.'

'Aye, sir.' Fraser grinned. 'Shall I need a pistol?'

'No. It's not brute force I need, but a diversion. Watch Elliott for me. He's in his room, I think. If he should come out, I need you to find a way of delaying him and to make as much noise as possible while you do it. That should give me enough warning to get Miss Elliott safely back into the house without being caught.'

'You'll make sure the side doors are open before you go out, sir?'

Ross grinned his response. Fraser knew perfectly well that Ross would secure more than one escape route before entering the danger zone. They had both learned the value of that, more than once.

'May I suggest a greatcoat, sir? Probably better to

cover that white shirt. The moon's still pretty bright out there.'

Fraser was right. There was no time to change. He needed to remain a shadowy figure, if he possibly could. Fraser was already fetching the greatcoat from the clothes press. In a matter of moments, Ross had donned it and was stealing quietly along the corridor and down the stairs to the garden door.

'Make haste, Morag.'

'I canna go any faster with ye jigging about like that, Miss Cassie.'

Cassie stood still while Morag fastened the last hooks on her gown. Then, full of impatience, she hurried to the window and opened the shutters just a crack. The garden was still full of moonlight. And in the distance, in the shadow of an old oak tree, she could just make out a tall dark figure. Was it Captain Graham?

It must be. Who else would be leaning against a tree in the colonel's garden at this time of night? It was certainly not James, for she would have recognised his silhouette immediately.

'He is waiting. I must go down.'

'Are ye sure, lassie?' Morag sounded anxious, but she was holding out Cassie's grey cloak, none the less.

'Yes, I'm sure. Don't worry, Morag. You can read his note for yourself, if you like. He says he wants to talk about how he can help me.' She pointed to the note on the table.

Morag fastened the cloak snugly round Cassie's shoulders and then picked up the note. After a cursory glance and a brief nod, she threw it into the embers. Ignoring Cassie's gasp of outrage, she said quietly, 'Best if there's nothing for the laird to find.'

The maid was right. Cassie paused on her way to the door. 'Morag, you must lock the door behind me. If my brother should come, you must refuse him entry. Tell him…tell him that I was feeling unwell, that I have taken a few drops of laudanum so that I can sleep. Say that it will not be possible to wake me.'

'But ye never take laudanum! He kens that fine.'

'Does he? I doubt it. He pays so little attention to what I do that he probably wouldn't notice if my eyes changed colour overnight.'

That surprised Morag into a nervous laugh.

Cassie touched her maid briefly on the arm. 'Don't worry. The chances are that he's had so much to drink by now that he's already passed out. And I'm sure that Captain Graham will have taken what precautions he can to ensure James is out of the way.'

'Aye. Mr Fraser will see to that.' Morag sounded very decided.

'Mr—? Oh, the captain's man. Yes, of course.' She opened the door a fraction and peeped out. The corridor was deserted. 'I'm going now. Lock the door after me.'

Cassie slipped out into the passageway and waited a few moments while her eyes became accustomed to the gloom. She did not dare to risk a candle. Behind her, she heard the click of the lock. Good.

Moving silently in her soft shoes, she stole along to the staircase, keeping close to the wall where the floor was less likely to creak. A few moments more and she had reached the ground floor and was standing on the path outside the garden door. James's chamber was on the other side of the house. He would not be able to see her from his window. Captain Graham had been careful in his choice of rendezvous. As was to be expected from a soldier.

Now, for the first time, Cassie paused to wonder whether she was taking a stupid risk. She was going to meet a man—a battle-hardened soldier—alone, and in the middle of the night. If they were caught together, her reputation would be in tatters. And if he chose to take advantage of her, she would have no defence. She could not scream, for that would only hasten her ruin. If she went forward now, her reputation, and her person, would be at Captain Graham's mercy. Did she dare trust him?

Of course she did.

She took a deep breath and squared her shoulders. She was sure she could trust him. He had saved her more than once and he had always behaved as a gentleman should. And now he was offering to help her again. Something must have happened in the last few hours. Earlier, he had refused to help her. Now he was volunteering to do so. What had he seen, or heard, to change his mind?

She hurried down the path to where he was leaning against the oak tree. There was only one way to find out.

Ross straightened as she approached, noting approvingly that she, too, was shrouded in a dark cloak. From the house, they would look like no more that two dark shadows.

'Miss Elliott. You have come.' He took her arm and guided her round to the far side of the great tree where they would not be visible to even the most determined watcher in the house.

'Captain Graham, have you…have you changed your mind about the money?'

By Jove, she was not mealy-mouthed. Good. They didn't have time for missish turns. They must agree a plan and then part, as soon as may be.

'Miss Elliott, I will gladly help you. First, the money.' He reached into his pocket for the little packet of money he had prepared and pressed it into her hand.

'Oh, but—'

'Don't worry, ma'am. It is a loan, as you requested. You may repay me at your convenience.' He squeezed the fingers that held the packet. 'Best to tuck it away out of sight, I think.'

'Oh. Oh, yes. Thank you.' She stowed it inside her grey cloak. Then, with a brief smile, she turned to go back to the house.

'Miss Elliott. Wait. A moment more, if you would.'

'Sir?'

Ross fancied there was a shiver of nervousness in her voice. 'Do not be alarmed, Miss Elliott. I just wanted to say…I… The money is only part of it. If you need my services, in anything, you have but to say the word. If you need an escort to reach your godfather's house, I should be more than happy to provide it.'

Even in the deep shadow of the tree, he could see that her eyes widened at his words. Her jaw dropped, too, just a fraction. But she quickly recovered. In seconds, her wide mouth was set in a very determined line. And she was frowning up at him. Clearly, she mistrusted his sudden change of heart.

'You may believe me, ma'am. Tell me how I may help you. You have my word, as a gentleman, that I stand ready to do whatever you need.'

The frown relaxed. It was as if he had stroked it away by running a finger across her flawless skin. But she was still breathing quite rapidly, still quite heated. From the warmth of her skin, he could just detect a hint of her lavender fragrance among the night-time scents of grass and honeysuckle. And now she was smiling up at him, a little hesitantly, but enough to reassure Ross that she was willing to trust him. He felt suddenly proud. And protective of her. She was a woman of strong character, but she had no chance against her brother's wickedness without a man by her side. He would be more than content to be that man.

'Captain Graham,' she whispered, 'I cannot tell you how grateful I am. But I must ask you: why have you changed your mind?'

Damnation! He had hoped she would not ask. He should have known that a woman like Cassie Elliott would not be satisfied with less than the truth.

And, in that moment, he decided that she deserved to know. All of it, if she wished.

'I had a…an encounter with your brother, ma'am. I now see that you do need to get away from him. No doubt your godfather will provide you with a refuge.'

She was standing very still, her shoulders held rigid. 'Tell me, sir. What, exactly, did James do?'

Ross had the impression that she was like a piece of fragile glass, ready to shatter at a touch. 'Forgive me for paining you, ma'am, but if you will have the truth of it…'

She nodded stiffly.

'Miss Elliott, your brother was very drunk, but…'

She made a dismissive gesture with one hand. No doubt she had seen her brother drunk many times.

'He offered you to me. As a wife.'

She did not move. She did not even blink. 'How much did he want?' Her voice was barely audible.

Dear God, she knew already. Perhaps Ross was not the first man to whom the blackguard had tried to sell her?

Ross swallowed hard, never taking his eyes off her strained face. 'Twenty thousand pounds.'

Chapter Nine

Cassie wanted to run. But her feet had become like part of the roots of the great oak tree, immovable, encased in the earth. If only it would open and swallow her up.

'Miss Elliott?'

His voice was low and full of understanding, but Cassie could not begin to look at him. She fixed her gaze on the deep shadows at her feet, hunching her body together, trying to make herself as small and inconspicuous as possible. If only he would turn away, give her space to run, to hide in the dark.

He did not move.

'Miss Elliott,' he said again, but a little more firmly. 'Pray do not be embarrassed by this, ma'am. I tell you only because you have a right to know the full extent of your brother's wickedness. And so that you will understand why I am totally at your service. I understand now why you have decided that you must flee.'

She dared one brief glance up at him. His face was full of compassion.

'And since no one else stands ready to help you…I will. Please believe me. I *can* help you escape. Sadly, there is no one else.'

The words echoed in Cassie's head like metal balls rattling round in a tin drum. *There is no one else. There is no one else. There is no one else.*

It was true. She had this one—slight—chance. Or none at all.

'Miss Elliott? Will you not trust me?'

There was something about his tone of voice, and the depth of conviction in it. And something else that she could not quite place. But it tore at her emotions, already stretched so tight they were on the point of shattering. She wanted to scream. Or weep. Or curse her brother to the end of time.

Captain Graham must have seen the turmoil in her features for, before she could utter a sound, he grasped her knotted fingers in his strong hands and held them. His clasp was warm, and gentle, and very reassuring. 'Do not be afraid,' he said. 'You shall escape. I promise.' He pressed her hands within his.

She had thought more than once that he had the merriest blue eyes. Now, in the gloom, it was impossible to distinguish any colour at all. His gaze was darkly intent and unwavering, willing her to believe.

'Miss Elliott? *Cassie…?*'

'I believe you, sir. And I do trust you.'

'Thank God,' he breathed. 'And now,' he went on, raising a hand and running his fingers through his hair, 'now we must plan.'

Cassie sensed the change in him. A moment ago he had been unsure, waiting for her to agree to trust him. Now, he was the soldier again, planning a campaign, deciding how to outwit the enemy.

'We must decide on a place where we may meet safely, without your brother. Will he allow you to leave home without him? To pay a call, perhaps?'

Cassie shook her head. 'No. You saw how it was at Mrs Anstruther's. My brother always insists on accompanying me. I go nowhere alone.' She paused, thinking. 'Unless…'

'Unless?'

Cassie shuddered. She would have to tell him yet more of the dark secrets she had hoped to keep hidden from the world. 'There is only one circumstance in which James might permit me to go out without him. If I were meeting Colonel Anstruther.'

'You mean Mrs Anstruther?'

Cassie shook her head miserably. 'No. I do mean the colonel. And without his wife.'

'But…'

'Captain Graham, I beg you to try to understand. My brother is deep in debt, as you must have known when he tried to extract such a price from you. It proves just how desperate he is. His creditors must be very pressing, for his real target has never been you, but the colonel.'

'Anstruther? But he is—'

'Yes. Colonel Anstruther. One of the richest men in Scotland. My brother has decided that I am to be the next Mrs Anstruther.' Cassie heard the sharp hiss of indrawn breath, betraying his shock. She ploughed on, desperate to complete the humiliating tale, even though it stripped her of every last scrap of dignity she possessed. 'I am afraid that James must have applied to you only because his creditors are at the door and, unlike the colonel, you are unmarried and available now. A husband in the hand, so to speak,' she added with a grimace of distaste. 'No doubt he would have hoped for much, much more from the colonel.'

To her surprise, he laughed, shaking his head. 'Miss Elliott, you are worth twenty times twenty thousand, with that brave spirit of yours. And you shall *not* be married by force to Colonel Anstruther, nor to anyone else. You have my word on that.'

In spite of her terrors, Cassie found herself smiling up at him. He was so sure that she, too, began to believe in possible deliverance. 'Sir, you are rash indeed, to make such a promise. I fear I must hold you to it.'

'Good,' he said firmly. 'Now, when and where shall it be? Clearly I must persuade my friend Anstruther that he needs to take us both to yet another of the fine sights of the area, somewhere your brother would never wish to visit. Was there not a church—no, an abbey—that you mentioned at one of our meetings, ma'am? I doubt your brother would wish to visit such a place.'

'The ruins of Sweetheart Abbey,' Cassie said, remembering. 'Sweetheart Abbey, built by the Lady Devorguilla in memory of her husband. She is buried there, with her husband's heart.'

'Is it far?'

'No. It is less than ten miles from Dumfries. A fairly easy ride. If you were to invite the colonel to visit it with you, my brother would almost certainly allow me to join you, in order to further the colonel's interest in me. I should need a suitable chaperon, of course.'

'Morag, I hope?'

She nodded.

'Good. Then I shall speak to the colonel over breakfast. With luck, your brother will be there to hear. He will probably take the bait.'

Cassie shook her head. 'I doubt it. Not after tonight's hard drinking. He rarely rises before noon after such a night.'

'Tomorrow, he will have to. All the colonel's guests are expected to leave a little after noon. I will ensure that the colonel's servants wake your brother in good time. He needs to have ample opportunity to hear us making plans. As do you. Then you may say, in all innocence, how much you long to see the abbey. I take it you have not visited before?'

'No.'

'Good. That's settled then. And when you come to the abbey, with Morag, you must bring only enough—'

'Oh, no! How stupid of me! It will not do. We must think of somewhere else.'

'Why? It sounded to be the perfect pretext.'

'It is not. I don't know what I was thinking of. Sweetheart Abbey is well to the south of Dumfries, quite near the coast, but on the wrong side of the river. There is no way from there to England, except by crossing the Nith. And the only bridges are in Dumfries itself. We dare not come back through Dumfries. My brother has too many spies there. And it would give him too much time to catch up with us. We must choose somewhere closer to the border. Or to the wath—that's the ford—at Annan.'

He groaned. 'You must be right, ma'am. We do need another solution. But I fear I have no knowledge of this country. You can light on somewhere else, surely?'

Cassie began to shake her head in frustration.

'Think, ma'am.' He was beginning to sound impatient. And more than a little desperate.

'I…' The answer came to her. 'Are you prepared to develop a sudden interest in ruined castles, Captain Graham?'

'Anything, ma'am, so long as your brother has no such inclination.'

Cassie grinned at him. 'Then I think I have the solution we need.'

Cassie leaned back in the corner of the carriage and tried not to smile across at Morag. It would not do to count on success. Not until she had reached her goal. And it would be safest not to tell Morag exactly what was planned until much nearer the time. Just as she had not told Morag the detail of what she and the captain had discussed under the oak tree. Morag could be trusted—of course she could—but she might inadvertently say or do something to give away Cassie's secrets, especially if she were confronted by Jamie in a rage, as he so often was.

Besides, he was now riding alongside the carriage, rather than far out in front as he usually did. He might be nursing a sore head, and riding gently as a result, but there was nothing wrong with his hearing.

'Mr Fraser tells me that the captain and the colonel are planning to visit some o' the sights,' Morag said.

'Oh? Yes, I recall that something of the sort was mentioned over breakfast. The captain is keen to make the most of his time here.'

'And ye said ye wanted to see them as well, did ye no'?'

Now who had told Morag that? One of the colonel's

footmen, perhaps, or even the captain's valet? Morag seemed to have become thick as inkle weavers with Fraser, judging by how often she repeated his opinions.

Cassie tried to look unconcerned. 'The colonel was talking about a number of sights worth visiting, such as Sweetheart Abbey. I merely mentioned that I had not yet had an opportunity to visit them myself.'

Morag frowned. 'Aye. Ye might as well be a prisoner in the gaol, for all the chances ye get to be away from Langrigg.'

'Shh, Morag.' Cassie put a finger to her lips, and nodded towards the shadow of her brother, riding alongside.

'Sorry,' Morag mumbled, reddening. Then dropping her voice even lower, she added, 'What harm would it do, if ye went wi' the gentlemen? Did ye not suggest it when ye had the chance? The laird couldna very well shout ye down at the colonel's breakfast table.'

'The colonel did invite me. I...I said that the abbey was probably too far for me to travel in the day. But there may be other invitations.' Cassie could still see the ferocious frown on her brother's face when the colonel had issued his invitation to the abbey. James had clearly not wished for either of them to waste a day on a ruined abbey. The colonel had probably seen that frown, too. Certainly he had not attempted to argue, merely adding politely that, if he and the captain should happen to be making a trip to somewhere nearer Miss Elliott's home, he would be sure to invite her to accompany them. Even James had been unable to grumble at that.

Cassie hugged her secret to herself. There *would* be another invitation—and soon—and she would have to move heaven and earth to ensure that James allowed her to accept it. Her first task was to prepare the ground. She must take every opportunity to remind James that there was only one way to promote her relationship with Colonel Anstruther. He had to allow Cassie to spend time with the colonel. And what better than a leisurely trip to see a local ruin?

She glanced out to see exactly where James was. Well within earshot. 'Colonel Anstruther is a most kind gentleman,' she said loudly, 'and an excellent host. I do find his company highly congenial. It is only a pity that we do not exchange visits more often.' From her corner, she nodded eagerly at Morag, willing her to take up the theme.

'Ye certainly seemed to be becoming fast friends, Miss Cassie, when ye was talking about the colonel's new garden. 'Twas as if ye'd kent one another for years. He's taken rather a liking to ye, I'd say, probably because ye ken sic a lot about plants and gardens. It seems to be a passion with him. 'Tis only a pity that his leddy canna leave the house to be there with the both o' ye.'

Cassie shook her head fiercely at her maid. That was exactly the wrong thing to say. James must not be reminded of the existence of Mrs Anstruther.

'Perhaps there will be another opportunity to further our acquaintance,' Cassie said quickly. 'I should certainly like to learn more of the colonel. He is very much the gentleman. And so knowledgeable. Do you know, Morag, that he was reciting the history of Sweetheart Abbey over the breakfast table today? His knowledge far outstrips mine, I must say, even though I have read a great deal about such places.'

'But ye've not been to the abbey.'

'No, that is true. It is too far. It would be a long journey and James is too busy to give up so much time to accompany me. For a visit closer to home, however, it might be possible for him to spare the time. In fact, he might even permit me to join the colonel without his escort. Colonel Anstruther is, after all, a perfect gentleman and can be trusted to behave honourably. And I would have you to chaperon me, naturally.' She glanced sideways to see whether her brother was listening. She was almost sure he was.

'Well, ye'd best hope that the colonel wisna offended by yer refusal of his invite the day, Miss Cassie. Maybe he'll not be making another.'

'That would be a pity. I should so hate to lose his friendship. It is seldom that one meets a true gentleman hereabouts. And the colonel is certainly one.'

'Aye, he is that. So ye'd best take care not to turn down another invite.'

Cassie nodded. 'I'm sure you are right, Morag. I shall…er…I shall mention it to my brother, I think. I know he holds the colonel in the highest regard. I am sure he would not like to lose the acquaintance of such a man.'

Morag was asking with her eyes whether the charade was to continue. Just at that moment, however, the carriage turned off the road on to the Langrigg estate and James spurred his horse in the direction of the house. It was over.

For now.

'Cassie, would you favour me with a few moments of your time?'

Cassie paused halfway up the staircase, struck by the politeness of James's request. 'Of course, James. If you will allow me time to change my clothes, I will—'

'Now, Cassie,' he snapped, taking a step into the hallway.

Just that single step seemed menacing. Cassie turned, assuming what she hoped was a confident smile. 'I will come immediately, since you wish it.' She walked calmly back down the stairs and into the little parlour.

'About Colonel Anstruther.' He began to pace.

Cassie took a seat by the empty grate and smoothed her skirts.

'You were very remiss in your dealings with him this morning. He was offended by the way you refused his offer.'

Cassie smoothed her skirts again, pleased to see that her hands were not shaking. 'Think you so? Oh, dear, how very stupid of me. It was certainly not my intention. I could see that you were against the visit, so I thought that it would be better if the refusal came from me. He could hardly pursue the matter once a lady had made her excuses.'

'No, he could not. But he could conclude that you were a mannerless harpy. Because of your stupidity— you do well to admit it—he may cut the acquaintance altogether. And then where will you be?'

Cassie ignored his last question. 'Forgive me, brother. Did I misread you earlier? I was so sure you misliked the idea of spending a day at the abbey. If I had—'

'Of course I misliked the idea. There are a million better ways of passing the time than trailing around after a milksop sister and two jaw-me-dead soldiers clambering over ruined piles of stone.'

'Then—'

'But you, of all people, should have known better than to offend Anstruther by assuming that I would not permit you to go.'

'Oh, does that mean—?'

'It means that I require you to seize every possible

opportunity for furthering your acquaintance with Anstruther. Good God, Cassie, even a chit like you should be able to see that the man is not going to ask for the hand of a woman he never sees. Do you understand that? Or are you completely witless?'

Cassie bowed her head. 'I am sorry if I have been stupid. And even more sorry if I have offended Colonel Anstruther. But I don't quite understand… What should I have said?'

He stopped pacing and planted himself in front of her chair, legs apart and hands on hips. 'If you had been less direct, had shown a becoming degree of interest in the expedition, you would have made it possible for me to say you could go with my good will, provided you were properly chaperoned. I would have been able to show that I trusted the colonel's honour, as a gentleman, to take care of you in my absence. My unavoidable absence.' James was now working himself up into a real temper. 'The colonel would have been flattered by my confidence. But you, you stupid girl, you prevented it. By Jove, I wonder why I still have patience with you. You thwart my plans at every turn.'

'I am sorry, James,' Cassie said meekly. 'I meant it for the best. Truly. Perhaps the colonel will issue another invitation to me? He did mention something of the sort.'

James narrowed his eyes and muttered something inaudible.

'Am I to take it that, if he should issue another invitation, you would wish me to accept?'

'Good God, is it not obvious? Of course I would wish you to accept, you stupid girl. You are to find ways of fixing the colonel's attentions. And soon. If he should invite you again, you will go. Whatever the destination and whatever the weather.'

'Oh.'

'Do you understand me?'

'Yes. I am to accept any invitation.'

'I'm glad to see that you understand your duty at last, Cassie. It has taken you long enough. But you always were a mutton-headed wench.'

She looked up at him, keeping her face expressionless. 'Would you wish me to accept for you, too?'

He shook his head angrily and resumed his pacing. 'No, of course not. I'm not going to dance attendance on Anstruther until I know the battle is won. Besides, he doesn't like me above half. Especially after— I'm better out of it. You'll take our own carriage, with Tam on the box, and Morag beside you as chaperon. That will be enough.'

She nodded, not daring to lift her eyes to his, lest he see the triumph in them.

'You'd better start praying that another invitation does arrive, my girl. Or I promise you that your life here will not be worth living.'

Cassie said nothing more. She rose and made her

way quietly to the door, keeping her gaze demurely lowered. But inside, her heart was dancing. Victory had come so much sooner than she had dared to dream. Her plan was working. And she knew she could rely on Captain Graham to fulfil his part.

Soon she would have her chance to escape.

Ross continued his wandering around the ruins. He was glad that he had come alone. The colonel would have been a source of much interesting information, of course, but Ross was more than content to be alone with his own thoughts.

He stood looking down the nave and into the presbytery where only the delicate tracery remained of what must have been a most beautiful window. If there had been stained glass, it was now replaced by the piercing blue of the summer sky. It might have been gloomy here, once, but now the roofless building was filled with light. Such an amazing ruin. And begun— according to the colonel—because Devorguilla, Lady of Galloway, had chosen to build a Cistercian abbey here as a lasting memorial to her beloved husband, John Balliol.

Ross walked slowly down the nave, though it was a grassy sward now. Somewhere here, the Lady Devorguilla was buried, along with the casket that contained her husband's heart. Ross stopped when he reached the threshold of the presbytery. The lady's grave must be somewhere here, where the altar would have stood. Ross would not tread on it. Let her sleep in peace.

He wandered back into the nave and then out into what had once been the cloister garden, skirting round the new church that leant against the side of the long wall. The church was a neat enough building, but totally out of keeping with the stark grandeur of the ruins. He strolled round to the east end of the abbey from where the new parish church could not be seen. Ross much preferred to see only the gaunt beauty of the abbey's red sandstone against the stark blue of the sky.

Why had be come here? He was not altogether sure. Possibly because of an interest sparked by the colonel's knowledgeable discourse. Or was it perhaps Miss Elliott's rather wistful description? A woman's love so strong and enduring that she would build an abbey to it. Was it possible for such a love to exist nowadays? After Julie, he had thought it was impossible. Yet he hoped he was wrong, for the sake of his friend Max, if not for himself. Ross did not expect to find love. Not now. Not after Julie's betrayal. How could he ever trust another woman?

He realised, with surprise, that Julie's image was fading. When he had left London, he had been unable to think of her without pain. Now he barely thought of her at all. What did it mean?

He shook his head, wondering at his own fickleness. Was it only a few weeks ago that he had sworn eternal fidelity to Julie in his heart? He sat down on a block of sandstone and dropped his head back for a moment to stare up at the sky. For once, there was not a single cloud to be seen. It might have been the south of France rather than the south of Scotland. He had first laid eyes on Julie against just such a pure, fierce sky. The picture she made had taken his breath away. Was that the reason why he had fallen in love with her?

He could not deny that Julie was a fine young woman—beautiful, brave and steadfast. Rather like Cassie Elliott, in fact. Both women had endured great hardships. Both women were worthy of a man's regard.

And yet there was a difference between them. He could see that now. Julie had been deceiving him. She had used his help, and his escort, to escape to her lover in England and to regain her noble status. It was Ross's own fault that he had been used, for he had been so besotted by her beauty and her courage that he had not asked even the most obvious questions. She had played him for a fool. He had put her on a pedestal, like a fine marble statue, and refused to see the slightest hint that the precious stone might be cracked.

Cassie Elliott, by contrast, could never be put on a pedestal. She was much too alive, much too real. Oh, she was beautiful—no doubt on that score—but, equally, she was damnably hot at hand. Yet she was honest through and through. She would never use Ross, or anyone else. Not in a way that was deceitful. She was the kind of woman, like the Lady Devorguilla, who would give her heart, fully and for ever.

The man who could win Cassie's love would be fortunate indeed.

For the first time in his life, Ross felt a tiny flicker of regret that he lacked the wealth and family that made a man a good catch. If he could have paid James Elliott's price for his sister, would he have done so? He shuddered. No. Never. Such a thing would be depraved, and wicked. Besides, Ross was not in search of a wife. And Cassie Elliott was not in the least suitable, even if he were. What gentleman would marry such a head-strong girl, with no dowry and a blood-sucking drunk for a brother? Cassie Elliott was probably destined to die a spinster, in spite of her remarkable qualities.

That unhappy thought sent a momentary shaft of pain through Ross's body. Poor girl, to be denied a home and children, simply because of a blackguard like James Elliott. She deserved better, did she not? Her behaviour was sometimes improper, to be sure, but it was Ross who had almost forced her to accept his escort when all she had wanted was a small loan. Now he was totally committed to helping her, but that was Ross's doing, not Cassie's. Indeed, something very similar had happened with Julie when—

A tiny seed of doubt began to take root. Was it possible that Cassie had contrived the situation, knowing that Ross was bound to offer to help her? Was she using him, as Julie had done?

No, it could not be true. Cassie was not like Julie. He was sure of it. Almost.

He shook his head to clear his thoughts, searching for the soldier's solution. It came. As ever, it was simple. He must keep his promise, but he must also ensure that he did not become personally involved with Miss Elliott's troubles. He would simply escort her to her godfather's house and leave her there. And he would maintain a proper distance between them throughout.

He looked up at the sky again. The colour no longer seemed pristine. The sun had lost its warmth. His friend Max had been fond of joking that Ross was the one who could always see the sunshine and the good in everyone. Max had been the one to see the black side. Now, after Julie, Ross was beginning to ape his friend. Love—unrequited love—was definitely a hard taskmistress.

But he must not allow it to blight his life. He knew that now. Having recognised his own weaknesses, he must set about putting his life back on an even keel. *After* he had disposed of Miss Elliott.

He must discover the truth about his father. He must. It was here somewhere, he was sure of that. His friend Max had roundly hated his own father. But at least Max had had a choice. Ross had had no father to hate. Or to love. And there had been such emptiness in his childhood after his mother's early death. Even at the end, she had refused to answer any of his questions. All Ross had were a few memories, grey and misty through the veil of time: an old man shouting at him in a broad accent while his mother cowered away, trying to protect Ross; a day on a beach, trying to skim stones across the firth; a long journey in a rickety carriage that smelled of damp, with only his mother for company. She had wept over him that night. He still remembered his boyish shock at the sight of her tears. And how he had slept in her arms.

Something must have happened to them in Scotland. As a boy of just three, he had not understood but, as a man, he could begin to read the memories, frail though they were. His mother had taken her son and fled from her husband. Why? What had he done to her? And how had she managed to hide from him until she died? Had he not been looking for them?

Ross shook his head. Too many questions and no answers. He could not begin to untangle the tale until he had discovered where his family came from. He must keep looking.

But first, he must fulfil his promise to Miss Elliott. He rose to his feet and began to walk swiftly round the outside of the transept. This place was affecting him strangely. It was peaceful and serene; and yet strangely disquieting, bringing back forgotten memories. He looked up at the greenery growing along the top of the ruined wall of the nave. It softened the stonework, even though it looked incongruous against the soaring arches beneath.

He would never forget this place, he realised. It was strong and steadfast. And very beautiful.

Somewhere in the back of his mind, a small voice responded, 'It has all the qualities of Cassie Elliott. You would not offer for her. Yet you willingly lay your service at her feet.'

Chapter Ten

Ross took his teacup and returned to his seat opposite Mrs Anstruther.

'That was a splendid dinner, ma'am, as ever. I cannot tell you how grateful I am to you and the colonel for your hospitality.'

Mrs Anstruther smiled broadly. 'Believe me, Captain Graham, it is our pleasure to have you here as our guest. Why, until you arrived, my husband hardly went anywhere, except on business. He would always find some excuse not to leave me. But now he is going about on pleasure trips. And I may tell you I am delighted to see it. I do thank you for it, sir.'

Ross returned the smile as best he could. 'You will be without us both again tomorrow, ma'am, I fear, for your husband has offered to take me to Caerlaverock.'

'Yes, indeed,' added the colonel from his place beside his wife. 'It is a magnificent castle. And well named, too. Lark's nest, in English. You will be impressed, Graham, I am sure. I am hoping that, on this occasion, Miss Elliott will join us there. Her brother can have no cause to object this time. It is hardly any distance from their home. And the invitation came from an impeccable source.' He beamed at his wife.

'Oh, my dear, I am so sorry,' cried Mrs Anstruther. 'I completely forgot to tell you. Miss Elliott did reply to my invitation. Just this morning, in fact. She sends her apologies. She would very much have liked to join you both at Caerlaverock, but is prevented by a prior engagement.'

The colonel frowned angrily. 'Humph. I take leave to doubt the existence of this prior engagement. Miss Elliott is well known as a recluse who never goes anywhere. Or rather, who is never permitted to go anywhere. I detect her brother's fell hand here, yet again. Do you not agree, Graham?'

Ross did not meet the colonel's eye. 'Perhaps some household duty keeps her at home tomorrow? She must have many tasks, as mistress of Langrigg. I am sure she would have accepted Mrs Anstruther's invitation if it had been possible.'

'There may yet be other opportunities,' Mrs Anstruther said brightly. 'I shall invite her again and again, until her brother finally relents. Mr Elliott will discover that I am not easily bested.'

The colonel laughed. 'I can certainly vouch for that, my dear.' He reached across and patted her hand.

'However, you can only continue to invite Miss Elliott while Graham is here with us. It would look most peculiar—and do the lady's reputation no good at all—if she were to be known to make excursions with only myself for company.'

His wife nodded sadly. Then she rallied. 'Well, we must make sure that Captain Graham remains here with us for many weeks yet, must we not?'

The colonel readily agreed.

Ross did his best to join in their cheerful conversation, but it was not easy. He was not a practised liar, and it was especially difficult to dissemble with hosts as generous as the Anstruthers. But, on this occasion, he would just have to do the best he could.

Until deliverance came.

'Excuse me, madam.' The colonel's footman stood bowing, just inside the drawing-room door. 'A letter has just come express. For Captain Graham.'

'Oh, dear.' Mrs Anstruther had turned visibly paler. No doubt she assumed, as most people did, that an express letter must be bringing bad news.

Ross rose from his seat and strode across to the doorway to take the letter from the salver. 'Thank you, Gordon.'

The footman beamed, clearly pleased that the guest knew his name. The smile was instantly wiped from his face, however, when the colonel rose from his seat and cleared his throat noisily. Gordon straightened his shoulders and raised his chin. 'Will you be wishing to send a reply, sir?'

'One moment.' Ross ripped open the seal and scanned the sheet rapidly. 'No. No reply.'

The footman bowed and silently withdrew.

'Not bad news, I hope, Captain Graham?'

'Not exactly bad, ma'am, but…troubling. I fear I shall not be able to remain here to enjoy your splendid hospitality. Some…er…business difficulties have arisen that will require me to return to London.'

'Oh, I am so sorry. When must you leave?'

'It would be best if I started out at once—'

'Surely not?' said the colonel. 'Can you not remain until tomorrow? Unless it is a matter of life and death, of course.' He looked a little embarrassed. It was clear that he did not want to pry into Ross's private affairs.

Ross shook his head. 'Not that, sir. At least, I fervently hope not. I thank you for your concern. And you are quite right. It is too late to start out now. Besides, it will take some time to prepare for the journey. I will leave tomorrow, as early as possible.'

'How will you travel? Shall you take the stage?'

'No, ma'am. At least, not initially. I think the best course would be to ride as far as Carlisle and take the London stage from there.'

The colonel nodded. 'Aye, true enough. You'll have a choice of coaches from there. You might manage to pick up the mail from Glasgow, if you are lucky. Don't worry about your baggage. I'll see that it's sent on, if you leave me your London address.'

'Thank you, sir. You are very kind, but I don't think it will be necessary for you to put yourself out to that extent. My man can ride with me as far as Carlisle and then bring the horses on to London by easy stages. If you would be so good as to send on the remaining baggage to Carlisle, he will take charge of it from there. I'll tell him to wait for the bags at the posting house.'

'That is an excellent solution, Captain.' Mrs Anstruther smiled up at him. 'You are to be commended for your quick thinking.'

'You should have learned to expect that from a soldier by now, my dear,' the colonel said with a wicked grin. 'There's no time for dithering on the battlefield, you know.'

Mrs Anstruther shook her head at her husband, but there was love and admiration in her eyes.

'If you will excuse me, ma'am, I will go and give my man his instructions. We may be travelling light tomorrow, but there is still much to do before we depart.'

'Shall I see you again before you leave?'

The colonel had moved to stand behind his wife's chair. He caught Ross's eye and shook his head faintly.

Ross knew that getting Mrs Anstruther ready in the mornings was a lengthy business. She did not normally appear at the breakfast table. No doubt she would make the effort if Ross were to encourage her, but it was bound to sap her strength. He did not need the colonel's hint to know what he should say. 'I would plan to be off as soon as it is light, ma'am. I'm sure even the servants would not be about so early.'

'But you will need to break your fast and—'

'Pray do not concern yourself, ma'am. We will be able to eat when we stop to rest the horses.'

'I'm sure the captain knows what he is doing, my dear. We had best say our farewells now and let him be about his business.'

'You are right, of course.' Mrs Anstruther stretched up a hand. 'My dear Captain Graham, it has been a great pleasure to have you here as our guest. I do hope that, one day, you will come to us again. You would be most welcome, as I am sure you know.'

'Mrs Anstruther, you have been more than kind.' Ross bowed over her thin fingers. He knew better than to suggest that their paths might cross in London. Mrs Anstruther would probably never leave Dumfries again. 'I am truly sorry that I have to leave so abruptly. Under your tuition, I was even learning to love plants.'

Mrs Anstruther laughed. 'Now that, sir, is what I believe you young people would call a bouncer.'

The colonel laughed too. 'I won't dare ask where you learned such language, my love. Though on this occasion, I think you may be wrong. Captain Graham was asking some extremely knowledgeable questions when we were at Castle Douglas.'

'Prompted by Miss Elliott, I fancy. That young lady is a real enthusiast. I only wish I might know her better.'

'Perhaps we will find a way. In due course,' the colonel said. 'I must say that I am glad, now, that she declined your invitation for Caerlaverock, my dear. Imagine her disappointment if she had been permitted to accept. For I should have had to put her off, now that Captain Graham will not be able to join me. I could not meet her there alone.'

Mrs Anstruther nodded her agreement.

'I am very sorry that I shall miss seeing the ruin, sir,' Ross said. 'You mentioned that it was well worth the visit. Shall you go by yourself?'

'No. I have visited often enough before. Without company—' he looked sadly down at his wife '—I should not enjoy it. Let us agree to visit it together the next time you come to Dumfries.'

Ross nodded. 'The next time. Agreed.' He bowed again. 'And now, ma'am, if you will excuse me? I leave behind my most grateful thanks for all your kindness. And for everything you have both done for me.' He looked meaningfully at the colonel. For a moment, he could almost smell the stench of Dumfries gaol in his nostrils. 'Now I will bid you both a good-night. And thank you again.'

* * *

Cassie cast a final warning look at Morag, assumed what she fervently hoped was an innocent expression, and stepped down from the carriage. She looked across at the majestic ruins of Caerlaverock, safe behind their encircling moat. Would she be safe soon? With Ross?

He was striding towards her. 'Well met, Captain Graham,' she said, dropping him a curtsy. 'It is another beautiful day, is it not? At least, so it seems to me.' She gestured towards Tam, still sitting on the box. 'Dour Tam there always looks on the black side. He's sure it will rain before long.'

Had the captain caught her meaning? It seemed he had. As he bowed to her, he frowned and gave a tiny nod in Tam's direction. He had recognised the danger she was warning him about.

'Has the colonel gone inside ahead of us?' Cassie asked airily.

'Ah, no, ma'am. I fear the colonel is not here. He was called away to an emergency on the farm, just as we were leaving. There was no time to send to tell you. The colonel sends his apologies and his hopes that you will enjoy the day, none the less.'

'Oh, I—'

'Miss Cassie.' Tam started climbing laboriously down from his seat. His face had gone rather red. 'The laird will be wanting ye t' go back to Langrigg. It's no' the thing fer a single lassie to—'

Captain Graham laughed shortly. 'Come, come, my man,' he said loftily, 'it is not for you to dictate to your mistress. Having come this far, I'm sure Miss Elliott would like to walk around the ruins.'

'But the laird—'

'Miss Elliott has her maid in attendance. Even her brother would not suggest that there was anything improper in our visit.' He beckoned impatiently to Morag to join them. 'Now, Miss Elliott, will you take my arm? Perhaps you would like to start with this extraordinary gatehouse?'

Cassie took his arm, conscious that her fingers were trembling. Would he notice?

He must have. Once his back was safely turned on Tam, he smiled reassuringly at her and pressed her fingers fleetingly. But he said nothing more, except to tell Morag to hurry along and to follow close behind them. Tam would have no reason for undue concern.

'Sir—'

'Is this not magnificent? And just wait until you see the Nithsdale apartments inside. I must admit to having had a quick look around before you arrived. It is everything the colonel promised.'

He walked her through the gatehouse and down the passage to the triangular courtyard beyond. 'It is magnificent,' he said in his normal voice. 'And we must spend a little time admiring it.'

'But should we not leave at once?' Cassie asked. She

was still feeling nervous. The sooner they started for the border, the better their chance of escaping without pursuit.

'Not yet, ma'am. Not yet,' he said softly. 'We must give Fraser time to deal with your brother's henchman before we make any move.'

'Oh. Oh, yes, of course. He won't hurt Tam, will he?'

'Not unless he has to,' the captain replied grimly. 'Though I will admit to an unworthy desire to treat him as he treated me, back there on the banks of the Solway.'

A vivid memory flooded Cassie's mind. Tam had been there, at that first meeting, helping James to truss the captain up and gag him like a common felon. Then he had been dragged off to Dumfries in the driving rain and thrown into gaol. Tam would be lucky to escape Captain Graham's vengeance.

'Now let us appear to be exclaiming over the wonders of the building, Miss Elliott. I shall indicate the various areas worthy of comment and you, if you please, will nod and do everything proper to demonstrate your interest.' He waved a hand in the direction of the single tower at the far corner of the ruined castle.

Cassie nodded obediently.

'Have you brought all you need for the journey?' he asked, still pointing upwards.

'Yes. In the carriage. A hamper full.'

'A hamper?' He was trying not to laugh.

'It seemed the safest choice. I told my brother I was bringing food and wine so that we might enjoy a picnic by the castle. Morag replaced the contents with my things once everyone else had gone to bed.'

'I hope you concealed the food well, Morag,' he said over his shoulder.

'They'll find it by the smell. By and bye,' Morag said with quiet satisfaction. 'But Miss Cassie'll be safe in England by then.'

'Pray God you are right, Morag,' Cassie breathed.

'It may be cold and wet on our journey, ma'am. I hope you have brought warm clothing.'

Cassie lifted the skirt of her travelling dress just a fraction and displayed a heavy walking boot. 'Not only stout clothing, sir, but boots also.'

'Very wise.'

'One thing, sir. Oh, you will think me a sad creature, but I cannot help worrying about Lucifer.'

'Lucifer? Your horse?'

'He has had to be left behind. And James hates him. Lucifer threw him more than once and James cannot ride him. I fear…I fear that, when James discovers I have fled, he may shoot Lucifer. For revenge on me. I will never forgive myself if he does.'

Captain Graham turned towards the more modern part of the castle and began gesturing towards the fine apartments that had been built within the ancient walls. 'Have no fear on that score, ma'am. Your brother will not do that.'

'How can you be sure?'

'Because he is not a fool. Even a blackguard like James Elliott knows the value of a horse like Lucifer. He may sell him, Miss Elliott, but he will not shoot him.'

'Oh. Oh, thank you, sir.' Cassie was so relieved she could have hugged him. Why had she not thought of that? James would not destroy something he could turn into hard cash. Of course he would not.

'Sir?' A man's voice came from the gatehouse. It echoed eerily from the gloomy passage there.

Captain Graham turned and took a couple of steps towards the voice. 'Fraser?'

Fraser stepped out into the sunlight. He was grinning. 'It's done, sir. Got him trussed up like a gobblecock. In the carriage where he can't be seen.'

'Miss Elliott is concerned that you might have hurt him.'

Fraser turned to Cassie. He was still grinning. There was nothing at all deferential about the captain's man. 'Well now, ma'am, let's just say that I ain't done no more than absolutely necessary. He'll be right as rain in no time…once someone finds him and takes the ropes off.' He looked up at the sky as if assessing the weather. 'Course he might get a wee thing wet while he's waiting.'

Cassie giggled nervously. She couldn't help it, though she told herself sternly that a lady should never laugh at another's misfortunes. Even if that other was Tam.

'We'd best bring him inside the castle, Fraser.' The captain's voice was curt. 'I can understand your desire to leave him out in the rain—he deserves to be drenched, just as I was—but I think we'll put him in one of the towers, if you can get him up there. If we leave him in plain view, he might be discovered much too soon.'

'Aye, sir.' Fraser produced a large pistol from behind his back. 'I'll bring him, shall I?'

'Yes. Take him up there—' he pointed to the stair-well by one of the gatehouse towers '—and prop him up against one of the walls. Make sure you tie his feet once you've got him up there. I wouldn't want him walking out by himself.'

Fraser said nothing. He just grinned again and disappeared through the massive gatehouse.

'Now, ma'am, we must leave as we planned. But first, tell me—what of your brother? Is he at Langrigg today?'

'No. After I'd sent off that note to Mrs Anstruther yesterday—luckily, it did not occur to James to ask to see what I had written—he gave me a long lecture on my duty to make myself agreeable to Colonel Anstruther today, and then he left. I assumed he was going to the brothel. That's usually the way of it when he says nothing about where he is going.'

'Miss Cassie!'

'Wheesht, Morag. I'm telling nothing but the truth. And Captain Graham has to know the risks we are running.'

'You are…er…admirably direct, ma'am. If your brother has gone…er…there, when is he likely to return to Langrigg?'

'Not early. Probably late afternoon. He often does that. Or he might even go to visit some of his cronies in Dumfries. Sometimes he does not return for two days.'

'We dare not hope for so much. But it seems that we may have a few hours' start. That should be enough.'

'Which route do you plan to take, sir?'

'As we discussed. It is safest to go round by the road, to Annan, and Gretna, and Carlisle.'

'You will not try the wath? It is shorter.'

'Only if the tide is in our favour. I do not relish the thought of being caught again with my back to the rising water.'

'No, but… Sir, if my brother should return early, he would follow us. We would be much quicker to take the wath. Forgive my stupid fears, but I cannot begin to feel safe until I am on English soil.' Cassie was conscious of the tremor in her voice but she could do nothing to control it. 'Please, Captain Graham, I—' She stopped, willing herself to be calm. 'There is no need to decide now. But let us take the coast road where we can, instead of the high road. Then we will be closer to the wath, if…if we should need to take it.'

'I…very well, Miss Elliott. We shall do as you wish. But you need have no fears about pursuers. I have already given Fraser instructions to act as our rearguard. He will ride a quarter of a mile behind the carriage. If anyone is following us, we will have ample warning.'

'Oh.' Cassie was a little reassured, but only a little. Her brother could muster a small army of ruffians if he needed to. What was Fraser—one man—against so many? But there was no point in betraying her fears. Morag was already nervous enough. Cassie needed to be able to depend on her maid. Reassurance was what she needed now. Adopting a deliberately mischievous tone, she said, 'My goodness. If Fraser is to ride behind, we will have no coachman to drive the carriage.'

The captain's grin reminded Cassie of a schoolboy out on a spree. 'Behold your coachman,' he said with a tiny bow. 'And now we must make haste. Come.'

He led them back through the gatehouse and across the bridge to where the carriage stood. Fraser was marching Tam across the grass at the point of his pistol. Tam's hands were tied and his mouth was gagged, but he glowered murderously at Cassie as he passed her. She shuddered. Heaven help her if Tam— or Jamie—ever caught her now.

Chapter Eleven

Morag grabbed for the leather strap to stop herself from being thrown on to the floor of the carriage. 'Oh, Lord preserve us,' she gasped. 'He'll have us in the ditch in a wee minute.'

Cassie smiled as confidently as she could. 'I doubt it, Morag. The captain is clearly an excellent whip. I admit he is driving very fast—argh!' She was unable to stifle a groan as the carriage went over another huge bump in the road, throwing her up in the air. She landed very heavily on the edge of the seat. She swallowed hard and clutched her strap even more tightly. 'Yes, it is fast. But if it's a choice between a dangerous carriage ride and being caught by my brother, I know which I'd prefer. Are you telling me you'd be happy to go back to Langrigg now?'

Morag was devoting so much energy to hanging on that she barely had the strength to speak. 'Canna go back,' she gasped eventually. Her expression betrayed her continuing terror. She had become ashen in the space of a few miles.

'We'll be on a better road soon,' Cassie said reassuringly. 'Look—' she nodded towards the window on the left of the carriage '—we're well past the Comlongon Castle wood now. We're almost at Ruthwell. It will be much easier from there to Annan.'

Morag groaned. 'If the next bit road isna so bad, he'll just go even faster. Oh, Lord, I think I'm gonna be ill.' She was beginning to turn green.

'Oh, no, Morag. You must not.' With her free hand, Cassie rummaged in her pocket for her vinaigrette. Where on earth had she put it? She couldn't have forgotten it, could she?

The carriage slowed a little, but only in order to make the sharp turn on to the Annan road. It soon speeded up again, but at least it was now rocking less than before.

Cassie's searching fingers finally found the vinaigrette and passed it to the maid. 'Use this, Morag. You'll soon feel better.'

Morag threw a baleful look at her mistress but did as she was bid. After a deep sniff, she was soon spluttering and her eyes were watering, but she no longer looked so queasy. She leaned her head back and closed her eyes for a moment. 'Oh,' she groaned, opening them again quickly. 'That's awful bad.'

Cassie stretched out a hand to touch Morag's shoulder

comfortingly. 'I could not have done this without you, Morag. You know that. I am so sorry it is making you ill, but truly, I do need you now. Desperately. And I shall never be able to repay your loyalty.'

Morag swallowed. Then she nodded. 'Dinna fret, lassie. I'll no' desert ye. No matter what.' She forced a tiny smile.

'Thank you, Morag.' That was heartfelt.

'What's the matter?' Morag cried a moment later. 'There's no need to ca canny here.'

The carriage was indeed slowing down. Cassie felt her heart thumping like a huge hammer in her breast. Had something gone wrong with the carriage? Or the horses? She lowered the glass just in time to see Fraser galloping up to them. That could mean only one thing. James was behind them. She closed her eyes and offered up a silent prayer. Please, please, don't let him catch us. Please.

Fraser smiled tightly at Cassie and called up to the captain on the box, 'Sir, there are three horsemen a fair way behind us. Can't see exactly who they are for the dust, but they're certainly in a hurry.'

'How long have we got, Fraser?' The captain was still keeping the carriage moving at a good pace. He had to shout to make himself heard over the noise of the wheels, but his voice was strong and steady. It gave Cassie a little confidence. If anyone could save her, it would be Captain Graham.

'They're a long way behind us, and they're not gaining much on us at the moment, sir, but your horses are tiring. I'd say we've twenty minutes, thirty at most. Why don't you and the lady take the two riding horses? You'd make better speed.'

'Aye, but he'd catch us in the end. I have a better plan. We'll need to get to the other side of Annan. Then I'll tell you what to do. Join us there.' With that, he whipped up the horses to even greater speed than before.

Cassie was thrown back into her seat. The carriage left Fraser behind and thundered on down the road to Annan. Whatever the captain's plan, it was probably her last chance of freedom.

Cassie expected Morag to be prostrate before they had gone another mile, but she had reckoned without the maid's doughty character. And her very real fear of James Elliott. Within the space of two minutes, Morag was cursing the name of James Elliott; in five, she was urging the captain to drive even faster. All sign of physical weakness seemed to have disappeared. The danger seemed to have concentrated her mind most wonderfully on the need to escape at all costs.

The carriage clattered through Annan, almost colliding more than once with the normal business traffic of the town. Cassie found herself blushing at some of the foul language that followed these near-accidents, but Morag paid no heed. 'Dinna fash yersel', Miss Cassie. The captain'll not let ye come to harm.'

For a woman who had been almost fainting away less than ten minutes before, Morag was transformed. If their situation had not been so desperate, Cassie might have laughed. She would certainly have teased her maid unmercifully. But there was no time for games. Soon, Captain Graham would have reached his rendezvous point. His plan—whatever it was—would have to be put into effect.

It proved to be remarkably simple. And more dangerous than Cassie could have imagined.

'Now, Fraser. Tie your horse on to the back of the carriage, alongside Hera. Take my pistols up on the box with you and drive like the wind for Gretna and the border.'

'Right y'are, Captain. Am I to shoot them if they try to stop me?'

Cassie gasped.

'No, Fraser. I don't want you hanged for murder. Fire over their heads if it will help you to escape. But only as a last resort. Your object is to make them think that Miss Elliott is still in the carriage. Keep them away from the windows for as long as you can. And you, Morag, try to block anyone from seeing in. Do your best to make that blasted hamper look like your mistress huddled in a corner. The longer you can fool them, the better our chances will be here.'

'What do you mean to do?'

'The tide is in our favour, ma'am. So you and I are going to cross the Solway. Now.'

'On foot? But surely it would be better to take the horses? We could—'

'No, Miss Elliott.'

The captain was on the verge of losing his patience, Cassie realised. But so was she. It was madness to pass up the faster option of riding across. Could he not see that?

'Your brother will already have seen one horse tied on behind the carriage and another following,' he explained crisply. 'If those horses disappear, he will know at once that you are no longer in the carriage. And it will not take him long to guess where we have gone. We need him to believe we are both still in the carriage, taking the dry route to England. We have to cross on foot.'

He was right. Cassie saw that immediately. She nodded and reached for the hamper.

'Bring a warm cloak, if you have it. Leave everything else.'

'But, sir, Miss Cassie canna—'

'Wheesht, Morag!' Cassie grabbed her long grey cloak from the maid's shaking fingers and stepped down from the carriage. 'Bless you, my dear friend. Try to keep ahead of them for as long as you can. Take care of her, Fraser. Bring her safely to me in England.'

'You can count on me, ma'am.' Fraser finished tying his horse on behind and scrambled up on to the box.

'Morag—'

'Miss Elliott! Come away! Now! We must let them go before your brother sees that the carriage has stopped.'

Cassie stepped back and raised a hand in farewell. Neither Morag nor Fraser had time to respond. The decoy carriage, drawn by its tiring horses, was already flying away on the road to Gretna.

They had to make the most of what cover there was, so it took them longer than Ross had calculated to reach old Shona's cottage. He would have been prepared to try the crossing without a guide, but Cassie Elliott was adamant. Shona could show them the quickest way. And steer them round the quicksands.

The gaunt old woman would not be rushed. She came slowly out of the cottage and looked across the firth, screwing up her eyes to judge the sands and the tide. Then she took the clay pipe from her mouth and waved it in the direction of the firth. 'Canna do it, Miss Cassie. 'Tis too late. There isna time to tak ye across and be back again afore the tide.'

'Shona, please! If I am found here—'

'Perhaps this will change your mind, old woman?' In desperation, Ross thrust a handful of guineas at her.

She ignored him and stared up at the sky. 'Rain,' she said. 'Aye. It'll be pouring down soon.'

'Shona, please, could you not take us just part of the way?'

The old woman didn't seem to be listening. She nodded to herself and disappeared through the doorway.

Ross allowed himself one curse of frustration. Then he seized Miss Elliott by the elbow and started to pull her towards the firth. 'We'd best get started on our own.'

'No' that way!' Shona had emerged from her cottage. She was carrying three stout sticks. 'Tak these.' She pushed sticks into their hands and gestured with her own. 'Come wi' me. And mak sure ye keep up.'

Suddenly the decrepit old woman had become strong and wiry, pacing out across the sand, only occasionally stopping to probe the edge of a pool. Miss Elliott followed immediately behind, though not treading exactly in Shona's footsteps, for that was dangerous—each step would sink a little more into the sand. Ross brought up the rear, watching carefully for any sign that the sand might be particularly treacherous. Now and then he would look up at the sky and at the coast of England, on the other side of the firth. It seemed close enough. But after fifteen minutes of trudging across, his legs were beginning to tire with the effort of fighting against the sucking sand. And the coast seemed no nearer.

Shona strode on, never once looking behind her to

see if they were following. As the water got deeper, she adopted an odd high-stepping gait that seem to make light work of the difficulties. But she kept looking up at the sky, which was growing ever darker, and down towards the sea from where the tide would soon come.

Miss Elliott said nothing. She simply plodded on behind Shona, copying her strange walk as best she could. She had sensibly kept her cloak high about her shoulders but she was now soaking wet up to her knees.

If only there were some way Ross could help her. But what could he do? If he offered to carry her, she would laugh in his face, with that deep-seated courage of hers shining in her eyes. Or else she would remind him that, with so much extra weight, he was bound to sink them both into the sand. She was an extraordinary woman. A diamond. She would not be cowed by this, or by anything. Had he really thought, for even a moment, that Cassie Elliott might be using him for her own ends? He should have known better. His disillusion over Julie should not have been allowed to colour his judgement of Cassie. For there was no comparison. None at all.

'Shona was right. It's starting to rain. Never mind. At least it's not a thunderstorm this time.' Cassie smiled over her shoulder at Ross. It was a smile of encouragement. And secret understanding.

Ross smiled back at the shared joke and trudged on, increasingly amazed by her hidden strength. He was beginning to feel that he did not know even a fraction of what Cassie Elliott was capable of.

Shona stopped suddenly, though she kept shifting from foot to foot, constantly feeling for firmer ground. 'I canna tak ye any further, else I'll no' get back.' She pointed with her stick at a large rock and a small hill behind. She explained that they must keep the two in line until the rock completely hid the hill. Then they must change course and head for the white rock, further to their right, away from Bowness. Once they reached that, they would be out of danger. And on English soil.

'Thank you, Shona,' Cassie said, breathing heavily from her exertions.

'Git on wi' ye, lassie. Ye've no' got long afore the tide. Remember, it comes up faster than a horse can gallop.'

Ross didn't waste any more time. He simply pressed a handful of guineas into the old woman's free hand and muttered his thanks as he started forward again. He was glad to see that Cassie was already moving. As a native of this place, she knew the dangers as well as anyone. Walking directly behind her, he could see that she was keeping the markers in line—and yet being careful where she trod. Where the direct line seemed to lead into deeper or faster-moving water, or to softer sand, she would move a little the other way. A moment later she would return to the line once more. She had learned Shona's secrets better than he would have thought possible.

'Can you go any faster, ma'am? If this rain gets any heavier, it's going to be difficult for us to see the markers. And it's going to get dark early.'

She nodded without turning and quickened her pace. She was now wet almost to her waist. As was Ross.

They were totally alone in the treacherous Solway.

Cassie could still see the rock and the hill. Just. Only another hundred yards or so and it would be time to turn. But the rain was getting worse, bouncing high off the pools. Not only was it getting dark early, but it was also getting misty. She forced her aching muscles to push on even faster.

'What was that?'

'I didn't hear anyth—' But then she did. It was the sound of voices, far across the firth. Men's voices.

'If it's your brother, he'll have horses. He can't have seen us yet, but he'll be able to move faster than we can. We must run.'

'But he's too late. The tide—' She stopped. Even through the mist she could tell that the voices were getting nearer.

'Run, Cassie. It's not far now. We can make it if you run.'

Cassie had already picked up her sodden skirts and was running towards the turning place. Once she tripped and fell her length, but she was back on her feet again before the captain could reach her. Terror drove her on, faster and faster.

At the turning point, she paused for only a second, to fix the route. She was almost sobbing for breath but she dared not stop. James was behind her.

It's not far. It's not far. We can make it. We can.

The white rock grew larger. There was one last stretch to cross. The water looked very deep. Cassie forced herself on. Straight on to the white rock. No time to go round.

She ploughed into the deep water. It pulled at her skirts though she tried to make her legs step high. She couldn't do it. She tried again. Her legs would not obey her. It was like wading through porridge.

A strong arm caught her round the waist and half-lifted, half-pulled her through to the shore. 'We're here,' he said hoarsely, gasping for air. He pushed her against the white rock for support, but her legs crumpled under her. She collapsed on the sand in a dripping heap.

He slid down beside her with a groan. 'A minute to rest, no more. We are not safe yet. We need to find cover.'

The sounds of voices, and horses, seemed suddenly very near. James must be ignoring the advancing tide. If he'd found Shona, he would have learnt the truth. Nothing would stop him. Not while he lived.

Cassie struggled to her feet. 'Which way, sir?

He grinned at her and hauled himself up. His face was filthy. All she could see were bright blue eyes, and white teeth. He grabbed her hand. 'Inland. Come on.'

'That clump of bushes. Try there.' Ross pushed her ahead of him through the low scrub. He looked over his shoulder. Nothing to be seen in the rain and the mist, but the voices were getting closer. Even though they were now a long way from the shore.

She took a few steps and disappeared.

'Wha—?'

Her head reappeared instantly, on a level with the ground. She was grinning. Almost laughing. 'Quick. Get in. Hurry, it's perfect.'

He slithered down beside her. The bushes concealed a large hollow, big enough to take them both. From above, there was nothing to see. Unless Elliott fell into the hole with them, he would never find it.

'Your guardian angel has my thanks,' he breathed, reaching out to pull her damp cloak around her. Her bonnet was long gone. Soon she would be shivering with cold.

'My guardian angel would be much less hard worked if I had a brother who was even half a man,' she cried angrily, venting her rage now there was a chance they might be safe. 'He's a disgrace to the human race. He—'

Ross tried to hush her. He needed to listen for their pursuers. In fact, he thought he could hear something. Closer than before.

'James Elliott should be dead and damned to all eternity,' she raged. 'He would be well served in hellfire. For he is the very devil—'

'Miss Elliott. Hush! I think I hear horses!'

She ignored him. 'And if he burns, it will—'

He had two choices. Silence her by brute force, or… He pulled her into his arms and kissed her.

Cassie had never felt so angry before. She was cold and wet. Her teeth were chattering. She was in fear of her life. And it was all James Elliott's doing. She wanted to curse him to the end of time. And she had the right. Captain Graham would not stop her.

And then he did. By simply kissing her.

The touch of his lips was hard at first, to silence her. She became rigid with shock. But then his lips gentled, began caressing her mouth. Suddenly, it was as if her chilled body had been sunk into a steaming hot bath. Every nerve, every bone, every inch of skin was burning. The danger that surrounded them melted away, and seemed to dissolve like Solway mist in the sunshine.

Cassie had never been kissed before. If this was kissing, it was wonderful. Something to make a woman forget the whole world. He continued to kiss and to tease. And, forgetting danger, forgetting propriety, Cassie returned his kiss with all the fervour she could muster.

'Cassie.' It was somewhere between a whisper and a groan against her mouth.

She could feel the heat of his fingers through her wet clothes. He pulled her even closer and she snuggled into him, willingly. He smelt of wet wool. And, somehow, of strong, protective male. This was a moment to—

'Cassie, listen.' Now it was only a tiny whisper.

Voices. And horses. Which direction? It was impossible to tell. The rain and the mist seemed to be doing strange things to the eerie sounds.

'Stay quiet. We'll be safe here.' He pulled her even closer, wrapping part of his own greatcoat over her cloak. She rested her cheek against his damp coat. She was almost sure she could feel his heartbeat, strong and solid, while her own was racing.

'We must gang back.'

Cassie started at the sound of that voice, suddenly very near. It was Ned. One of James's henchmen.

Ross stroked her hair gently. He didn't seem to have noticed how wet and tangled it was. His touch helped to calm her fears. Discovery was so very close.

'Feart, are ye?' That was James's voice. Just at hand.

Cassie tried to cower down into the hollow to make herself invisible. Ross held her up, taking the weight that her trembling legs could not carry. And then he kissed her again. Not to silence her. Not this time. This kiss was as gentle as thistledown blowing in the wind. For the length of his touch, her fears evaporated.

'Go back if ye must.' James again. 'I'll no' leave until I find her. I know she's here. She must be.'

'But ye'll be too late to get across the firth, maister.'

'There's time yet. I'll get across fine. But since you two are so hen-hearted, ye'd better start back.'

'We canna leave ye here alone.'

'I'm not alone, Ned. I have two loaded pistols for company. I'll not leave till I have to. And there's time yet to find her.'

Cassie's gasp of terror was muffled by Ross's damp coat. He put his lips to her hair. She could feel his warm breath, willing her to be strong.

'We'll go then, maister. An' wait for ye at Annan side.'

'Stop havering, man. Just get on with it.'

James's men said nothing more. Cassie could hear the sound of their horses as they started back across the firth. Now she and Ross were alone, waiting.

James was alone, too, searching. But he had pistols. With bullets enough for both Cassie and Ross.

Chapter Twelve

Ross cursed silently, pulling Cassie even closer into the shelter of his own body. Elliott had pistols. Ross had given both of his to Fraser. A soldier should have known better than to give up all his weapons. At the time, it had seemed the obvious course, for Fraser needed them to keep the pursuers at bay. Now that the pursuers were here, however…?

There was no point in wasting time over might-have-beens. The danger was here and now. His task was to protect Cassie. With his life, if need be. She was nestling in his arms like a wet and frightened kitten, seeking his warmth and comfort. Her every move showed how much she trusted him. That thought made him feel suddenly very proud. And very afraid.

Ross absently stroked Cassie's tangled hair, trying to soothe her, to keep her calm and quiet. He had no real fears that she would give them away. She had too much courage for that. In a tiny, disconnected part of his mind, he understood that he was holding her close, and stroking her body, because he wanted to. Because he had been longing to do so. Because he desired her.

The muffled sound of a horse forced him to focus on the danger around them rather than the stuff of dreams. Ross strained to hear the tiniest sound. Had he imagined that faint jingle of harness? With the mist swirling around, it was impossible to be sure of anything. Except the slightly trembling body in his arms.

She moved a little, starting to raise her head from his chest. Was she about to speak? That risk was too great. Ross hurriedly kissed her again, telling himself that it was the only safe way to ensure her silence. But he was lying. And he knew it. Especially when she began to respond to him and the kiss deepened into one of mounting passion. It was lunacy! Kissing her here, in the shelter of some sodden bushes, patrolled by a madman with pistols?

Yes, here! For if James Elliott found them, and killed them both, Ross wanted his last memory to be one of passion with Cassie Elliott. And, judging from the urgency of her response, she wanted it, too.

The presence of death does strange things, he realised. And he was not sorry for it.

He became vaguely conscious of another sound— the heavy breathing of an exhausted horse. Then it receded. Or he thought it had. It was impossible to be sure. Elliott might still be out there, only a few yards away. There was nothing to be done but wait. No matter how long it took. He would continue to hold Cassie safe in his arms. And they would wait.

It had been fully dark for a long time. There was no moon. In their leaf-shrouded hiding place, it was impossible to see anything at all.

Cassie was not afraid. Not while she was in Ross's arms. She knew, in the depths of her being, that Ross was going to save her. She did not know how. But the last shred of doubt had disappeared when he had finally torn his mouth from hers and murmured her name. His voice had been so low that she barely heard it. But she had felt the word vibrating through her body. Like a promise to be fulfilled.

He had been holding her close, supporting and warming her weary body, for hours now. He seemed to have the strength of ten. Should he not be as exhausted as she?

He brushed her hair back and put his lips to her ear. 'Cassie, I think he must have left by now.' His voice was barely a thread. 'There has been no sound for hours. He *must* have gone back.'

Cassie was not so sure. She reached up to pull Ross's head down to hers, so that she could whisper as he had done. 'What if he has decided to stay until the next tide? He may still be here somewhere, searching—waiting for us to make a move.'

She felt a shudder of response run through his body. She could sense the frustration consuming him. And the fear. Fear for her. He would not do anything to risk her safety. If risks were to be taken—and Cassie knew they could not simply remain to freeze to death where they were—she must be the one to say so.

'Sir, do you not think we should try for a better hiding place? If we stay here, we risk being discovered as soon as it is light. There must be tracks, must there not?'

He nodded against her hair. She could feel that his lips were smiling. She did not stop to wonder why. 'If we leave now, no one will be able to see us. It is too dark.'

'You are a brave woman, Cassie Elliott,' he whispered. 'But have you thought? If the mist has not lifted, we may start wandering in circles.'

'At least the walking would keep us warm.'

He made a sound low in his throat. Cassie fancied it might have been a laugh. Then, 'Stay here. I will return as quickly as I can.' He heaved himself out of their hollow and was gone.

Cassie hugged her cloak around her body, trying vainly to make up for the loss of his warmth. And his protection.

He returned more quickly than she had expected. To her surprise, he slid back down beside her and pulled her into his arms. As if she belonged there. He put his lips to her ear once more, but this time he did not speak. Not until he had placed a gentle kiss, first on her earlobe and then on her cheek. 'Don't be afraid, Cassie. I will protect you. I promise.'

She nodded. She knew that.

'There is no moon, but the sky is clear, so we will have the starlight to guide us. As far as I can tell, we are alone.'

She bit her tongue to stop herself from asking whether he was sure. She did not want him to think she doubted him. And, in any case, he could not say more than he already had. She hesitated a moment, then put a hand to his cheek. It was no longer wet, but she could feel the grime and the day's growth of stubble.

'Shall we go?' He sounded as light-hearted as if he were asking her for a dance.

'Yes. Perhaps we might find someone to help us soon?'

'We dare not risk that until we are much further from the shore. Your brother may have paid watchers here.' As if he had sensed her disappointment, he added, 'Later, when we are well inland, I'm sure we shall find help. But, for now, we must make what speed we can on foot.'

Cassie stifled a groan. Her stout boots had been soaked in the Solway. They were still wet, but they were already stiffening and cracking with the salt. Walking would rapidly become very painful. She put the thought aside. The captain's boots—Ross's boots—would be no better. If he could walk, then so could she. Barefoot, if need be.

She allowed him to help her out of the hollow. 'Take my hand, Cassie, and don't let go. If we become separated in the dark, we may not find each other again.'

The touch of his hand was warm and reassuring. Like her, he had lost his gloves somewhere along the way, so she could feel the calluses on his palm. In a strange way, that made his strength seem even more real.

He had been right about the stars. That faint glow did allow them to distinguish the rough shapes of bushes and trees. Animals, too. In one field, behind a stone dyke, Cassie made out the shapes of fat sheep lying on the ground. Still chewing, probably. One of them was certainly awake, for it turned its head as they passed. But none of them bothered to come to investigate the shadowy figures moving silently along in the lee of the wall.

After less than a mile, Ross stopped abruptly. 'Listen!'

Cassie listened intently, but all she could hear was the sound of a brook.

'Are you not thirsty?' There was a quiver of laughter in his low voice.

'I… Yes. Yes, I am.' She had not thought of it till now, but her throat was parched.

'Come. Take care where you walk. The bank may be slippery.' He led her towards the sound, gripping her hand firmly. 'Here. Sit down on this stone. At least it is not as wet as the grass.'

He let go of her fingers, but returned an instant later with some cool water in his cupped hands. She drank greedily. Nothing before had ever tasted quite so good. He continued to offer more and more until she shook her head and pushed his hands away. 'You must drink too.'

While he was slaking his thirst at the brookside, Cassie quietly pulled off her boots and ran her fingers over her feet. Her stockings had been shredded by the cracks in the leather and her heels and toes were blistered. She took off the stocking from one leg and threw it down on the grass. She was just starting on the other when he came back to her. He could not see her bare calves, could he?

She felt, rather than saw, that he picked up the discarded stocking. 'We must not leave any traces.' She thought he put it in his pocket. 'Do you wish to remove the other one, too?'

'I…I cannot. Not while you are watching.'

He said nothing. But he did turn his back for a moment.

Quickly, she removed the second stocking and pulled down her skirts again.

'I'll take that one, too,' he said, and pocketed it. 'Shall I help you on with your boots?'

'N…no,' she stammered, blushing in the darkness. 'If you would please turn your back once more…'

Cassie knew she must sound unbelievably missish to him, but there was more than propriety to consider. The moment he had turned away, she began trying to force her blistered feet into the unyielding leather, biting her lip against the pain. It was no use. She should never have taken her boots off in the first place. Her feet were too swollen and painful to wear those boots again now. She would have to go barefoot.

Swallowing hard, she stood up and dropped her skirts once more. Mindful of the captain's advice about the stockings, though, she picked up both her boots in her left hand and hid them behind her skirts. It was still much too dark for him to see what she was doing, thank goodness. Just as well, for he was the kind of man who might offer to carry her! 'I'm sorry to have been so slow, sir. I am ready to go on now.'

As he turned back towards her, she stretched out her right hand to clasp his. 'Will you lead the way, sir?'

They had been walking steadily for about half an hour when the sky clouded over again and the rain began. At first it was like damp mist—something Cassie called smirr—but it gradually became heavier and heavier. In no time, their half-dry clothes were soaked again. And they were both freezing. They would have to find shelter.

Ross glanced up at the sky, to take his bearings by the stars, but it was too late. There were no longer any to be seen. Instead, he tried to keep going in the direction he had chosen earlier, when he had been able to take a rough fix. They would only be able to inch forward now, feeling their way at every step.

He knew they must stop very soon. If they kept going in the rain and mist, they might lose their bearings completely. He was fairly sure they had been going roughly south-west, towards Sir Angus's house, which lay west and some miles inland from Bowness. Ross reckoned that they had made good progress in the terrible conditions, but he had to admit to himself that, for all their efforts, they had probably covered no more than a couple of miles.

In the dark, Cassie gave a little gasp of pain. It sounded dangerously loud even amid the thunder of the rain.

'What's the matter? Are you hurt?'

'No, no,' she said quickly, but he did not believe her. Cassie Elliott could tread in a man-trap and she would still deny she was hurt.

He took a step back towards her and put his arms around her, under her cloak, drawing her into what little warmth he had to offer. 'Tell me the truth, Cassie,' he said gently, but firmly. 'Why did you cry out?'

'I...I hurt my foot. I must have stepped on a

jagged stone. In the dark. But I am better now, truly. Let us go on.'

He ignored her plea. Instead he knelt down in front of her on the wet ground. 'Which foot?' Silence. She was going to be stubborn. 'Which foot, Cassie? We are not moving from this spot until I find out what is wrong.'

She let out a long sigh. 'The left,' she said at last and raised her skirt a fraction so that he could feel for damage to her boot.

'Good God!' If there was anyone within a quarter of a mile, they would have heard that anguished cry. 'What on earth have you done?' he groaned, but much more softly. 'How long have you been barefoot? Tell me, Cassie!'

'Since we stopped by the stream,' she whispered.

Ross could not find the words to upbraid her. And it would be wrong to do so, in any case, for her motives had been good ones. As for her courage, it was boundless.

'We must find somewhere to shelter.'

'No! I can go on. I—'

'But I will not. I cannot judge the direction without stars or landmarks to guide me. We must stop, and shelter, till the weather clears.'

'Oh.' She had stopped protesting.

'Now, Cassie. Stay where you are for a moment. Take this—' He rummaged in a pocket and produced something that he pushed into Cassie's hand. It felt like a piece of string. 'Tie it round your wrist. Here, let me.' He did so. 'Now I will leave you for a little and try to feel for some shelter. I thought I saw a dyke earlier, before the rain closed in.'

'Oh, but—'

'Hush. I have the other end of the string. There are several yards of it. I promise I will not go further than that. If I am unable to find anything, I will carry you for a little, and then we will try the string again.'

'But—' She was protesting again. He decided the quickest, and simplest way to silence her was the tried and tested one.

He kissed her.

Cassie groaned.

Ross pulled away on the instant. 'Cassie, my dear, did I hurt you? I am so sorry—'

She laughed—a woman whose feet were torn to shreds, and who was freezing to death, to boot—she actually laughed. 'Ross,' she said slowly, using his given name for the very first time and starting a strange glow in his belly, 'you are a fine soldier, I am sure, but you are sadly lacking in…er…certain other respects.'

'Oh.' It was all he could think to say.

'I shall wait here on the end of this flimsy piece of string, since you ask it of me, but I will have the rest of that kiss first.' She reached up to put her arms round his neck, pulling his mouth down to hers. Just before their lips touched, she whispered, 'And I will *not* be carried.'

* * *

It took several essays with Ross's clever piece of string before they found the dyke. Each time, Cassie hobbled along behind, holding Ross's hand and stubbornly refusing to be carried. It was a purely practical matter, she said. If he was carrying her, he wouldn't be able to feel his way. And then they would both be lost. She had no desire to be carried straight into a tarn, even by a heroic soldier intent on saving her feet. He had laughed, groaned, and surrendered. After kissing her yet again.

'Ah, the guardian angel again.' Ross's questing fingers had found that the dyke adjoined a high wall. A house, perhaps? More likely a barn or some kind of rough shelter for animals. Even if it was just a wall, it would give them some better protection from the wet. If it had a roof, it would be a palace.

By the time he had felt his way to the end of the string and then returned, he had made up his mind. Without saying a word, he lifted her into his arms.

'No, Ross! You can't! I won't let you!'

'I don't think you have a choice, Cassie.' He hoped she could hear the smile in his voice.

'But you'll have us in a ditch!'

'No. I know where we are. Reach out your hand. Towards the dyke.'

She exclaimed in surprise at finding a high wall.

'Now, if you'll just keep your hand touching the

wall while I carry you. Tell me as soon as the wall ends. I know it's not far.'

Cassie was so engrossed in doing her part of this task that she forgot to protest about being carried. They reached the end of the wall and followed it round one corner and then another. It was some kind of dilapidated barn. Part of its front wall was falling down. But it was shelter of a sort.

Ross carried Cassie inside, still following the line of the wall. In the far corner, he sensed that the ground was dry underfoot. At least part of the roof might still be intact. He set her down just as she started to protest once more.

'Put me— Oh. Thank you.'

'My pleasure, ma'am.' He grinned at her, even though he knew she could not see his face. 'At least this corner is dry, which is a relief.' He squatted down and felt around. 'We're really in luck. There is some hay here. It must be a store for some animals hereabouts.'

'That sounds wonderful. I admit I should very much like to sit down. It has been…er…a tiring day.'

Ross could not control the laughter that burst from him. 'Cassie Elliott, you are quite unbelievable. I may tell you that I've seen seasoned soldiers with less courage. And who complained a great deal more.'

'Have you? I—' There was a distinct catch in her voice. 'Thank you.' She moved to sit down.

'No, not yet. Let me spread this hay first. There isn't very much of it, but I fancy I can fashion a seat big enough for both of us. It's almost like being back in Spain, now I come to think of it. Though the rain was sometimes warmer there.' He finished spreading the hay and took off his coat to cover it. He hesitated. His coat was probably much too wet. Better to risk the scratching of the stalks than to invite a dose of the ague. 'If you are ready, ma'am, your *chaise longue* awaits.' He reached up for her hand and pulled her down beside him.

'Nothing less than the best velvet will do, you know.'

'Ah, forgive me, I was unaware. 'Tis only silk damask, I fear. Would you have me change it?'

'Immediately,' she said, snuggling into his side.

She was bearing up bravely, but he could feel that she was shivering with cold. No wonder. 'Cassie, would it not be best to remove your cloak? It is very wet.' As she started to struggle with the ties, he said, 'Let me help you, my dear.' He put his hands to her neck, touching the cold and slightly clammy skin until he found the fastenings and untied them. Then he lifted the cloak away. 'If I can find a hook of some kind, I'll tie it to the wall. It might dry a little. I'll need that string.' Gently, he untied it from Cassie's wrist. 'And my knife, too. I hope I still have it. It was some-where in my coat.'

He started to search through the pockets of his coat, but stopped with a curse so violent that Cassie gasped. 'Forgive me. I did not mean to shock you, but I am an idiot. Just look what I have found.'

'I would if I could, but I'm afraid my cat's eyes seem to have deserted me for the moment. What is it?'

'My brandy flask.' He started to unscrew the top. 'This will help to ward off the chill, Cassie. You need to get warm.' He pulled her against him and put the flask to her lips.

She pushed it away, with a cry of protest. 'Ugh! I can't drink spirits. You will make me drunk.'

'Cassie, you are as stubborn as a Spanish mule. You are soaked through, you're shivering with cold, you haven't eaten all day, but you refuse the only thing we have that might help?' He picked up a handful of hay and thrust it at her till it touched her skin. 'You could always eat the hay, of course, but since you are not a horse, I venture to suggest that the brandy would do you more good.' His anger was perilously near the surface now. Did she not understand the danger she was in? He almost wanted to shake her. And to force the brandy down her throat.

Very gently, she opened his fingers and removed the wisps of hay. 'I'm sorry,' she said quietly, putting her hand in his. 'I didn't mean to vex you. I know you have my best interests at heart.'

'Then, will you—'

Without letting him finish, she took the open flask from his hand and swallowed a large gulp.

'Cassie, you can't—' It was much too late. She was already coughing and spluttering as the spirit burnt its way down her throat.

'I—' Her voice was a barely audible croak.

Ross quickly set the flask down and pulled Cassie into his arms, kissing the top of her head. His anger had evaporated on the spot. He only hoped she would not realise that he was laughing.

But she had. 'You rogue,' she wheezed as soon as she had a little control of her voice again. 'You're laughing at me.'

'Well, you did rather remind me of a frog.'

'Oh? I'm happy to admit that I am wet and cold, as frogs are, but I didn't think I was green.'

He laughed again, but this time she was laughing with him. 'You may indeed turn green if you stay as wet as you are. Seriously, you must get warm. I dare not build a fire, just in case. So we shall have to make the best of what we have. Lie down here with me. My coat can cover us. It's heavier than your cloak and perhaps not so wet on the inside.'

She did as he bade her, apparently without a qualm. Most other ladies would have had a fit of the vapours at the thought. But most other ladies would not have been alone with a man in the first place.

He pulled her body close against the length of his own, trying to warm every inch of her. He tucked the coat around her as best he could. His boots were sticking out, but her poor injured feet were, mercifully, covered.

'Are you feeling any warmer now?'

'Yes. Much,' she whispered. 'I can certainly feel the effects of the brandy.'

'Good.' He held her even closer. 'Try to go to sleep if you can.' He tucked her head under his chin. Her hair had come down around her shoulders in a mass of damp, tangled curls. Exactly like the first time he had ever seen her. A sodden gown and a mass of tangled hair.

She moaned a little.

'Cassie?'

'It is nothing. Truly.'

This time her body was betraying her, for she had started to shake uncontrollably. The noise of her chattering teeth was incredibly loud in the dark silence.

'This is no good. We must get you out of those wet clothes. There's no other way.' Ignoring her stammering protest, he threw off the greatcoat and pulled her up so that he could start undoing her gown.

'Sir, you cannot—' she managed between shivers.

'This is no time for propriety, Cassie. If we don't get you dry, you'll never recover from this.' He was running his hands down the back of her gown as he

spoke. 'Dammit. Where are the fastenings on this confounded garment?'

'I can do it.' She started to fumble, somewhere at the
front, under her breasts.

Chapter Thirteen

Cassie managed to make her trembling fingers obey her for long enough to undo her gown and petticoats, though she could not prevent Ross from helping her out of them. She tried not to think about what she was doing. If she did not get dry and warm, she was going to be very ill. And then she would never reach her godfather's. Compared with that, what was a little impropriety?

'Now your stays, Cassie.'

Cassie gulped between shivers. 'You will have t…to help me. The laces. At the back.'

She felt his fingers struggling with the damp laces. And failing to undo the knots. 'I can k…keep them on,' she said faintly.

'No. They are just as wet as your gown.'

She felt his fingers on her back and then her stays gave way. Heavens, he had used that knife to slit them!

'You will have to arrive at Sir Angus's without stays, I'm afraid. But it's better than not arriving at all.' He rose. 'Stay there. I'll try to hang up your things, or spread them out at least.'

Cassie picked up the greatcoat and huddled into it. In a moment, he was back. 'Now your shift, Cassie.'

'Wha—? No. No, I cannot.'

He reached across and took a handful of the material. 'It's thin enough. It will dry if we spread it out. But if you keep it on it will help you to freeze.'

For a moment, Cassie thought he was going to pull it from her body. But he did nothing. He simply waited. Then, 'Be sensible, Cassie. It is for the best. You know that.'

He did not need to force her. He knew exactly how to make her comply. With a slight shrug, Cassie wriggled the shift from under her bottom and took it off. At least he could not see her naked body in the dark.

'Thank you.' He took it from her and moved to spread it out. 'Now, lie down on the hay and we'll try to get you warm.'

Cassie waited for him to spread the greatcoat over her. He did not. Instead she heard some sounds she could not place, and then he was lying beside her once more, pulling her against his big body and covering them both. She gasped. 'Sir, you—'

'My clothes were as wet as yours, Cassie. They had to go, too.'

'But—'

'Sleep now. We have a fair way to go, as soon as it

is light.' He sounded very firm, almost matter of fact. Which was very strange, coming from a man who was naked from the waist up.

Ross lay still for a long time, holding Cassie until the shaking stopped. She was certainly much warmer now. At length, she drifted into sleep and he dared to let out the breath he seemed to have been holding for hours.

It was not easy to hold a naked girl in his arms, trying to prevent his body from reacting to the temptation she offered. And Cassie Elliott—even wet and shivering—was a luscious armful. He had told himself that he could not remove his damp breeches because he did not dare to remove his sodden boots. That was true. As far as it went. But it was only half of the story. He could admit now that he was afraid to lie naked with Cassie in his arms.

He tried to divert his thoughts, to plan what they should do when dawn came. He would have to find some way of binding up Cassie's feet. Bits of her stays, perhaps, tied up with string? No, absurd. But he might be able to hack off part of the tails of his greatcoat and use those. The cloth was fairly thick. It might fit the bill, for a while. If only he knew how much further they had to go. And whether they dared to seek help.

Cassie moaned softly against his chest, but did not wake.

That settled it. It would be inhuman to ask her to walk. He would have to seek help, no matter what the risk. He still had money enough, a purse of guineas and some slightly damp banknotes. If he could find someone in this godforsaken landscape, he would offer them a king's ransom for a horse, or a cart.

'Ross?' Her voice sounded drowsy. And tempting.

'You're safe, Cassie. Go back to sleep. It's still dark.'

'Mmm.' She snuggled up against him, rubbing her cheek against his bare skin.

He managed to suppress a groan. But his body was reacting, no matter how much he willed it to behave.

'Mmm. It feels so warm, so safe.' She turned slightly in his arms. 'Ouch!' She sat up. If she had been half-asleep before, she must be wide awake now.

'What is it, Cassie?'

'Something bit me. I think.'

It was still too dark to see so Ross ran his hands over their makeshift bed. He pulled out a piece of sharp straw and touched it to her hand. 'Not a bite, I think, just a piece of straw. But if you wait here a moment, I will fetch your shift. It should be dry enough now and it will protect your skin.'

Cassie sat hugging her knees while she waited. She felt so much better now, having slept a little. Her feet still hurt, but she was determined to ignore that. Besides, she had been enjoying the extraordinary sensation of being naked in the arms of the man she loved.

She gasped aloud.

'Cassie, what is it?'

'N…nothing.' She swallowed hard. She was burning all over. Did she really love him? How had that come about? She barely knew him. These tangled thoughts continued to tumble around in her brain while he sat down beside her and helped her into her shift.

'You will feel better now that you are at least partly clad,' he said with a smile in his voice.

'Thank you,' she murmured automatically. But something inside her wanted to shout *No! No, I want to be as we were. Breast to breast and skin to skin.* Good God, she was clearly a total wanton. She shivered a little at the thought.

'Cassie, you are getting cold. Come back under the greatcoat. Let me warm you.'

How could she let him hold her now, now that she knew? She slid back into his arms, nonetheless. It would be foolish to do anything else in the chill of the night. He drew her close and tucked her head against his shoulder. His scent was all around her, caressing her skin like a silken wrap. She could feel the rasp of his stubble against her temple. Deliberately, she moved to feel it more. It was proof positive that he was here, and that he was real. It might be all she would have, for if James caught them, he was bound to kill them both. Cassie was sure of that. She wriggled a little, trying to bring Ross even closer.

He groaned. 'Cassie, please.' His voice sounded deeper than normal, and hoarse. 'Please try to keep still.'

'Oh. I beg your pardon. Am I stopping you from going to sleep?'

He groaned again. 'I…er… Cassie, it is…not easy for a man to sleep with a woman in his arms, especially one like you.'

What did he mean? 'I don't understand. Am I hurting you?'

'Oh, Cassie.' He laughed softly. 'I had forgotten what an innocent you are, in spite of your soldier's courage. My dear, when a man has a beautiful woman in his arms, it can be…er…a struggle to control his body. Forgive me,' he added quickly. 'I do not mean to embarrass you.'

Cassie might have been embarrassed if it had been light, but here, in the dark, tucked up close beside him, she felt as if they were in a fairytale castle, with high walls all around, protecting them from the horrors of the world outside. Jamie was out there somewhere, prowling with his pistols. But as long as the dark lasted to protect them, he could not come near. She pressed a tiny kiss on the skin at the base of Ross's throat.

She did not want the dawn to come.

'Cassie, please… It is difficult enough already. If you do that, I may not be answerable for my actions.'

She smiled against his skin. And kissed him again. Touching him was magic, too.

'Cassie, you don't know what you are doing. Please stop.'

She lifted her head and began to feather tiny kisses down the length of his jaw.

'No!' He threw back the greatcoat and started to sit up, but Cassie would not let him go.

'Don't leave me, Ross. Please. Stay with me.'

'I cannot.' His voice was harsh, and strained. 'If we continue to lie together here, we will end up making love. We must not do that. My duty is to escort you to safety. I cannot dishonour you. It is best if you stay here, under the greatcoat. I will put on my other clothes and walk about. That way we will both be warm. And away from temptation.'

Cassie hesitated for only a second. She could not allow Ross to leave her enchanted castle. The moment he did, Jamie might shoot him down. They had only this one night. And, accepting now that she did love Ross, Cassie was burning for him. She knew well enough what happened between a man and a woman—she was a country girl—and she knew, too, that Ross Graham was the only man she could ever love. She would have none of his notions of duty and honour.

She sat up behind him and wrapped her arms around his waist, pressing her breasts against his naked back. She cursed the thin shift. She wanted no more barriers between them.

'Cassie! Stop! You don't know what you are doing, what you are risking!'

She leant her cheek against his back. She could feel the tension in his muscles. 'I do know, Ross,' she said softly, but very firmly. 'I know exactly. I know that, tomorrow, my brother may shoot me, or both of us. I know that tonight I want to be in the arms of the man I love.'

She heard his sharp intake of breath. His body froze, every single muscle now rigid. She rubbed her cheek gently against his back. 'Do you not believe me? It *is* true. I understand it now, though I did not before. I want us to be together, Ross. Now.'

He moaned slightly.

To Cassie, it sounded like a rejection. She tried to swallow the sob that rose in her throat. 'I...I had not thought you would not want me. I am sorry, I—'

'Oh, Cassie.' He turned round in her arms and pulled her close. 'You goose. Of course I want you. Desperately. You are proud and brave and beautiful. And I desire you with every fibre of my being. But I cannot.'

Cassie smiled then. She put a hand to his cheek, gentling him. 'There is no dishonour. I love you, Ross Graham. And I give myself willingly. I need you to make love to me.' She drew his head down and kissed him, trying to show him the depth of her passion and to ignite his own.

He moaned again, but this time it was a response. 'You

are a witch, Cassie Elliott,' he breathed. It seemed that he, too, had realised that there was magic in this place.

He kissed her until her mind was reeling and her body was screaming for more of his touch. Her breasts had begun to ache. The thin stuff of her shift rasped across her erect nipples like rough-hewn wood on finest lawn. She knew she could not bear it a moment longer. 'I must take this off,' she gasped, breaking their kiss for a second. She ripped the shift over her head and would have cast it aside, but he took it from her hand.

'Sit up a moment, Cassie,' he said. 'There are better uses for this.' He smoothed the shift across their bed of hay and laid her down on it. The shift felt transformed against her skin—from coarsest sackcloth to sheerest silk.

Cassie reached up to pull him down to her. He was fumbling with his breeches. 'They are damp,' she said chidingly. 'You should have removed them before.'

He gave a strangled laugh. 'If I had done so, I would have made love to you hours ago. And if I do so now… Oh, Cassie, it will be too late to change your mind. Are you really sure this is what you want?'

She put her hands over his. 'Yes. I am sure. I cannot see you, but I need to touch you. All of you.'

That was more than Ross could bear. With clumsy fingers, he unfastened his breeches and pushed them down. Then he pulled Cassie close. He expected her to recoil in fright at her first contact with a fully aroused man. But she did not. She moved her body slightly, so that her breasts teased the skin of his chest. It was a most glorious torture. There was no going back now.

He kissed her beautiful mouth, darting back and forth with his tongue until her lips opened to admit him. She was an apt and willing pupil, for soon she was kissing him with more passion than he had ever known from a lover. He put his hands to her breasts, teasing both nipples until they stood in hard peaks between finger and thumb. Tempting. Too tempting to miss.

He moved to take one of her breasts in his mouth and began to suck. Hard. Cassie moaned with pleasure. He smiled against her delicate skin and began to suck even harder, at the same time allowing his hand to drift down her belly to the junction of her thighs. When he cupped her, she did not resist. She opened to him like a flower to the sunshine. Oh, she was beautiful. And so very desirable.

Her hands were on his back now, moving up and down, her nails digging into his flesh with every pull of his mouth on her breast. He moved his fingers into her moist warmth and caressed her. This time the groan came from the depths of her belly and her nails dug deep into his back.

He returned to her mouth and began to kiss her more passionately yet, his tongue keeping pace with the movement of his fingers at the core of her. She had begun to move against his hand, in rhythm with his touch. She was more than ready.

Without lifting his mouth from hers, he moved to cover her fully and made ready to take her. He hesitated. It took all his self-control, but he waited.

She would have none of it. She smoothed her fingers down his back and put her hands on his naked buttocks. Then she pushed, at the same time rising up to meet his thrust.

Her cry was instant, swallowed in his kiss.

He froze. He had hurt her. He must stop.

In that single moment, her body had gone rigid, but now it softened again and she began to kiss him back. Her hands started to stroke the skin of his bottom.

Once more, he moved within her and she responded, more strongly than before, rising to meet his every thrust. Stronger. Faster. And then she cried out his name. A second later, he too reached the moment of ecstasy and collapsed on her quivering body.

Cassie beamed into the darkness, loving the feel of his weight upon her. Her body was humming with pleasure and sated passion. She had known— somehow—that it would be like this. And this memory of her magic castle could not be taken from her. Not while she lived.

Tentatively, she stroked his shoulder. He raised himself on his elbows. 'Forgive me. I am too heavy for you.' He rolled over on to his side, bringing her with him and holding her close. 'Thank you,' he whispered.

She beamed again. Then, realising he could not see, she tried to think of something to say in response. No words came. Feeling suddenly very shy, she said nothing at all. Instead, she touched a gentle kiss to the corner of his mouth.

'Sleep now,' he said huskily, pushing her head down on to his shoulder. 'We will speak of this later.'

Cassie woke to find that it was still dark. Ross was lying beside her, but he was awake. She could tell from his breathing. There was no other sound to be heard except the dripping of rain outside.

'Ross?'

'Mmm?' He seemed to be staring up into the darkness, his right hand tucked behind his head. His left was still under Cassie's shoulders. She doubted that he could have any feeling left in it.

'What are you thinking?'

'Oh, nothing much. About unanswered questions, I suppose. Who I am. And where I really come from. And how I come to be here. Making love to a beautiful Scottish lass.'

She put her fingers to his lips. She had guessed right. He was smiling. 'Do you really know nothing about your family?'

'Almost nothing. I was sure my father's family was here. I have searched, but… I asked Colonel Anstruther and various others about the Graham family from Dumfries, but no one could tell me anything. One strange thing did happen, however. When I visited the church at Ruthwell, a few days ago, I saw a crest on an old gravestone. It seemed somehow familiar. Unfortunately, the stone was so old and worn that no one could tell me exactly what the inscription had been. Though they were sure that the name had not been Graham. So I am no further forward in my quest. Perhaps I shall find the answer at Longtown. You did say, did you not, that the inn there was called the Graham Arms?'

'Yes. I am sorry you have found so little. It must be difficult to feel alone in the world. And rootless.'

'No, Cassie, I am not alone. I have no family, to be sure, but I have friends, good friends. Whereas you…you have no one.' He stroked her hair back from her forehead.

'I—' Her voice cracked. For a moment she could not speak. 'I have good friends, too,' she managed at last. 'Morag, and Alasdair. And Colonel and Mrs Anstruther, now. And…and you.'

He dropped a kiss on her hair. 'Mmm.'

Cassie could think of nothing more to say. She was increasingly conscious of her nakedness. And of the fact that she had offered herself to him. Nay, she had thrown herself at him like the veriest trollop. He was holding her close. But what did he really think of her? It did not matter that she loved him. She should never have told him so. For he did not love her. That was clear. If he loved her, he would have said so. Surely he would? But he had not.

'Poor Cassie,' he murmured, stroking her back. 'Such a hard life you have had.'

Cassie swallowed hard. He was going to start talking about her family. She sensed it. And he was bound to ask about her mother. She ought to tell him. A wave of revulsion engulfed her at the thought. She could not tell him. It was impossible. Had she not already been brazen enough, telling him she loved him? And forcing him to make love to her? He must already have decided she was no better than a harlot. If she told him about her mother's fate—condemned for a lunatic and a wanton—it would serve only to confirm Cassie's own depravity. He would despise her. That was a thought she could not bear.

'I… You…' She racked her brain, trying to think of some way to turn the subject away from her family. 'Were you many years in the army?' she said at last.

'Yes. Max and I joined together, when we were very young.'

'Max?'

'He is my closest friend. We grew up together. After my mother died.'

'Oh.' So he did have family. Of a sort. 'Did you see much of the world in your years of service?'

He made a strange sound, deep in his throat. 'It's a strange life in some ways. There are hardships, but the greatest of friendships, too. What matters most to any soldier is his comrades. We shared everything. Laughter and childish jokes. Horses and hunting for our next meal.' He paused, clearly remembering. There had been a smile in his voice. But when he spoke again, it had vanished. 'We saw the snow, and the mud, and the driving rain, and the burning sun of the Peninsula. We met all that together. But…there was so much death. Too many of my friends, brave men all, lying in their own blood.' He shuddered. 'Forgive me. I should not have spoken so. Especially to a lady. I was not…er…not thinking clearly. Forgive me.'

Cassie said nothing. His pain was too obvious, too raw. He needed comfort, not words. She put her arms round him and drew his head down on to her breast, stroking his hair, just as he had done for her.

'Oh, Cassie,' he breathed, lying still for a second or two. 'Oh, Cassie.'

And then he was kissing her again, and the passion was filling them both, until it spilled over and carried them up into the shining sky above the magic castle where their world exploded into stars.

* * *

The first grey light of morning woke Ross. For a moment, he imagined he was back in Spain, rising with the dawn to assemble his men and march out towards the next battle. But, in Spain, he had not slept with a warm and yielding female body tucked beguilingly into his. Cassie. Beautiful Cassie, passionate Cassie.

She loved him. He did not understand how that could be, how such a woman could offer him the gift of herself. He had not deserved her. But he had been unable to resist. Could any man? The thought that she might have given herself to any other man gnawed at his gut. He—Ross Graham—had taken her. And he was honour-bound to keep her now.

Stealthily, he raised his head so that he could look at her in the gathering light. They had spent so many hours together in the dark, feeling their way, feeling for each other. Now he wanted to feast his eyes on the woman who had made love to him so passionately.

She lay, curled into his body, with her cheek cradled on one hand. Her slow breathing fluttered against his bare chest, with a trust, an intimacy, that touched him deeply. What was he to do now? He had promised himself that he would deliver her to her godfather's house and then leave. He had promised himself that he would keep his distance from her, lest she, too, be using him. He almost laughed at the absurdity of it all. Surely a woman did not use the man she loved?

For she did love him. Somehow, Ross knew that he could be absolutely certain of that. When he had loved Julie, it had led to nothing but heartache. He had lost her to another man, the one she had always loved. Cassie must not be allowed to suffer as Ross had done. He would not desert her now. It was a matter of honour.

He grimaced at the latest turn of his thoughts. What on earth was he doing? Trying to convince himself, by cool argument? Utter madness! He *could* not leave her now.

He barely suppressed a shudder at the thought of such weakness. Was it love?

No! He would have recognised it. It was certainly not what he had felt for Julie. He had admired Julie's beauty and her courage. She had been like a white goddess, somehow untouchable, almost forbidden, a woman who must not be sullied by contact with earthly things. With Cassie, his greatest desire was to hold her close, to shelter and protect her, and—he admitted ruefully—to continue to share the passion they had discovered together. But with Cassie, he would laugh, too, and they would face the dangers of the world together.

At that moment, Ross realised that he had never once mentioned, to Julie, the horrors he had seen on those bloody campaigns, nor the depth of the loss he felt about his missing family. But he had confided in

Cassie, as easily as he confided in himself. Almost as if she were part of him.

He shook his head in bewilderment. For a man of thirty-four, it was passing strange that such grown-up feelings should arrive so late. Yet this sudden emotional bond to Cassie was very strong. And he knew, deep in his bones, that it would grow with every day they spent together.

But it could not be love. He was armoured against that.

He gazed down at Cassie's beautiful face. This wonderful woman had given herself to him, in love. Strong emotions welled up within him. He was unable to resist the temptation to place a tiny kiss on her smooth white forehead.

Not tiny enough. Her long dark eyelashes flickered against her cheeks. She gave a tiny purr and opened sleepy eyes. 'Ross?' she murmured.

'I am here, my sweet. It's dawn. We must be on our way soon.'

Her eyes widened as the reality of their situation hit home. And then she blushed, a glorious rosy red. She could not hold his gaze.

'Stay there a moment,' he said, trying to adopt the matter-of-fact tone that would spare her further embarrassment. Under cover of the greatcoat, he finished fastening his breeches. 'I will fetch your clothes. And then I will go outside while you dress.'

He sat up, leaving the greatcoat tucked around her to preserve her modesty. She murmured something that might have been thanks. But as he moved towards the ramshackle entrance to their shelter, she burst out laughing, a golden peal of merriment that lifted his spirits to the skies. He turned back to see her head poking out over the collar of his coat and a single bare arm pointing at his lower body.

'Boots!' she managed at last, between whoops of laughter. 'You never took off your boots!'

Ross, too, began to laugh. 'I did not dare, Cassie, for then there would have been two of us, limping along barefoot.' He looked down at himself. His breeches were filthy and barely dry, but at least he was decent. Cassie could look at him without needing to blush even more.

He gazed across at her laughing face and made a silent vow. The next time he made love to Cassie Elliott, it would be in a proper bed, with fine white sheets and silken covers. And she would be his wife.

Chapter Fourteen

Ross had quickly reconnoitred the route while Cassie was dressing. There appeared to be quite a substantial river some way ahead of them. As far as he could tell from such a distance, the only means of crossing it was a single-track bridge. If James Elliott was still on the English side of the Solway, that would be where he would lie in wait. They would have to be immensely careful when they came to approach the crossing point.

Beyond the bridge, there seemed to be houses, possibly a village. If he and Cassie managed to reach it safely—Ross offered up a fervent prayer for that— there would be a fair chance that the immediate danger might be over. He would be able to risk looking for someone to take them to Sir Angus's house.

Taking one last, very careful look around for hidden dangers, Ross retraced his steps. He found Cassie fully dressed, trying to force her injured feet into her boots. 'No, Cassie!' He knelt down, catching her hands and forcing her to stop. 'You really will injure yourself if you do that. I have a better plan.' He picked up his greatcoat from the hay and began to hack large pieces from it with his pocket knife.

Cassie watched, bemused, as he then proceeded to cut away the soles of her ruined boots.

'Now, sit on the hay and give me your foot.'

It was not a request. He was back to being a soldier again. Giving orders. Cassie bit back the retort that leapt to her tongue and did as she was bid. She sat, fascinated, while he wrapped the cloth round her foot, added the leather sole beneath, and then bound the whole snugly together with string and the laces from her discarded boots.

'Now the other one.' He did the same again, with deft but gentle fingers. 'Stand up, and see how it feels.'

The result was strange, to be sure. But it might enable her to walk, a little way at least. 'Much better than before. Thank you. Do you think these makeshift boots will take us all the way?'

Ross patted her ankle and rose to his feet. 'The laces will soon wear through if we meet rough ground. Let us hope we do not. Come now. We should go. But before we do…' He handed her his flask. His stern look dared her to refuse.

'Thank you, sir,' she said demurely. This time she only sipped the fiery liquid. Once. Twice. That was enough.

'You learn quickly, Cassie,' he said with a smile, putting the flask to his own lips and swallowing. Then he returned it to the pocket of his mutilated greatcoat. 'There is enough left to warm us just once more, if the rain should return.'

He led her out into the field. 'Draw your cloak around you, Cassie. Its dull colour will serve to make you less conspicuous. And stay behind me. Like my shadow. We must go forward quietly, and with great care. It is safest to assume that our pursuers lie in wait for us at every turn.'

A shiver started to run through Cassie's body, but she mastered it enough to look up at him and to nod firmly. 'I am ready,' she whispered.

They trudged forward in silence for perhaps half a mile. There was no sign of life, neither human nor animal. The sky was leaden. The sun had no chance of penetrating the gloom. It felt more like winter than high summer.

'How are your shoes, Cassie?' He grinned at her over his shoulder.

The leather sole was flapping a bit with each step, and she had to lift each foot much higher than normal in order to walk. He must be able to see that perfectly well, but Cassie simply grinned back at him and said, 'They are the most comfortable dancing slippers I have ever worn, sir. You should set yourself up as a souter.'

He frowned at the unfamiliar word.

'A shoemaker, I should say.'

The frown disappeared. 'Maybe I shall. And you will make a fine souter's wife, I dare say. I shall have you cutting out the leather and writing up my accounts with the best of them.' He turned away from her and continued walking.

He was teasing. But not about the marriage. Not about that. Cassie felt suddenly chilled to the bone, as if she were back in the salt mist of the Solway. Ross Graham had clearly decided that Cassie was to marry him. Of all the arrogant, high-handed, odious—! He did not love her. He had not even asked for her hand. He had simply assumed that, by taking her virginity, he had acquired the right to decide her future. How like a man! Cassie was not sure whether she was about to weep, or to scream.

Anger won. How dare he treat her like a…like one of his underlings, required to obey without question? She took one swift pace towards him, grabbed his hand and pulled him back round to face her. Then she slapped him with all the strength in her right arm. 'It is enough that my brother treats me like a chattel,' she spat. 'Now you are no better.' Feeling the tears pricking behind her eyelids, Cassie gathered her skirts and started to run across the field, away from their line of march.

'Cassie!' Ross put a hand to his cheek. His little

Cassie was much stronger than she looked. He started after her, but not so fast that he would catch her before her anger had begun to subside. For she was right. Or partly right. He admitted to himself, rubbing his cheek a little sheepishly, that he had been unfeeling. But she, on the other hand, had been downright foolhardy, shouting at him at the top of her voice when any number of enemies might be within earshot. No one had appeared, however, so it seemed they were still safe. Really, the situation was totally ridiculous. A young woman in homemade boots trying to run across a muddy field. Followed by a grimy man in a tattered coat. It was his fault she was fleeing. Of course it was. But if she could see how they both looked…

The tension had been building in him like water behind a dam. He could hold it no longer. It burst through—as laughter. She heard it and turned. Her expression was a mixture of fury and humiliation. His nervy laughter died on the spot.

'Cassie! Wait!' He began to run. He heard her strangled 'No!' Then she was running away from him again.

He overhauled her just as she tripped over her ungainly boots and fell her length on the grass. For a moment she was too winded to speak. But by the time she had recovered her breath, Ross had thrown himself down and caught her to him. They tussled in a tangled heap of filthy clothes and limbs. This time he did not make the mistake of reasoning with her. As soon as she opened her mouth to berate him, he kissed her. She struggled. But not for long. The touch of their lips ignited the fire of passion in both of them, like lightning striking the tinder of a bone dry heath.

Just before he lost all power of coherent thought, Ross tore his mouth from hers. 'Cassie, my sweet Cassie. Forgive me. I would not have hurt you for the world. I…I need you. And I truly want you to be my wife. Will you?'

She hesitated, looking at him with eyes so dark he could have drowned in them. He held her gaze, willing her to respond. Then, at last, she nodded.

He wanted to whoop in triumph. Instead, he kissed her again, long and hard. And she responded with equal passion. Their bargain was sealed.

They moved in the shadow of a hedge until they neared the river. It was clearly too wide and too fast-moving to ford. Besides, Cassie's feet were in no fit state to walk through water again. Ross pushed her deep into the cover of the hedge. There was hawthorn in it. She could feel the thorns digging into her flesh. She bit her lip hard, forcing herself to ignore the little stabbing pains.

'Stay there while I check the bridge,' he whispered.

She could see the concern on his face. He was afraid to leave her. Perhaps he did love her, even though he had not said so? He was caring for her, certainly. At the last moment, he turned back and touched a finger to her cheek, before moving off again. He crept forward, bent into a half-crouch, moving like a shadow. Cassie closed her eyes. And prayed.

In less than ten minutes, he returned. He was smiling. Quite jauntily. While she was still impaled on a hawthorn bush!

'There is no sign of your brother, or any of his men.' He helped her out of her hiding place, carefully removing the thorny branches that had been pinning her down. 'Poor Cassie. You have been in the wars. But I have good news, at last.'

Her spirits rose. A little. He did care. A little.

'I have found a carter who will carry us. There is no need for you to walk any further.' With that, he picked her up, ignoring her cry of protest, and started for the bridge, carrying her as if she weighed nothing at all.

'Put me down, Ross! I can walk just as well as you!'

He shook his head but said nothing. And he tightened his grip on her. Confound the man, he was much too used to getting his own way. In everything.

Cassie did not struggle any more, for his arms were clamped round her like a vice. She struggled instead with her own thoughts. He had said he needed her. That at least was true. She had heard it in his voice. And he had asked her to be his wife. But that might simply have been a means of getting his own way. She could see perfectly well that he was not a man who was easily diverted, once he had decided on a course of action. And it appeared that he had definitely made up his mind to marry her. Because they had lain together? Because, without marriage, she was ruined? Was marriage the price his sense of honour demanded, in return for his one night of passion?

She had no way of knowing. And that hurt. She began to question why she had accepted him, but that answer came soon enough. It was because he had been kissing her until her senses were reeling, until she could no longer tell what was sky and what was earth. She could no more have refused him than she could have flown across that river on her own wings.

He had said he needed her. And he had asked for her hand. She must cling to that. It might be all she would ever have.

A treacherous voice reminded her that she still had not told him of her mother's fate. Would he have offered for her if he had known that? That little worm of doubt settled in her gut, twisting and gnawing. She did not know. And she never would. Not now.

'Ah, here is our carriage.'

The so-called carriage was a very dirty farm cart drawn by a single ancient horse. The carter threw them a strange look. No doubt he thought she was a mad woman, dressed as she was, and carried in the arms of a man who looked like a cross between a ruffian and a beggar.

'My wife and I were caught by the tide in the Solway. She lost her boots and cannot walk, as you see. But you said that you were going near Whitemoss House, did you not?'

'Aye, sir. It's on my way. I be going to Langrigg.'

Cassie gasped. Even Ross paled.

'Langrigg, you say?' Ross said, after a moment.

'Aye, sir. D'ye ken it? Village t'other side o' the abbey. Was ye wanting t' gang there?'

'Er…no. No, thank you. If you would simply take us to Whitemoss House, by Newton Arlosh, we should be obliged to you. And I promise it will be worth your while.'

'Thank 'ee, sir.' The man touched his greasy cap and climbed up on to the front of the cart.

Ross lifted Cassie on to the back of the cart and made them both as comfortable as he could. 'The carter offered us seats beside him, but I refused,' he whispered. 'It's less than five miles, he says, and we still have to plan what to say to your godfather. I should have thought of that before.'

Cassie thought he sounded cross with himself. No doubt he was berating himself for being carried away by passion when he should have been planning their campaign.

The cart started forward at an easy pace. The carter was singing to himself, in time with the plodding hooves.

'Now, lean against me, Cassie, and keep your head

down so that no one can see your face. If anyone speaks to us as we go by, you must not look at them, or say a word. Do you understand?'

She nodded. He was right, of course, but did he have to be quite so imperious? He sounded like a sergeant-major with a raw recruit.

'We must stick as closely as possible to the truth. And you will have to do much of the telling, I'm afraid. You can say that you were coming to see him, with Morag, of course, to…er…consult him about your future. You had to come in secret because your brother was totally opposed to any such visit. Sir Angus does know about James, I suppose?'

'Yes.' As soon as the word was spoken, Cassie realised, with a guilty pang, that she sounded like a mutinous child. And she was behaving like one, too. But Ross seemed not to have noticed. He was intent on concocting their story.

'I happened to be in Annan and offered to escort you both across. Unfortunately, on the day, the crossing proved too treacherous for the carriage. Morag refused to go on foot. But you…er…you—'

'I behaved like a spoilt child and insisted,' Cassie said, with renewed spirit. This was a part she could certainly play. And now was no time to let her doubts get in the way. She pushed them aside. 'Don't worry,' she said confidently. 'Sir Angus has not seen me for years. He has no reason not to believe that of me. I'll spin him a tale about taking Shona for a chaperon and only discovering, too late, that she would not stay with us.'

'Good. Very good. And then, of course, we had to struggle ashore and were soaked in the process. You also lost your boots.'

'Did I?'

'You did. You are like a tiresome child, Cassie. And frequently stupid and headstrong.'

'Oh. Undoubtedly. And then what happened, pray?'

'We were unable to hire any horses, but managed to persuade this good carter to bring us to the edge of Sir Angus's estate. Now, just a few hours later, here we are.'

'A few hours?'

'Oh, yes, Cassie. Mark that. We crossed on this morning's low tide. Last night, you were safely tucked up in bed at Langrigg. The Scottish Langrigg.'

She had to smile then. He seemed to have thought of almost everything. Except for one thing.

She put her lips to his ear and lowered her voice even more. 'Ross, you told the carter we were man and wife. Did you plan to say the same to my godfather?'

'No, of course not. He would know it was not true. I lied to the carter—' he looked over his shoulder, but the carter was still singing lustily and seemed to be paying no attention to his passengers '—because no lady would be travelling alone with a man unless she was married to him.'

'We might have been brother and sister.'

'Do we look like brother and sister?'

It was true that they did not. Their colouring could not have been more different. 'We must just hope, then,' Cassie whispered, ignoring his question, 'that the carter does not start telling the world about the dirty tramp and his wife he carried to Newton Arlosh.'

Ross nodded. And shrugged. The damage was done.

'So, as far as my godfather is concerned, Captain Graham and Miss Elliott are…the merest acquaintances?'

'Yes. No!' He shook his head vehemently. 'No, Cassie, I do not think we could convince him of that. Let us tell him that I am a good friend of Colonel Anstruther's and that you are much in the habit of visiting the colonel's wife. We have become well acquainted during your visits there. We share a mutual interest, in…in—'

'Plants and gardens?'

He smiled at last. She saw the tension leave his clenched jaw. 'Aye, if you like, my dear. As long as you are sure that your godfather does not have the knowledge to test my claim. For I will soon be discovered as a fraud if he does.'

Once they had settled on their tactics, Cassie relaxed against Ross's shoulder and closed her eyes. Ross did not wonder at it. After all she had been through, her body must be exhausted.

Ross was glad of this chance to put his own thoughts in order, soothed by the rhythmic rumbling of the cart. This road, in contrast to others they had used, was remarkably free of bumps and holes. The gradual slowing of Cassie's breathing told him she was asleep. He hoped she would not wake before they reached Sir Angus's house. She needed her rest. He resisted the temptation to stroke her hair back from her forehead, lest he wake her, as he had done once before. No, let her be.

A muffled crack brought his senses to the alert. He looked cautiously all round, but could see nothing to account for the noise. Perhaps the horse had trodden on a twig? That had to be the most likely explanation. There were low hedges and dykes edging the fields, but the land was very flat, with hardly any trees to be seen. A man could hide behind the hedges, but there was not enough cover for a horse. If James Elliott was waiting hereabouts, he was on foot. That seemed highly improbable. More likely that he had given up and gone back across the Solway to join his gang of ruffians. And to think of another way of seizing Cassie.

Don't be too sure, too soon. That inner voice had saved him more than once, in Spain. He knew better than to ignore it. He continued to scan the fields carefully, looking for the slightest sign that the animals were restless or wary. A nervous sheep, or a startling bird might be the only warning he would have of an attack. Until he could deliver Cassie safely to Sir Angus at Whitemoss House, she would remain in real danger, for Ross had only his fists to defend her if it came to a fight with Elliott or his men. At Whitemoss House, he would be able to borrow a pistol. And he was sure he would be able to rely on Sir Angus's servants, too.

Provided he could rely on Sir Angus himself. What if he did not believe their cock-and-bull story? Might he refuse to offer Cassie shelter? No. Impossible. He was her godfather. And Cassie had assured Ross that her godfather knew all about James Elliott's wickedness. Sir Angus could not turn her away. The real danger was that he would see through their flimsy story and insist on knowing the truth. If that happened… Well, if that happened, Ross would simply admit that they had been together for a day and a night. And then he would formally ask for Cassie's hand. Sir Angus was sure to agree. A man of the world would bow to the inevitable.

But Cassie would be furious. With both of them.

Poor Cassie. She did not begin to understand the risks they were taking. If she knew how many times his heart had been in his mouth… He was almost sure he had managed to conceal how much he feared for her safety. She had probably concluded he was quite without feelings.

If only she knew!

The cart began to slow. 'Here y'are, sir,' said the driver over his shoulder. He nodded to a long driveway on their right, flanked by bushes and, further on, by fine trees. 'Whitemoss House. 'Bout half a mile up yonder.'

The tension in Ross's gut began to lessen. Almost there. He would soon have Cassie safe. Just another half mile along the drive to the house. Just another half mile of careful watching.

'Cassie. Cassie, my dear. We have arrived.'

She opened her eyes and blinked against the light. Then she looked round inquiringly. 'But where is the house?'

He smiled reassuringly and pointed. 'At the end of this drive. A few hundred yards more, and you will be able to rest, and have your hurts tended.' He jumped down and lifted her on to her feet. 'Wait by the bushes, my dear, while I settle our debts.' He began reaching into his pocket.

Cassie's feet had stiffened while she slept. It hurt to put one foot in front of the other. But if Ross saw that, he would insist on carrying her all the way along the drive. She could not allow that. She walked slowly across the road to the bushes by the entrance to Sir Angus's estate, forcing herself to ignore the pain as she moved. She must not allow it to show on her face. She must smile at him. After all, they had almost gained her freedom. And Ross had told her he needed her.

Yet there had been precious little sign of it since. She might have been a servant, considering the way he had been ordering her about.

The cart was moving off again. The driver was singing even louder than before. No doubt he was delighted with his unexpected windfall.

Ross came to stand beside her, watching the disappearing cart. 'Come now, Cassie,' he said with a smile. 'Just a little further and you will be safe.' He made to pick her up.

'No! It is too far. And besides, you will need your hands free. What if James should be lying in wait for us?'

He nodded, looking serious once more. 'You are right. And the sooner we are knocking on your godfather's door, the happier I shall be. Let us make a start.'

Cassie refused to let herself limp. What were a few blisters, after all? She could do this. She could.

It took longer than she expected—Ross had not told her the truth about how far it was—but at last they could see the house, a low, ivy-covered building with gleaming windows and a wide front door at the top of a flight of white steps. From where they stood, the avenue approaching the house cut through sweeping lawns bordered by magnificent lime trees.

Ross heaved a sigh of relief. 'We are safe now.'

'What do you mean?'

'There is no more cover between here and the house. Your brother cannot be here.'

It was only then that Cassie understood the fears that had been driving him. Was that why he had been so sharp, so uncaring? She smiled tentatively up at him.

'And now, my dear Miss Elliott, we had better try what we can do to make you a little more presentable. If Sir Angus sees this dishevelled little hedge-bird on his doorstep, he may send for the constable.' He helped her to straighten her clothes a little. There was nothing to be done about the clumsy cloth boots. She could only hope that her skirts would hide them.

'Let me tie back your hair.' He combed it back with his fingers and plaited it roughly. Then he secured the end with yet another piece of string.

'Where did you learn to plait hair?'

'Ah, my dear, a soldier learns many skills in the course of his travels. But a lady would not wish to know how I acquired that one.' He grinned wickedly at her.

She smiled back. She could not help it. Ross—her Ross?—was now being light-hearted and teasing once more. And caring? Perhaps.

'And finally, your dirty face, m'dear. You daren't meet your godfather like that.' He took a damp hand-kerchief from his pocket, explaining that he had dipped it in the river for just this purpose, and proceeded to wipe the grime from her face. 'There,' he said. 'Much better. No, wait. There's a little smudge on the end of your nose.' He bent to drop a kiss on the tip of it and then stepped back, eyes dancing. 'Now you'll do.'

He offered her his arm, for all the world as if they were in a ballroom. 'Madam, will you walk?'

She dropped him a tiny curtsy and took his arm. She could not stop smiling. Not just at his teasing—though that was wonderful, and heart-warming—but at his gentle consideration for her. He must love her. Why else would he behave so?

He would say the words soon. He must do, surely?

Chapter Fifteen

Just as they reached the end of the drive and the grand entrance to Whitemoss House, a tiny shaft of sunlight broke through the heavy clouds. It caught the front of the house close by the door, making the white steps gleam and the window panes sparkle like gems. Ross put a hand under Cassie's elbow and ushered her up to the door. 'Look! The house is smiling a welcome to us. You will be safe now.'

Cassie felt more than a little nervous, none the less. Even with Ross's reassuring bulk at her back. She straightened her spine and glanced over her shoulder at him. He did not look totally confident either. But they had no choice now. They must go forward. She reached up for the huge brass knocker, lifted it and let it fall. The noise echoed as if the whole house behind the door were one vast hollow. And the echo went on and on.

'Chin up, Cassie,' Ross whispered.

At that very moment, the great door was opened by a very superior butler. He looked at Cassie, down a very long nose, as if she were something dropped on the doorstep by a marauding cat. 'We feed beggars at the kitchen door,' he sneered. 'The scullery maid will see to you.' He made to close the door in Cassie's face.

Cassie's nerves were drowned by a flood of indignation. She would not permit any servant to treat her so. 'We are here to see Sir Angus Fergusson,' she snapped. 'Pray tell him that Miss Cassandra Elliott, his *goddaughter*, has arrived, with Captain Ross Graham.'

The butler goggled. Her educated speech did not match her appearance. Not at all.

Cassie swept past him into the cool hallway. The butler was still rooted to the spot by the open door. 'Perhaps you would show us into a saloon where we may wait? I am not in the habit of being left in the hall, like a tradesman.'

That last sally did the trick. The butler bowed Ross into the house and quickly closed the door. Then he showed both of them into a book-lined library that opened off the hall. 'I will inform Sir Angus of your arrival, miss.' With a tiny bow, he scuttled out.

'Remind me never to try to get the better of you when you are acting the great lady, Cassie. Very impressive.'

Now that the initial skirmish was over, Cassie's nerves

were returning, and worse than before. 'I…I…' she stammered. 'I suppose I have spent too long as mistress of a household. Servants have to know their place.'

'Quite. And that butler now knows his—under Miss Cassie's foot. Do you think that I, too, shall soon be under the cat's foot?'

He was trying to tease her out of her nervousness. Cassie felt a warm glow starting somewhere around her heart. He was such a thoughtful, considerate man. As a husband, would he be—?

The door was thrown open to admit a man of middle height and remarkable girth. 'Cassie? Is it really you?' He stopped in his tracks, frowning at the sight of the extraordinary pair who had invaded his library. 'Cassie?' he said again, in a voice filled with uncertainty.

Cassie ran to him and seized both his hands. 'Oh, Godfather. I am so glad to be here at last. I did not know where to turn. You were—you *are* my last hope.'

Sir Angus's frown cleared. 'Cassie. My dear child. What on earth has happened to you? You look like— Well, never mind that. Where is your maid? And who is this gentleman with you?'

'Godfather, may I present Captain Ross Graham, late of his Majesty's Fifty-second Regiment?' Ross bowed politely. 'Captain Graham was kind enough to escort me to you when I…' She pulled Sir Angus towards the sofa and almost pushed him into it, settling herself close by his side and tucking her hand into his. 'Oh, Godfather, I fear you will think that I have been very foolish.'

Sir Angus began to look concerned. He threw a very stern look towards Ross, as if trying to assess his part in whatever folly Cassie was guilty of.

'Please let me explain,' she gushed, allowing neither man a moment to intervene before she launched into the tale that she and Ross had prepared. 'I had to come to you, sir. James is determined to sell me to the first man who will offer enough to pay his debts. He says it is my duty to agree. And he will lock me in the asylum if I do not.'

'Good God!' Sir Angus was outraged. He had turned almost purple. 'Sell you? Impossible! You are gently born. A lady leaves her home only when she marries.'

'Oh, it *is* marriage he has in mind, sir. Not…er…not anything else. But he does not care who the man may be, provided he is willing to pay.'

Sir Angus's outrage was visibly lessening. 'If your brother is proposing an honourable alliance, with a gentleman, I do not see that you need concern yourself with the details of the marriage contract, Cassie.'

Oh, dear. Cassie quickly changed tack—and allowed herself an untruth. What choice did she have? 'My brother does not intend me to marry a gentleman. And I am sure that no gentleman would agree to James's demands. A gentleman would expect a dowry, surely, not an account for merchandise delivered? James has mentioned several possibilities, all of them in trade. One of them is rumoured to have smothered his father in order to gain control of the family shop. Oh, Godfather, I should rather go to the asylum than marry such a man!'

'You shall do neither, my dear. Marry a shop-keeper? Certainly not. The very idea! Outrageous! I would not have thought even James Elliott capable of anything so base.'

Cassie reached up to kiss his cheek. 'Thank you, dear Godfather. I was sure you would understand. But now I am here, I don't know what to do next. I am much in need of your advice. I know it will be sound, for you have always had my best interests at heart.'

Sir Angus nodded and patted her hand. 'Quite so. Quite so.'

'I'm sure you will agree that I cannot return to my brother now, not after what he has threatened to do. But, you see, I have no money of my own. And nowhere to go. What should I do, Godfather? He will be here soon, demanding that I return to Langrigg immediately.'

'No need for any hasty decisions on that score, m'dear,' Sir Angus said gruffly. 'All in good time. All in good time. You are safe here for the present. More to the point, though, how is it that you are travelling, unchaperoned, with a gentleman who is not related to you? It is not at all the thing, you know, for a young lady such as yourself to—'

'Oh, that!' said Cassie dismissively. 'That was *such* a chapter of accidents, Godfather. I swear you will never believe what happened. It was just like a romance.'

Sir Angus cleared his throat, probably to scold her for her taste in reading.

Cassie did not allow him time to say a word. 'It was like this. I crept out of Langrigg with Morag, my maid, very early this morning, and we drove to Annan so that I could cross the Solway to see you. I knew we would have to take the short route so that James would not catch up with us. You know how adamant he is that I should not be allowed to see you. Or even write to you.'

'Aye. Your brother nurses the old feud.'

'We happened to come across Captain Graham in Annan. He is an old friend of Colonel Anstruther's, by the bye, and very respectable. We have met often of late at the colonel's house.' Cassie put her mouth to her godfather's ear and added, in a whisper, 'The Captain can be a bit stuffy, but I don't hold it against him.' Reverting to her normal voice, she continued, 'Captain Graham said that a lady and her maid could not cross alone. He insisted on escorting us. He went on and on at me until I agreed. In fact—' she threw an arch look at Ross '—it was because of that delay that everything went wrong.'

'Miss Elliott, that is unjust. I—'

'No, sir. It was certainly your fault that we were delayed. If we had started earlier, as I wished, we could have driven across. It was because of you that I had to go on foot. And without Morag.'

'That is not so,' Ross said brusquely. 'When the guide said it was too late to drive across, you could have given up the idea. Tried another day. Your woman was very wise to refuse to go. Just look at what happened when you did try.'

Cassie shook her head vehemently and turned back to Sir Angus. 'I could not go back to James, Godfather,' she said, with a distinct catch in her voice. 'He would have locked me up at Langrigg. Or sent me to the asylum. I should never have been able to reach you. And you are my only hope of avoiding a…a *mésalliance*.'

He patted her hand again. 'Yes, yes. I quite understand that. But you should not have crossed without a chaperon. Think of the damage to your reputation, my dear.'

'Oh, but I did have a chaperon, Godfather. I had Shona, the guide. I thought she would be just as good as Morag. Better even, for Morag does not know the way across the firth and is afraid of the quicksands, besides. Only…only Shona would not stay with me as I had assumed she would. She insisted on going back to Annan as soon as we were close enough to the

English shore. She abandoned us!' Cassie thought she had put just the right note of outrage into that. 'She should have stayed with me until I had a chance to get a message to you. Don't you agree, sir?' she added, trying to sound suitably aggrieved.

'I think you have been remarkably foolish about this, Cassie. I had not remembered you as quite so headstrong, I must say.'

'Oh. Oh, dear. Please do not be cross with me, Godfather. I will try to be more sensible in the future. Truly I will.'

He softened immediately. 'Very well. But you still have not explained how you come to be in such a sorry state.'

'Oh, that is easily done. After Shona abandoned us, we had to make our own way ashore. The tide was coming in, incredibly fast, and we were almost caught by it. Running across sand is very difficult, you know. I fell into the water more than once. And it was only by abandoning my valise that we managed to avoid being drowned.' She waved a hand in Ross's general direction. 'Captain Graham did help me ashore. I am grateful for that, of course. But it is a pity he didn't succeed in rescuing my baggage, too. I don't even have a clean gown to wear.' She scowled at Ross as if all her misfortunes could be laid at his door.

'It seems to me, Cassie, that you should be thanking the captain, rather than complaining.' Sir Angus rose and crossed to the fireplace to pull the bell. 'I take it, sir,' he said to Ross, 'that you had the dev—the deuce of a job to bring my goddaughter here in one piece?'

'Yes, indeed, sir. And luck was against us all the way, I fear. We could not find horses to hire anywhere. We had to walk as far as Kirkbride before we found a carter to bring us here. Miss Elliott is very cold and probably still quite wet. Might I suggest—?'

'No need, sir, no need. I will get my housekeeper to take care of her. Immediately. A hot bath is what she needs. And a change of clothing. You, too, I dare say?'

'I can think of nothing better. Thank you.'

The door opened to admit the butler. This time, his face was a picture of concern. Cassie only just managed to hide her amusement as Sir Angus gave his orders and the butler hastened to assure them all that nothing was too much trouble for the master's goddaughter.

Presentable at last, Cassie sank gratefully on to the sofa by the fire in Sir Angus's sitting room. She could hardly believe that Sir Angus had been so welcoming—or so ready to swallow their Banbury tale. Yet it was wonderful to feel secure at last and free from fear. And to be surrounded by the warmth of Ross's regard. It did not matter that their future was uncertain. Somehow she would ensure they could make their way together. She knew that she—they—would succeed. She had enough love for both of them. Her love *would* conquer all obstacles, she was sure of it. Almost.

She reached out a hand to pull Ross down beside her. He ignored her. 'Ross?' Another little flicker of doubt touched her heart. He was not even aware of her presence. He was staring at the wall alongside the fireplace.

'Ross?' she said again, rather more forcefully. 'What is it?'

He turned to look her full in the face. His own was ashen. Then he turned back to stare at the wall once more.

Cassie jumped up and grabbed his hand. It was cold and a little clammy, as if he were starting a fever. He must be ill! No wonder. His clothes had been soaked. 'Ross! Please sit down. You are unwell. You—'

The door opened to readmit Sir Angus. Cassie dropped Ross's hand as though it were a red-hot coal, praying her godfather had not seen. She could feel her face flushing hot. She dare not risk alienating Sir Angus by a vulgar display, for she truly needed his support now. If he did not continue to take her part, she could be lost, back in James's power. It would be best to pretend, for the moment at least, that she and Ross meant nothing to each other. If Sir Angus ever discovered what had happened… No, he must never learn that. Never. It was enough that James had called her 'harlot' when it was not merited. Now…

'I hope you are well settled in to your bedchambers,' Sir Angus said genially. 'You look much more the thing, both of you, now that you are no longer in those filthy clothes.'

His normal bluff manner seemed unchanged. Perhaps he had noticed nothing, after all? Cassie hoped her blush was subsiding. 'Thank you, Godfather. It is very warm in here, do you not think?' she added hastily, beginning to fan herself with her hand. 'Do you always have a fire at this season?'

'Aye, when the wind is in this direction. I'm afraid this house can be very draughty. No amount of work by the men seems to be able to prevent it. I have discovered that the best remedy for that—and for being cold and wet—is a good fire and a good brandy. Will you join me, Captain?'

Cassie was glad to see that Ross seemed to have recovered his wits enough to remember his manners. He bowed slightly to his host. 'Sir, you are very good, especially to unlooked—for travellers such as ourselves. I would enjoy a brandy very much.'

'As would I, Godfather.' Cassie smiled up at Sir Angus in what she hoped was a winning way. She was determined to lighten the atmosphere. Ross's voice had sounded so strained.

'You may have Madeira, Cassie. Or ratafia, if you wish. Brandy is not a drink for ladies.'

'Oh.' Cassie threw a laughing sideways glance at

Ross and then said, demurely, 'I should very much like a glass of Madeira, Godfather. I hope it is as efficacious as brandy for warding off the chill?'

'You, child, are a minx.' Sir Angus smiled down at her, in spite of his words. Then he poured the glasses and handed them round. It was an easy, friendly gesture. Cassie was glad that her godfather had not summoned a servant. It suggested that he felt comfortable with Cassie. And also with Ross.

But Ross was not comfortable. He was still standing near the fire. And every few seconds he would half-turn to stare again at the wall.

'Is there something about those miniatures that interests you, sir?' Sir Angus rose from his place and came to the fire.

Ross pointed at a miniature of a youngish lady wearing the dress of perhaps thirty years before. 'That lady in the blue striped gown, sir. She interests me greatly.' His voice was barely above a whisper.

'She was a very handsome young woman, I will admit. And the likeness was well taken, too. I do not wish to pry, sir, but may I ask the reason for your interest in her?'

Ross swallowed audibly. 'That lady was my mother.'

Chapter Sixteen

'I suggest you take a seat, sir,' said Sir Angus once their initial stuttering confusion had been resolved. 'There is much to discuss, and the telling may take some time.' He raised an eyebrow at Cassie. 'Perhaps you should return to your chamber, my dear? A rest will do you good. I can send for you when the captain and I have finished with his private business.'

Cassie hesitated. She could not insist on staying.

'There is no need, sir,' Ross said quickly. 'Miss Elliott already knows something of my family history. We discussed it at Mrs Anstruther's. I have no objection to her hearing more.' Before Sir Angus could respond, Ross helped Cassie to her place on the sofa.

Taking a seat close by her side, he said, 'As Miss Elliott knows, I came to Scotland partly to find out what I could about my early life. My mother died in London when I was just a boy, and there was no one else to tell me about my family. I knew only that they came from the area near Dumfries. So far, I have been unable to discover anything, apart from a mysterious ancient carving in Ruthwell church that no one can explain. But it is clear from that miniature that you have some knowledge that relates to me. If you could throw light on my ancestry, I should be more than grateful to you, sir.'

'Aye, I can do that, though it's a melancholy tale.'

Cassie frowned, wondering what was to come. It did not sound promising.

'First of all, I must tell you, sir, that your name is not Ross Graham.'

Cassie saw how the blood immediately drained from Ross's face.

Sir Angus nodded slightly. 'It is Ross Graham Fergusson.' He paused, taking a sip of his brandy and letting that startling piece of information sink into his listeners' minds.

Ross was the first to recover. 'Does that mean that you and I are in some way related, sir?'

'Aye. But distantly. Distantly. However, that is how I come to know something of your history.'

'I should be most grateful if you would tell it to me, sir.'

'Yes, please, Godfather,' Cassie added. 'If the mystery is to be solved, it will be—'

Sir Angus reached across and patted her hand.

'Wheesht, lassie. If you don't interrupt, we will make more progress in the telling of this tale.'

Cassie sank back in her seat, biting her lip. She was reassured by Ross's solid warmth beside her, leaning ever so slightly into her. He wanted her to know that they were facing this discovery together. Whatever it might turn out to be.

'The lady in the portrait was born Margaret Graham, the daughter of a prominent Edinburgh lawyer. She married a husband who was much older than her, a man by the name of James Ross Fergusson, a distant relative of mine.'

'James *Ross* Fergusson,' breathed Cassie. 'I see.'

Sir Angus ignored her. 'James Ross Fergusson was the youngest child—and only son—of a landed Dumfries family. And you, sir, are his only child.'

Cassie clapped her hands together. 'So Ro—er—Captain Graham *does* have an inheritance after all? Why, that is wonderful!' She beamed across at Ross, trying to convey how delighted she was on his behalf. A moment later, she remembered the part she was meant to be playing. Oh, dear. They were not supposed to be intimate friends.

Sir Angus did not seem to have noticed Cassie's slip. 'There is an inheritance. On paper. But, in practice, there is nothing. I'm afraid your inheritance is well beyond reach. Indeed, that was why your mother went to such lengths to conceal herself and her child. She understood, as the Dumfries family did not, that it would be throwing good money after bad to seek to regain her son's inheritance. She knew she could never succeed and that she could be bankrupted in the doing. She was a canny woman, your mother, sir. London educated. And, as her father was one of the cleverest lawyers in Edinburgh, I have no doubt she learned much at his side. You have a great deal to be grateful for, my boy.'

Ross felt he would need to know a lot more of this strange story before he accepted Sir Angus's airy judgement. And, in any case, the old man's tale was becoming more and more difficult to follow. 'Sir, exactly what did my mother do? And why did she do it? Can you tell me that?'

'I need to tell you, first, a little about your father and your grandfather. Your grandfather, also James Fergusson, was a supporter of the Pretender, and followed the man they now so readily call Bonnie Prince Charlie. Your grandfather fought for him. And so did your father, even though he was barely fifteen years old at the Battle of Culloden. Your grandfather died on that bleak moor. His lands were forfeited to the crown the following year. So your father was left with nothing to inherit. Perhaps just as well, for he'd have handed it all over to his prince, so besotted was he with that romantic and forlorn cause.'

'He followed the prince into exile?'

'Aye, he did. He was under attainder. He'd have been arrested and executed for treason if he had returned to Scotland. And he hated the Hanoverians. Always. The more so a few years later when his lands were annexed for good. You can't really blame him. He would have been barely into his majority at the time, and there he was, an exile, seeing his inheritance swallowed for ever in the maw of his London enemy, leaving himself for ever penniless and rootless. I believe he spent many years serving as a mercenary in various European armies.' Sir Angus took a slow and thoughtful sip of his brandy.

Ross felt as if a lead weight had settled in his gut. He had sought his father. And found a traitor! Trying to sound as normal as possible, he said, 'But he must have returned eventually. Else how did he meet my mother?'

'He returned about fifteen years after Culloden, I think. He called himself James Ross Scott, then, for there was still a price on his head.'

Cassie gasped. Then, under her skirts, she laid her hand on his. It was balm to his bleeding wounds. He had been sure she must be repelled by him now. Could she love him still, in spite of this?

'It meant little by then, my dear,' Sir Angus continued. 'The government was secure enough by that time and certainly didn't want to stir up trouble by arresting people like the captain's father. I'm sure they spied on him, to make sure he wasn't up to mischief. But apart from that, they let him alone. Like many others who had…er…chosen the wrong side, he was quietly accepted back into society. And he prospered. In trade, I'm afraid, but without his lands, nothing else was open to him. Eventually, he was comfortable enough to re-establish himself as a gentleman and to take a wife. He must have been well nigh fifty by then. He couldn't afford to delay any longer.'

'How did he meet my mother?'

'I'm afraid I don't know that. I assume he met her in Edinburgh, where he often went on business. Come to think of it, her father may have been his lawyer there. That would certainly explain it.'

Ross nodded. He was finding it increasingly difficult to speak without betraying his emotions.

'Her name was Margaret Graham. And you were their only child—Ross Graham Fergusson. Your family lived in a fine new house in Dumfries. And your father prospered, until the government decided to return some of the forfeited lands.'

'I don't understand. The lands were returned?'

'Only some of them. The government returned some of the estates to their original owners. In 1784, I think it was. But your father's estate was not among them. I don't know why. Perhaps he had not spent enough time, or money, on toadying to those with the power to make such decisions. Whatever the reason, it was clear then that his estate was gone for ever. There was no chance of regaining it. Your father died that same year. I was told it was an apoplexy, as a result of his fury at the wicked wrong done to him by the government. I can well imagine that was the cause. He had a temper, most certainly.'

That old man—shouting—must have been Ross's father. Dead for over thirty years. And Ross's only memory of him was of anger. And of his mother's fear.

'My poor mother. What did she do, alone with a child of just three?'

'Her father had insisted on generous marriage settlements. He was also trustee for your inheritance from your father. The widow and child would have lived comfortably enough, except…'

'Except?'

'Your father's family—he had two older sisters, both married—wanted to go to law to make the government return the family lands. They didn't have the money to pursue the case, of course. They wanted *your* inheritance to pay the legal costs. Your poor mother was plagued by them, and their huge broods of children, day in, day out. She resisted strongly, and as long as she had her father's support, she succeeded. But once he died, she had no hope of continuing to resist the family pressure, for she had no one to take her side. So she did the only thing she could. She sold everything and fled with you to England, to her other trustee, a London lawyer by the name of Gent. I now believe that he sheltered your mother and helped you both to hide from your father's grasping family.'

'And she changed her name back to Graham.'

'She must have done so. It appears she was determined not to be found.'

Ross nodded. There was a lump in his throat at the memory of his mother. He would not have believed such courage and devotion was possible. She had even carried her secrets to the grave, in order to protect the son she loved. If only he could see her, now that he was a man, and tell her—

'When did she die?'

Ross had to clear his throat to reply. 'When I was eight. I was brought up by a dear friend of my mother's, Miss Mary Rosevale. I believe they had been at school together, in London. Miss Rosevale was already bringing up her own nephew and she kindly took me in. Max and I grew up almost like brothers. Eventually, we even joined the army together.'

'You are still close friends?'

'Yes, sir. Very close. Even though my friend is now much risen in the world. He served with me as plain Captain Rosevale, but now he is the Earl of Penrose.' Ross felt he was starting to regain his composure. It was easier to talk about Max. And the touch of Cassie's hand on his was healing, still. She was an amazing woman, too.

'Indeed? I have heard of that affair. It was the talk of London a few months ago. Probably still is.' Sir Angus sipped his brandy appreciatively. 'Am I right in thinking that the new Earl of Penrose has snared the family wealth as well? The rumours of that have reached us even here.'

'The earldom is not well endowed. That is true, sir. But the earl is not marrying his cousin for her money, I can assure you of that. Theirs is a love match.' He glanced quickly at Cassie. He could not help it.

Sir Angus grunted. 'New-fangled notions. Don't hold with 'em, m'self. In my day, we married where we were bid.'

That was too much for Cassie's self-control, it seemed. 'Godfather,' she burst out, 'I did not tell you earlier, but James's latest idea is to marry me to Colonel Anstruther, who must be old enough to be my grand-father. You wouldn't approve of that, would you?'

'Anstruther? But, surely he already has a—' Sir Angus cleared his throat loudly. 'Are you sure, Cassie? Colonel Anstruther is no tradesman. No. Most defi-nitely a gentleman, not at all the kind of man to stoop to James's notion of a bride-price. Still…it would be a good match for you, no doubt of that. Anstruther is ex-tremely wealthy. And he has no children of his own. So—' He coloured a little. 'But it is not to be thought of. Not now. Wicked—and ill bred—to suggest such a thing. Once the colonel becomes a widower, perhaps. And once there has been a decent interval of mourning.'

Ross cursed silently. Sir Angus was no longer reacting as Cassie had hoped. It was her own fault, of course, for mentioning the colonel at all. She should have allowed Sir Angus to continue to believe that James was about to sell her to a shopkeeper.

Ross leaned forward, pressing his warmth against Cassie as he did so, trying to provide reassurance. She had played her part so convincingly. Until now. Ross swallowed hard, forcing himself to focus on Cassie. He would have to distract Sir Angus. Somehow. But how? It was not an easy thing to divert an old man from the prospect of a match as rich as Croesus for his goddaughter. Especially when the alternative had just been shown to have a very unsavoury history.

Ross's gut churned again at the thought of what he had just learned. A traitor's son. And he had dared to aspire to Cassie's hand? Yet what else could he do? He had taken her honour. He had to restore it…by giving her the protection of his name. Graham. That was his name. And he would keep it so. It was an honourable name, belonging to an officer and a gentleman. A name with no taint.

'Sir,' he began quietly, 'what you have told me about my family puts most of my questions to rest. It is truly a sad history—what a grasping family they must be— but, at least, I now know who I am and where I came from. Thanks to you, I have learned that I have no ex- pectations beyond what I had when I came to

Scotland. And that I am the son of a sometime trades-man, who was a traitor, to boot.' He placed his glass on the mahogany side table with great deliberation. Then, rising to his feet, he said proudly, 'Nevertheless, I am not without friends, or influence. I am a gentle-man; I hold the king's commission.'

Sir Angus looked a little puzzled at his guest's be-haviour, but he nodded his agreement. To a man of his upbringing, an officer was most certainly a gentleman, whatever his family history.

Ross cleared his throat, not daring to look at Cassie. 'I can assure you, sir, that I am comfortable enough to support a wife. With your permission, I should like to pay my addresses to your goddaughter.'

Cassie gasped.

Sir Angus ignored her. He rose to his feet, glass in hand. 'Captain Graham, this is most irregular. One does not make such a request when the lady herself is present. And you should address yourself to James Elliott, not to me. Since Cassie's father is dead, James stands in his place.'

'I could not make such a request to a man who tried to have me hanged.'

'What?'

Ross quickly explained that he had rescued Miss Elliott when her horse had bolted in a thunderstorm. For his pains, he had been accused of abduction and thrown into gaol.

'But that is even more outrageous!' cried Sir Angus. The brandy was shaking in his glass. 'James Elliott is certainly not everything a gentleman should be, but to do such a thing to an officer…! I cannot believe it.'

'It is true, Godfather.' Cassie spoke quietly, stepping forward to put a hand on the old man's arm.

He looked down at her for a long moment. Then he frowned in puzzlement. 'But if the captain… What were you doing, Cassie, riding alone in a thunderstorm?'

'I… Godfather, I was coming to you. I had no choice. James was threatening to send me to the Bedlam. That very day.'

'What? No, no, that makes no sense at all. If he thought he could cover his debts by marrying you off, he would never have thought of such a thing. No one—not even the basest shopman—would marry a woman out of the Bedlam. James must have been in his cups when he made such a threat. Or driven to it by anger. Which was it, Cassie?'

The blood drained from Cassie's face. 'He was furious with me,' she whispered, staring at the floor. 'He said I was unchaste.'

Ross's sharp intake of breath was very loud in the sudden silence. It hissed between his teeth, for his jaws were clamped tightly together. There was no other sound for a long time.

'And was he right?' Sir Angus asked. His voice was quiet but very firm.

The blood rushed back to Cassie's face till her cheeks were flaming. Ross held his breath, waiting.

'I…'

'Look at me, Cassie,' Sir Angus said.

She raised her eyes to his. 'Sir, he accused me falsely. He found me with a love poem, sent by a boy of fifteen.'

'Who was he?'

Cassie shook her head. 'I cannot tell you his name, Godfather. He is only a child, after all, and does not deserve the punishment that James intended for him.'

'You would defend him?'

'I refused to give James his name. He will not be thrashed by my doing.'

By Jove, what a woman she was! His woman! With difficulty, Ross forced himself to stand motionless, and mute. He wanted to cheer, to kiss her until she was mindless, to— But now was not the time.

'Ah.' Sir Angus stroked his chin. 'Yes, I see. He is a gentleman's son?'

'Yes.'

'And for this, James Elliott would confine you to the Bedlam?'

'He said he would. He said he would marry me to a tinker, if he could find one rich enough. He said that if my injured reputation got about, he would confine me for the rest of my life. As my mother was.' Cassie felt she was choking as she spoke those last few words.

Sir Angus reached out a hand and patted her shoulder. She felt herself relaxing a little. She had succeeded in arousing his sympathy again, at last. It was only a pity that she had had to embroider the truth in order to convince him.

Sir Angus looked past Cassie to Ross, who was still standing motionless, his jaw set grimly, as he seemed to have done throughout Cassie's recital. It was impossible to know what he was thinking. 'And you, sir, wish to pay your addresses to my goddaughter, even having heard all this? Even having learned, at first hand, what a flighty, headstrong child she is?'

Ross did not hesitate. 'I do, sir.'

'Even knowing about her mother?'

Cassie held her breath. Sir Angus was going to tell Ross the awful truth. Would he reject her once he knew?

'Sir Angus, I know only what is common knowledge and what was said here, just now—that Mrs Elliott was taken to the lunatic asylum and died there.'

'You are determined to marry Cassie and you do not know?'

Ross straightened his shoulders. 'I am determined to marry Cassie, sir. For better, for worse.'

Sir Angus almost recoiled from the force of Ross's words. 'Of course, of course,' he blustered. 'In any case, there is nothing to fear. Cassie's mother was no lunatic.'

'Then, why—?'

'She… Forgive me, my dear, if this gives you pain,

but the captain has the right to know. Cassie's mother, sir, was cruelly used by her husband. To spare Cassie's feelings, I will say no more than that. Eventually, she attempted to escape from her husband, in company with another man.'

'Oh, no!' Cassie gasped. She had never believed it, and yet it must be so. Her godfather would not lie about such a thing.

Sir Angus threw her a compassionate glance before continuing. 'Cassie's father caught her and had her taken to the asylum for a wanton. No one could do anything to save her. In the end, she died there.'

'I see,' Ross muttered, stony-faced.

'As to your desire to offer for Cassie,' Sir Angus continued, obviously more at ease now the distasteful history had been related, 'I fancy, from what she has said, that you are not the husband that James Elliott would have sought for her.'

'No, sir, I am not. I am neither wealthy enough nor weak enough to suit Elliott's purposes. If he looks to touch me for money, he will be sadly disappointed.'

'Hmm.' Sir Angus looked troubled. He sat down once more and began to swirl the brandy in his glass, staring thoughtfully down at it. Ross and Cassie resumed their places on the sofa, both staring straight ahead. Silence reigned for what seemed a very long time. At last, Sir Angus raised his head. 'Remind me, Cassie. How old are you?'

'I shall be twenty-three next birthday, Godfather.'

'Yes. I thought it was so. You must forgive an old man's poor memory. But, if you are of full age, your brother has no rights over you. I do not understand how he intended to compel you.'

Cassie heard herself laugh. It was a harsh, mirthless sound. 'Easily, Godfather. He kept me a prisoner. He allowed me no access to money. He ensured I had no chance to make friends who might support my interests. And he would have been happy to start rumours about my chastity, if it had served his purpose. He made it perfectly clear that, if I resisted his marriage plans for me, I should be committed to the Bedlam as a wanton. I believed him. That was why I was coming across the Solway to you. I could think of no one else who would take my part. You will not send me back to him, will you, Godfather?' She could not conceal the note of pleading in her voice. Or was it fear?

'You shall certainly remain with me for the present, my dear. Your brother cannot take you from here by force. I dare say he would not try. He must know by now that you are no longer in Scotland. And he has precious few to do his bidding on this side of the Solway.'

'Thank you, Godfather,' Cassie breathed, feeling the tension draining out of her body at last. 'Thank you.'

The old man smiled. 'And since you are of full age,

I think it best if you decide for yourself how to respond to Captain Graham's addresses. Let me say only this: you do not have to marry Captain Graham—or anyone else—in order to secure your safety. I will be happy to give you a home with me. And to provide for you after my death, too. You do not need to return to Langrigg. Ever.'

'Oh, Godfather!' Cassie threw her arms round the old man's neck and kissed him soundly on the cheek. 'Thank you, sir. From the bottom of my heart, thank you!'

Sir Angus unwound her arms and put her from him. He was blushing a little. 'No need for thanks, my dear. No need at all,' he said gruffly. 'An old bachelor like me enjoys having a young thing about the place. You will make me feel alive again. And where else would I leave my money?'

Cassie could not find words to thank him properly. She felt as if the thunder clouds had lifted and both body and soul were being warmed by the brightness of the sun.

Behind her, Ross cleared his throat. He looked very stern. 'Your offer is most generous, sir. But might not James Elliott continue with his charges of impropriety, if Miss Elliott remains here unchaperoned? Might he blacken her name just for revenge? Between us, we will have removed his last hope of paying off his debts.'

'I am an old man, sir,' Sir Angus said stiffly. 'And I

am Miss Elliott's godfather, besides. There is no impropriety in her remaining here.'

Ross was silent. The point had been made, and the risk was clear to them all, in spite of Sir Angus's hasty denials. Cassie could not remain in any man's house unchaperoned. She must not accept his offer. She must not!

The silence continued, awkwardly. Ross saw that Cassie's heightened colour persisted. Was she thinking about the possible hurt to her reputation if she stayed with Sir Angus? He doubted it. It was not her way. If she was considering Sir Angus's offer, it would be as a way of escaping her brother, of being free. Did she want to be free of Ross, too? Of the traitor's son? He must find a moment to be alone with her—and soon—to find out the truth of that. He had to know. For his part, he would assure her that his intentions were unchanged, that he wanted, above all things, to make her his wife. He could only pray that she loved him enough—still—to accept him. She could never be safe with Sir Angus. Marriage—marriage to Ross—was her only sure refuge.

The door opened to admit Sir Angus's butler. He seemed flustered. Looking around at the assembled company, he said, 'Excuse me, Sir Angus. Would it be possible for me to have a private word with you? Some urgent news has just arrived. I think you should hear it as soon as may be.' The man was almost hopping from foot to foot in his impatience.

'Private business…?' Sir Angus's tone, at first un-convinced, soon changed, probably as a result of the very serious look on the manservant's face. 'Ah, yes, I see. My dear, would you…?'

'Perhaps Captain Graham and I should take a turn in the garden, Godfather?' Cassie said, rather too brightly.

Ross breathed a sigh of relief. He needed a chance to be alone with Cassie, and now it was being offered to him on a plate.

Sir Angus nodded. 'Yes, do. You can go out through the French windows there. But make sure you take a shawl, Cassie. The wind is quite sharp today. I'm sure this business—whatever it is—will not take long. And then we may sit down to dinner together.'

Cassie dropped him a tiny curtsy. Then, retrieving her shawl from the back of the sofa, she took Ross's prof-fered arm and allowed him to lead her through the window and down the steps into the knot garden beyond.

She smiled impishly up at Ross as they walked down the gravel path. His heart turned over. If she planned to spurn him, she could not smile at him like that, could she?

Chapter Seventeen

'I fear I suffer from insatiable curiosity. It is a sin, is it not? Yet I cannot help wondering what is so urgent—and so serious—that my godfather must send us out of the room.'

Cassie was trying to hide her nervousness behind a bright façade. To be honest, she was afraid to be alone with Ross just at present. As long as they were with Sir Angus, she could tell herself that Ross did care for her, that every look and word was an expression of that feeling, rather than a sign of doubt or—worse—distaste for the daughter of a wanton.

Oh, God in heaven, he knew now! Surely he would spurn her? What man in his senses would marry a penniless girl whose mother had perished in an asylum? What man would want his children tainted by such a mother?

'Cassie?'

She jumped. His voice sounded odd. Strained. She

started away from him, but he would not let her go. With his free hand, he covered hers, where it was trying to pull away from his arm. His touch was gentle, and warm, but Cassie's skin prickled under the firm contact.

'Cassie, my dear, what is it? Tell me what is wrong. Please.'

She said nothing. She could not bring herself to look up at him.

'Do you not trust me any longer, Cassie?' His voice was suddenly very low, almost inaudible. As if he had barely the strength to make his words heard.

That crack in his voice almost broke her heart. She looked up into his eyes. 'Of course, I trust you, Ross. How could it be otherwise?'

'I thought you might have changed your mind, now that Sir Angus will make you his heir. Have you? Is that it?'

'No! How could you think such a thing?'

'I…I…' He smiled. It was an enigmatic smile. What was he thinking? 'I felt sure that, when you discovered that you had allowed the son of a traitor to make love to you, you would—'

Cassie felt herself reddening all over again as he spoke. She stopped him with an impatient gesture. 'I regret nothing that we have done together, Ross. Nothing. But I—' Gently, but firmly, she detached her hand from his arm and took two steps away. Turning back, and seeing the sudden anguish in his face, she said quickly, 'You are not the son of a traitor. All that is long forgot. In Scotland, no one asks about such things. They have been buried deep for decades, and we all know better than to rake them up. They mean nothing now. Besides, you are Captain Ross Graham, an officer and a gentleman. You could pay your addresses to anyone. Anyone!'

For almost a minute he stood staring at her, his jaw working. Then, 'Is that truly what you believe, Cassie? Truly?'

'Yes, of course it is,' she said a little crossly. Why was he so determined to focus on ancient history? Why would he not tell her the truth about what really mattered?

When he still said nothing, she burst out, 'Oh, ask anyone if you do not believe me. Ask my godfather. Ask Colonel Anstruther. They will all tell you the same. No one cares any more.' A huge surge of emotion threatened to overwhelm her. She turned away, battling against her tears. She must return to the house, before she broke down completely. She started away from him.

'Cassie. Cassie, wait.'

His hand was on her shoulder. It was gentle and warm, not controlling. She could shrug him off with barely a shiver.

'Cassie, forgive me.' Behind her, his voice was low. She fancied it was shaking, just a fraction. 'Forgive me, I have been so swept up in my own concerns, my own disgust at what I have learned, that I have not given you a chance to tell me what is wrong. You have told me what it is not. So now, will you tell me what it is that is troubling you? Please?'

He let his hand slide slowly, caressingly, down her arm until he reached her fingers. Then he took her hand in his and held it. She welcomed his touch, her heart swelling at this evidence of his kindness, his regard… But still she could not turn to look into his face.

She gulped and let the words come out in a great rush. 'I know I did not tell you the whole truth about myself. I allowed you to propose marriage to me without making you aware that I…that I am the daughter of a lunatic.' His fingers tightened convulsively on hers, but she would not be stopped. 'And my mother was a wanton, too. Please believe me when I tell you that I did not know about *that*. I had always believed that my mother was unjustly imprisoned.' She whirled back round to face him and wrenched her hand from his. 'It seems I was wrong. My father did have cause.'

Ross reached out to take her hand again, but she did not dare to touch him. Instead, she clasped both hands tightly together in front of her.

He sighed deeply. She glanced up at his face, expecting to see disgust, or anger. But his expression seemed to have lightened. What on earth—?

'Exactly when, in our dealings together, were you supposed to have told me about your mother's fate?'

'I…ah…well, I could have—'

'Perhaps you could have mentioned it when we were leaping across sinking pools in the quicksand? Or when we were cowering under that bush, soaked to the skin, and praying that your brother would not discover us?'

'I…um…'

'Precisely so. And later on, when we were huddled together, trying to keep each other warm, perhaps you should have told me then?'

'Yes. I could have—'

'Cassie, you are no lunatic, but your memory is clearly defective. I have a very clear recollection that I had found other uses for your delicious mouth by that stage. I do not believe talking played any part in it.' He grinned at her. It was sunshine after rain.

'Oh, you are impossible, Ross Graham. Why will you not listen to me?'

'Because, my sweet, you are talking nonsense. Utter nonsense. Your mother was not mad. You have your godfather's word for that. Poor lady, she suffered at the hands of a cruel husband. I could not blame her for trying to escape. Nor should you.'

It was not enough. He had overlooked the greatest risk. 'What if I were to take after her?'

'Why should you? Are you suggesting that I would

treat you as your father did your mother? Good God, Cassie, what sort of man do you take me for?'

'Not a cruel one. Never that,' she whispered to the gravel at her feet. He had seemed amused before, but now he sounded very hurt. She had not intended that.

This time he did not try for her hand. He reached her in a single stride and pulled her roughly into his arms. When she opened her mouth to protest, he laughed delightedly and captured her lips.

Cassie did not try to pull away. She could not. This, after all, was what she wanted more than anything, to be held, and kissed, by Ross Graham, the man to whom she had given her heart. She breathed in the warm male scent of him, letting the intoxication of his nearness fizz in her blood. She was almost dizzy as she began to return his kiss with a fervour equal to his own. He had taught her the joys of passion, but she now showed him that the pupil could match the master, perhaps even surpass him.

Ross groaned, deep in his chest, as her tongue touched his, teasing, retreating, and teasing again. He pulled away just long enough to take a breath, and gasp, 'I swear you are a witch, Cassie.' For a second, he put a hand to her hair, stroking the silken curls as if they were the most precious treasure in the world. Then he lowered his mouth to hers once again.

For a long, long time, they kissed. It seemed to Cassie that her soul was melding with Ross's, that they were becoming one, a single spirit. It felt…oh, it felt like utter bliss. He was still stroking her hair, and one strong hand was splayed across her back. His fingers seemed to be branding her there. The heat was searing her skin, in spite of her clothes.

'Cassie. My sweet Cassie,' he whispered. He had torn his mouth from hers and was gazing down into her eyes. His own were unfocused and dreamy. Were hers the same? She was certainly no longer sure of who or where she was. But why had be stopped kissing her?

'Ross? What is it?'

'Nothing. Except that I hope you are now properly convinced of my intentions, ma'am.'

'I… You mean that you truly *do* want to marry the daughter of a lunatic?'

He shook his head wearily. 'Our positions are clear enough. You are *not* the daughter of a lunatic. But you *are* being asked to marry the son of a traitor. For that, it appears, is what I am. That being so, I think the benefits of the union would be all on my side. If you would agree to take me. Will you, Cassie?'

She looked up into his eyes. They were focused now, and full of doubt. He was afraid that she was going to reject him. How could he possibly think that? And for such a reason? She had given herself to him, because she loved him. Her path was set. Nothing could alter it, except Ross himself. 'Do you not know that I love you,

Ross?' Her voice was very low, and it shook, just a little.

'I…I have to believe you do, for you have told me so. And I know you would not have allowed me to make love to you if you did not. That gift was the greatest proof of love a man could receive. Do you mean to marry me? Truly?'

'If you are sure that you want me for your wife. Only if you are absolutely sure. I should have told you about my mother before, when you proposed the first time. I should have given you the chance to withdraw then. What if our children were tainted with madness?'

Ross took her by the shoulders and shook her. Not violently, but enough to make his point. 'By Jove, Cassie Elliott, you are a stubborn woman. How many times do I have to tell you that your mother was *not* a lunatic and that there is no taint of madness to be carried through to future generations? You are a perfectly normal young woman—though as stubborn as a Spanish mule—and a traitor's son, such as I, would be honoured to take you as his wife.'

A tiny smile hovered at the corner of her mouth. 'Very well then, Captain Graham, son of a traitor, I accept your offer of marriage.'

Ross wanted to shout his triumph from the rooftops. She had accepted him. Truly accepted him at last!

And in the full knowledge of his family's murky past. He felt as if a huge burden had been lifted from him. There could be no doubt, now, that she did love him, in spite of what he was. He was truly blessed.

He resisted the temptation to kiss her again. He wanted her too much. If he kissed her now, there was a real risk that they would end up tangled among the box hedges, making love in full view of Sir Angus's household. He must now try to behave as a gentleman should, curbing his overwhelming desire until they were safely wed.

And that must be soon. Very soon.

Tucking her arm under his once more, he led her through the garden. 'We must be wed as soon as possible, Cassie. I shall ask Sir Angus to allow us to be married from this house. That would be the safest course. You will still be in danger until my ring is on your finger. I would do it tomorrow, if only we could get a special licence. But that is impossible, so far from London.'

She squeezed his fingers and looked up at him with mischief in her eyes. 'We could always go across the border to Gretna Green.'

'No, ma'am, we could not.'

'Oh? Why not? It would be just as quick as a special licence.'

'Lord preserve me from logic-chopping women,' he said with a grin. 'There are at least two good reasons, madam.' He took a deep breath and began to count on his fingers, like a tutor explaining a lesson to a particularly dim child. 'First, because it is dangerous for you to set foot in Scotland without being safely wed. And second, because of the damage to your reputation from a Gretna wedding. Just imagine—an innocent young lady carried off to Gretna, obviously the dupe of the unscrupulous half-pay officer she had married, all unaware that he was the son of a traitor.'

Cassie's eyes widened at that. She made as if to speak, but then shut her mouth again without saying a word. A tiny frown marred her beautiful face.

He pulled her closer. 'You do understand, don't you, my dear?'

'Yes,' she said softly. 'You are right. A Gretna marriage could well damage your reputation, and we—'

'*My* reputation?'

'Yes, of course. And I will not permit that to happen. Everything must be done with the utmost propriety.'

He shook his head. 'I can see that marriage to you is going to be something of an adventure, Cassie. Even if you do promise to love, honour and *obey*.'

'I am sure you will never require me to do anything idiotish, so there will be no call for me to break my vow, will there?'

'Idiotish?' He struck his forehead with his open palm, trying not to smile in response to the wicked glint in her eyes. 'You have my full permission, ma'am, to disobey any command of mine that should prove to be idiotish—'

'Oh, good.'

'—in the opinion of any right-thinking man.'

Cassie burst out laughing. Her joy was so clearly written on her beaming face that Ross put his hands on her trim waist, picked her up and whirled her round and round.

'Stop, stop! You are making me dizzy. Put me down, you impossible man!'

He did so, setting her on her feet but leaving his hands where they were. 'You make *me* dizzy just looking at you, my dear one. And the touch of you…' he squeezed her waist gently '…the touch of you drives me wild. Oh, Cassie, if you knew how much I want you, here and now, you would certainly run for cover.'

She did nothing of the sort. Instead she pressed her body against him, reaching up to wrap her arms around his neck. 'I shall not run from your passion, Ross,' she said huskily. 'Not ever.'

Ross groaned aloud. He could not help it. The picture conjured up by her words was just too tempting. His whole body was now humming with desire. A few moments ago, he had been impatient for Sir Angus's business to be over so that they could share their joy with him and begin to plan their wedding. Now, painfully aroused as he was, Ross could only pray that Sir Angus would be further delayed.

'Oh, God, Cassie, do you know what you are doing to me?'

She smiled. It was a smile filled with knowledge. And satisfaction. She knew exactly what she was doing. And she was proud of it.

Ross stopped fighting his own desires. She was offering herself for his kiss. What man in his right mind would refuse?

To his surprise, it was not a kiss of passion that they shared. It was a kiss of much deeper meaning—commitment, and mutual devotion. It went on and on. Ross was feeling weightless, as if he could float away to Arcadia with this amazing woman in his arms. Never, in all his life, had the touch of a woman affected him so profoundly.

When at last Ross broke the kiss, he held her into his body as if he could shield her from all the world, as if to make them one. And Cassie leaned into him, trusting, loving, giving of herself. For a long time, neither moved.

'Hurrumph!'

They sprang apart at the sound. Even in the deep shadow of the house, Ross could see that Cassie had turned bright pink. Poor girl, she blushed so very easily. It would be a joy to tease her, once they were man and wife.

'Humph!'

In spite of her blushes, Cassie was clearly not to be daunted. She was brimming over with happiness, and she was determined to share it. She tucked her hand possessively into Ross's and tugged him towards the steps, where Sir Angus stood in the open French window. 'Godfather! Oh, Godfather, you shall be the first to learn of our happiness. Ross and I are to be wed, as soon as may be. Oh, Godfather, you cannot believe how happy I am!'

When Sir Angus did not speak, Cassie stopped in her tracks. 'Are you not glad, sir? Oh, please do not be cross. I do not mean to shun your generous offer of shelter, but you see, I love him. And I want more than anything in the world to be his wife.'

Sir Angus smiled, but it looked a little forced. 'I am pleased for you, my dear child. And I congratulate you, Captain Graham. I hope you will be very happy together.'

'Oh, thank you, Godfather.' Cassie kissed him on the cheek. It was rather more demure than her previous effort, Ross was glad to see.

'But, come inside. Come inside, both of you. We should not be discussing such momentous events on the garden step.' Sir Angus turned back into the room.

Ross put a protective hand in the small of Cassie's back and shepherded her inside. He sensed danger. His soldier's awareness had not deserted him. There was something very wrong. But would Sir Angus tell him what it was? Ross could feel the tension tightening his gut. He had only just secured Cassie for his own, and until the knot was tied in church, there was still a risk that she might be snatched from him. It was a thought he was not prepared to contemplate.

All three resumed their seats, but it was different from before. Cassie was leaning into Ross and clearly no longer cared whether Sir Angus noticed or not. She was relaxed and overflowing with happiness. Ross, meanwhile, was too worried to let his feelings show. He felt, somehow, that Sir Angus was about to deal a blow to their plans. The old man was sitting very upright in his chair, his hands tightly gripping the arms. Unlike Cassie, he was far from relaxed.

A tense silence reigned for several moments. Ross determined to break it. 'Sir, I am sorry that it will not prove possible for your goddaughter to come to live with you as you wish. She—'

'Think nothing of that, my boy,' Sir Angus said with a thin smile. 'I take back everything I said about marrying where one is bid. If Cassie is happy with you, then you have my blessing.'

'Thank you, sir.'

'Oh, thank you, Godfather,' Cassie breathed at the same moment.

'But, Cassie, my dear—' Sir Angus had clasped his

hands in his lap and was now staring down at them. 'My dear, I have dreadful news. Oh, Lord, there is no way to soften this blow. My dear child, I have to tell you that your brother is dead. He drowned. Yesterday. In the Solway.'

Cassie's eyes widened for a second. Then she struggled to her feet. 'It is my fault,' she whispered. 'I wished him dead. I prayed for it. And it has happened. Oh, God forgive me.'

'Cassie! Child!'

It was too late. Cassie had sunk into a dead faint.

'Don't look so concerned, my boy. The doctor says she will soon recover.'

'Of course, sir.' Ross's response was automatic, but he was not so sure. Her body would recover, certainly, but her mind? He would never forget her fervent prayer for deliverance and for the damnation of her half-brother. No doubt she would never forget it either. And she would carry the guilt for the rest of her life. It made no difference that it was not her fault in any way. Her conscience would tell her that it was.

'I am glad of this chance to speak privately to you, however, Captain Graham.'

Sir Angus seemed to have noticed none of Ross's inner turmoil. Nor that the timing of Elliott's drowning did not fit with Cassie's tale of her escape. Good. Ross would not tell Sir Angus the whole truth unless he had absolutely no other choice. Too many grubby secrets had been revealed already.

Sir Angus was absently drumming his fingers on the arm of his chair. 'With Cassie's brother gone, there is no one to act for her. I feel I must take on the role. In the matter of…er…settlements and so on.'

'Thank you, sir. I am sure Cassie will be most grateful when she learns of your kindness in this. I am not a wealthy man, but I can assure you that we shall be perfectly comfortable. Cassie will not want for anything that is due to her station.' Ross proceeded to a brisk description of his financial position and the settlements he was proposing. By the time he had finished, Sir Angus was beaming with pleasure.

'That is all very satisfactory, sir. Very satisfactory indeed. You say you are not wealthy. Well, well. Let me just say that, by her brother's lights, you are certainly very comfortably situated. Perhaps he should have seized on you as a suitor.'

Ross nodded slightly, but said nothing. Sir Angus's remark was true enough but, in the light of Elliott's death, it was really not a remark a gentleman should have made.

Sir Angus seemed to become conscious of his *faux pas* for he cleared his throat loudly and abruptly changed the subject. 'It is important that you understand my goddaughter's financial position, too, Captain Graham.'

Ross looked at him in surprise. 'I had understood that Cassie would come to me with nothing. Nothing at all. Is that not the case?'

'Possibly. But there may be something. The Langrigg estate is not entailed. That being so, Cassie should inherit everything. There is no other heir.'

'Ah, yes. I see what you mean.' Ross waited for Sir Angus to continue. He did not wish to appear eager to learn of Cassie's inheritance. If there was actually anything left to inherit.

'There is the Langrigg manor and a good deal of land. I do not know how much income it produces. Nor whether it is mortgaged. I should think it may well be. And there are bound to be debts, considerable debts. James Elliott did not invest in his land. He invested only in his own selfish passions. His gambling and his women were very expensive, I believe.'

'I shall pay his debts, of course.'

'Including his gambling debts?'

'Yes,' Ross said flatly. 'He was Cassie's brother. I would not have her suffer the slightest unease because some debts of honour were left unpaid.'

Sir Angus snorted. 'I should find out the extent of them first, if I were you. It might cost you far more than you imagine. You surely would not prejudice your wife's future comfort just to pay her worthless brother's debts?'

'I will investigate the extent of them, as you suggest, sir. But they *will* be paid.'

Sir Angus did not argue any more. 'Assuming she does inherit the Langrigg estate, what will you do with it? Shall you live there?'

'That will depend very much on Cassie. My own estate in Wiltshire is small, but very pleasant. However, if Cassie wishes to spend part of the year at Langrigg, I should be happy to agree.'

'Not the winter months, I suggest,' murmured Sir Angus with a hint of a smile.

Ross grinned in response, and nodded. 'I take your point, sir. I shall try to persuade her that the best time to visit is in the summer, when her garden will be at its best.'

'What will you do about the wedding?' asked Sir Angus after a pause.

'That will depend on Cassie.'

'I fear that Cassie is in no fit state to make any decisions at present.'

'Probably not. God, I wish I had carried her off to Gretna instead of crossing the Solway.'

'No. No, Captain Graham, you do not. Remember Cassie's history. Remember what happened to her mother. If Cassie is to be able to take her place in society, at your side, there cannot be anything havey-cavey in your marriage.' He lifted a hand to forestall Ross's protest. 'Oh, we could have succeeded by marrying her from my house. I have some standing in the community, after all. But a Gretna marriage would not be tolerated. You must know that.'

Ross nodded. He did know that perfectly well. He had said as much to Cassie in the garden. But he did not know—not really—about Cassie's history. After a moment, he said, 'Sir Angus, Cassie has not told me of her mother. And judging from her reaction earlier, I am persuaded that she did not know the whole. You said that Mrs Elliott was not mad, but the victim of her husband's cruelty?'

'Aye, that was the way of it.' He paused, a deep frown on his brow.

Ross sat very still, waiting.

'I can see that you are determined to hear the worst of the family you would marry into. Well, you have the right. You have dealt with James Elliott. His father was much the same. Cassie's mother, Elizabeth Fergusson, was a second wife and much younger than her husband. She was beautiful, too, and Elliott was a jealous man. After Cassie was born, he persuaded himself that his wife was unfaithful. He may even have believed that Cassie was not his own get.' He stopped, gazing vacantly into the fire. 'I always wondered whether that was why he banished her to that Edinburgh seminary for so many years. He seemed to hate the child. And her brother soon learned to do the same, I fear.' He shook his head sadly.

'Cassie's mother, sir?' Ross prompted gently.

'Ah, yes. Poor Elizabeth. She had only to smile on another man, no matter how young or old, for Elliott to accuse her. And he beat her, cruelly. Sometimes she was confined to her bed for weeks, until the bruises subsided. Eventually, she could stand it no longer. She did take a lover and she tried to escape from her husband. She did not succeed. James Elliott caught them and had her taken to the asylum. There was no one to help her.'

'But the lover…surely he tried?'

'He could not. He was dead. They said his neck was broken in a carriage accident. But I never believed it. He was murdered, by James Elliott. For revenge. That man had to control everything and everyone. It was he who should have been in the Bedlam.'

There was so much bitterness in his voice. There was something more here, something hidden.

'You were related to Cassie's mother, I take it, sir?'

'Yes. Distant cousins. Very distant. We shared a great-grandsire.'

'Does that mean that I, too, am related to Cassie?'

'Yes, but no more closely than I am. There is no impediment to your marriage, if that is your concern.'

Ross nodded thoughtfully. The hidden factor must relate to something else. 'I am surprised that Mrs Elliott was given any opportunity to meet a lover. Surely James Elliott would have been most vigilant, given his insane jealousy?'

'Aye, but he could not shut his doors against the family. I was his daughter's godfather.'

'It was you? But you said—'

'It was my brother.'

Chapter Eighteen

'Let me come with you, Cassie.'

'No!'

'But you should not be alone.'

'I *need* to be alone.' She knew she ought not to be short with Ross. He was not the cause of her troubles, or her guilt. She had brought that on herself. He was trying to support her. And she was rejecting him. She turned back to him. 'Forgive me, Ross. I do not mean to be rude. Or ungracious. I know that you have the best of motives, but… Forgive me, I *need* to be alone.' The tears were threatening to overwhelm her again. She picked up her skirts and ran for the sanctuary of the garden.

As she reached the steps, she heard his long sigh behind her. He was deeply unhappy. But he would not follow her. He was too much of a gentleman to intrude in her grief.

She stopped running at the end of the knot garden

and turned, just to check. She was alone. She had known it would be so. She stood, for a long moment, gazing around, trying to focus her mind on anything but her morass of tangled emotions. She tried to concentrate on the geometric perfection of the clipped hedges and fancy gravel.

It was not her own preferred style of garden, but it was certainly effective. Sir Angus—no gardener himself—had opted for the classical styles of his youth and entrusted their care to a team of trained men. If she were going to stay at Whitemoss, Cassie would use all her feminine wiles to persuade her godfather to change it to something more to the modern taste. But she was not going to stay, was she? She was going to marry Ross Graham, was she not?

Cassie shook her head, in bewilderment. She was no longer sure of that, or of anything else.

She walked back to the centre of the knot garden and sat down on the little bench, automatically settling her black skirts around her. At least the housekeeper had been able to provide Cassie with a gown that made her feel as if she was properly in mourning. It did not fit well—not well at all—but no matter, for who was to see her, hidden away here, miles from anywhere? Her inner voice reminded her that Ross had seen her. And what did he think of her? Red puffy eyes, pasty complexion, and a gown that resembled a corn sack. What's more, she had barely spoken half a dozen sentences to him since the news had come.

He wants to help you, Cassie Elliott, yet you push him away.

'I can do no other,' she groaned aloud. 'My brother is dead. And I am responsible.' She sat twisting her hands together, as if the act could somehow undo the past. It could not. Of course it could not. She would have to learn to live with what she had done.

Shaking her head, she rose and walked slowly out of the knot garden and towards the woods beyond. The sun was getting hotter. It was not like Solway weather at all. She would feel better under the cool canopy of the trees. No one would disturb her there.

The stately trees seemed to welcome her in. She reached out her fingers to touch the lowest branches of a short hazel, and then a magnificent beech. How beautiful they were. And some of these trees must be well-nigh a century old, perhaps older. That Holm oak beyond, for instance, looked to have stood in the Whitemoss garden for longer than the house itself. No doubt these trees had looked down on many a weeping woman, over the decades. Whatever those women's troubles, the trees would still have been looking down after their pain was long gone. As Cassie's troubles, too, would pass.

Had she been indulging her grief these last two days? She walked back under the trailing canopy of the beech and stroked its rough bark. The great tree's strength and permanence soothed her, as if it could speak. *You have had your moment now, Cassie. You have shrieked your grief and guilt to the skies. Enough now. You must live with what you have done and embrace life once more. For no one can go back and change the past. All that is left is to shape the future. Running away from it will shape nothing.*

Cassie continued to stroke the bark for a long time. And then she leant against it, resting her head against the trunk so that she could gaze up into the branches. They reached up to the sky, with pride and confidence. And a great lust for life. Yes. It was time for her to do the same. She had to start taking control of her life once again.

And she must make her peace with Ross. She had hurt him. She had no doubt about that. And he, being a man of inner strength and understanding, had allowed her to snap at him, to reject him, without ever voicing a word of complaint.

She loved him. Of course, she did. But he could be pardoned for doubting it, of late.

Did it matter to him, a man who did not love her in return? She rather thought it did. He did care for her. She was sure of that. Only a man who cared—and a good and decent man—would have behaved as Ross had done. It was time she told him so, and thanked him.

She would spend just a few more minutes collecting her thoughts in this tranquil green space and then she would return to the house, to find him. Then she would tell him.

She walked slowly back out on to the main path and a little further into the wood, gazing up at the trees and marvelling at their variety. There were native rowans and pines, but also younger, smaller trees that must have been imported and planted here by Sir Angus or his predecessors. In another thirty or forty years, this wood would be even more splendid.

Perhaps, in thirty years, she and Ross would be able to return here, with their children and grandchildren, to walk once more down this winding path? That picture warmed her heart.

Cassie's reverie was interrupted by a rustling in the undergrowth. Rabbits? Or a bird, rooting for worms?

The noise grew louder. A twig snapped. That was no bird.

'Who is there?' Cassie cried, turning towards the sound.

'Come and sit down, Captain Graham. How is she?'

Ross shook his head and took the chair opposite Sir Angus. 'No better, I fear, sir. I cannot persuade her to talk to me.'

'No, and nor can I. I tried again this morning, when she first appeared, just after breakfast. She simply shook her head and turned her back on me. She was muttering something about needing to be alone. At least, I think she did. To be honest, I did not think it was directed at me. More at the floor at her feet. We cannot allow this to continue, sir. We will have to find some way of shaking her out of this all-pervading gloom.'

Ross shook his head. 'I don't see how we can. She is a grown woman. She has convinced herself that her brother's death was her fault, that her prayer for his damnation was answered. She believes she might as well have killed him with her own hand. It is nonsense—we both know that—and she is sensible enough to know it, too. Or rather, she will be. Eventually. I think we must give her more time.'

'You risk indulging her too far, my boy, if you will permit an old bachelor to advise you. What sort of a marriage will it be if you do not exert your authority? A husband must be master of his own household.'

'I shall be,' Ross said quickly. 'But Cassie needs more time now. And she shall have it.'

Sir Angus said nothing. It must have been obvious that Ross's mind was made up on the issue and that nothing would move him.

Ross leaned back in his chair and gazed across at the miniatures on the wall. His mother's portrait hung there still. He was glad he knew the whole truth now. Surprisingly, it no longer seemed so dreadful, compared with the horror of Elliott's death. But he was relieved that he had no need of his family. He could set himself to forgetting the whole sorry crew. All except his mother. He began to muse on what he now knew of her life, and her sacrifices for him, her only child. She had been a brave and steadfast woman. Much like Cassie, in fact.

He smiled towards the portrait. *You would have approved of Cassie, Mother. She will make a good wife and—God willing—a good mother to our children. I am only sorry that you will never see them. If you are looking down on us now, Mother, I ask you to bless Cassie and to help her through her torment. I need her to come to me with a glad heart, and a willing hand.*

For a moment, he almost thought that the portrait nodded. A strange fancy, indeed.

'Excuse me, sir.' It was Sir Angus's butler. He was now well used to the visitors and treated them both with proper respect. 'Your man, Fraser, has this moment arrived, Captain, with two horses. He has taken the baggage up to your chamber.'

'Excellent. I can certainly do with a change of clothes. I am hardly presentable in these.' He glanced ruefully down at his coat and breeches, borrowed from one of Sir Angus's gamekeepers.

Sir Angus smiled. 'I have seen worse, my boy. No doubt you have, too, in the wars?'

Ross nodded. Ever since he had come north, he

seemed to be fated to ruin his own fine clothes and spend his time wearing ill-fitting cast-offs instead.

The butler made to leave.

'A moment,' Ross said. 'Tell Fraser to lay out my clothes. I shall be upstairs in a few minutes.'

The man bowed and withdrew.

'It has taken your man long enough to get here, Graham. I hope you will upbraid him suitably.'

'That will depend, sir. He had much to dispose of, along the way. He was left with the carriage and horses and the various valises. It will be interesting to learn how he dealt with all of those. And with James Elliott's men, too.'

'They were probably too busy trying to haul their master's body out of the quicksand to bother too much about a mere servant. It would have been different if they had been able to lay hands on you, or Cassie, of course.'

'Mmm. I'm sure you are right, sir. Now, if you will excuse me, I shall go upstairs and discover for myself what Fraser has been doing for the last two days.'

'Fraser! At last! I had almost given you up. What took you so long? And where have you left Morag? Miss Elliott needs her.'

Fraser turned back from laying out the clothes he was removing from Ross's valise. They looked much in need of pressing. 'Well, sir, I doubt I could have got here any quicker. Not without shooting those beggars from Langrigg so's I could come across by the ford. Or drowning Morag in the Solway. She's a stubborn woman, is Morag, just like her mistr—'

Ross tried not to smile. 'It is not your place to criticise your betters, Fraser,' he said, trying to sound stern. It did not work.

'No, sir,' Fraser replied with a grin that said everything. He would continue to criticise his betters—in private at least—as he always had. Ross would be the only one to hear it. And Ross might well be the butt of it himself.

'I am just laying out your things, sir. They will need sponging and pressing, but you should be presentable by dinner time. How is the mistress? Er…Miss Cassie, I mean?'

'Not good.'

'Oh, dear. What—?'

'Never mind that now. Miss Elliott is safe here. Tell me. Where is Morag? What happened with Elliott and his men? Is Hera sound? What did you do with Elliott's carriage?'

'One thing at a time, sir. One thing at a time.' He began to fold Ross's small clothes, ready to put away. 'I left Morag at the inn at Longtown. It didn't seem sensible to bring her all this way, seeing as I didn't know for sure that you and the mistress was actually here. Besides, she's the devil of a woman when it comes to horses. And by that time, there was only the two of us and the two riding horses. I left the carriage at Gretna. Didn't want to be taken for a horse thief by driving it across the border.'

'You brought Morag across the border on horseback?'

'Aye, sir. And a more difficult task I've rarely met with. She don't like horses. Nor they don't like her, neither. In the end, I took her up behind me, for Hera would have nothing to do with her.'

'What did you do with the bags? Your horse could not have carried two, and the valises as well.'

'I tied them across Hera's saddle.'

Ross burst out laughing. 'She will not have thanked you for that. Very much beneath her dignity to be used as a pack animal.'

'Aye, and so she told me when she tried to kick me in the cods. Didn't miss by much, I can tell you, sir.'

'You shouldn't have been surprised, Fraser. A high-born aristocrat like Hera does not take kindly to being used like a menial. Did she…er…get you at all?'

'No, sir.'

'Hmm. Honours even then.'

'Aye.'

'I shall obviously have to go and make my peace with her. I had better make sure I have an apple or a carrot in my pocket when I do. But, enough of that. What of your pursuers? Did they catch up with you?'

'Not precisely. James Elliott was well in advance of

his men. He got close enough to see inside the carriage. He has—had—a fine raking grey with a remarkable turn of speed. It's a wonder he didn't catch us sooner.'

'How did he know Miss Elliott was not in the carriage? Morag was supposed to make that hamper look like a cowering body.'

'Aye and she tried well enough. But the moment Elliott saw that *you* were not in the carriage, he knew that Miss Cassie could not be there either.'

Ross swore. Yes, of course he would!

'Elliott didn't even attempt to stop us. He just turned tail and raced back to Annan. I thought he might send one of his men after us, but he didn't.'

'No. He wouldn't. He needed every man to pursue us across the Solway.'

'But he couldn't get all the way across. The tide would have been coming in.'

'It was. But he had horses and we were on foot. He did get across and not so far behind us. If we hadn't happened on a place of concealment… Well, I won't think of that. We did find a place. And James Elliott did not discover us. He tried, though. He even sent his men back ahead of him, to escape the advancing tide. I presume they all got back safely, those ruffians?'

'Aye, sir.'

'You saw them?'

'No, sir. I would have been wrestling with Morag

and Hera by then. But news travels fast. Everyone on the Scottish side of the Solway seemed to know how you had escaped. The news was all around, before nightfall. Even Elliott's accident.'

'Indeed? It's a wonder that the rumours have not yet reached Whitemoss, then. As far as Sir Angus is aware, we crossed in the early morning, not the evening. I would not have it noised abroad, Fraser, that Miss Elliott spent a night alone in my company.' He raised his eyebrows.

Fraser looked somewhat pained. 'You know you can rely on me, sir.'

'Yes, I do, Fraser. I apologise. I was not thinking. My concern for Miss Elliott's reputation made me forget just how discreet you are.'

Fraser nodded, mollified.

'It's too late to send you back to Longtown tonight, but I should like you to go to fetch Morag at first light tomorrow. I'm sure Sir Angus will lend me his carriage for the journey. He knows how much Morag's presence will reassure her mistress.'

'Is it wise to send me off, sir? Don't you need me here to help protect Miss Cassie? If her brother should come, he might—'

'But her brother is dead, Fraser, drowned in the Solway. You said you knew.'

Fraser shook his head. 'That's not how I heard it, sir. James Elliott was caught by the Solway tide, right enough, and his horse was swallowed in the quicksand. But the man himself survived. Those men of his may be the scum of the earth, but they're loyal. And they understand the quicksands. They pulled him out.'

'Oh, God! Cassie! He'll come for her!'

'That's what I was trying to tell you, sir. Elliott will be recovered enough now. He was only half-drowned, more's the pity. He'll be here any day. We need to protect Miss Cassie—'

Ross barely heard the last part of Fraser's impassioned speech. He was already throwing open the door and dashing down the corridor to the staircase.

Cassie! Where was she? He had last seen her going out into the knot garden. She would be safe enough there, surely? Even Elliott would not dare to attack her so near the house. But it was at least an hour, maybe two, since she had gone out. She might be anywhere by now.

He took the stairs three at a time and almost collided with the butler in the hall. 'Tell your master Elliott is still alive!' he shouted, pushing the man out of the way and racing for the garden door. A quick glance round told him that Cassie was no longer in the knot garden. He ran through it and out into the wood beyond. If Elliott had found her here…

It did not bear thinking about.

'Cassie!' he yelled at the top of his voice. 'Cassie! Where are you? Cassie!' There was no response.

Ross saw that Sir Angus was scuttling along the

path towards him. The butler and a number of male servants were following.

Ross ignored Sir Angus's questions and simply took charge of the men. 'Spread out through the woods and search for Miss Elliott. She may be anywhere. It is imperative that we find her.' He told the men off in various directions. 'If you see any signs of intruders, come back at once and report to me.'

'Captain Graham! Sir!' Sir Angus was now insisting on being heard. 'What on earth is going on? My man gave me some incredible story about Elliott. Did he not drown after all?'

Ross shook his head impatiently. He needed to join the search. He needed to find Cassie. 'According to my man, Fraser, Elliott did not drown. He was rescued at the last moment. It will have been an ordeal, of course, and it must have taken him time to recover. But he has had two days now. I fear…I fear very much that he has taken Cassie.'

Sir Angus swayed on his feet. 'Oh, no. Not again,' he muttered weakly.

'I beg your pardon, sir?'

'Don't you see? Cassie's father took Elizabeth from my brother. Both of them died. Now James Elliott has taken Cassie from you.' He shook his head hopelessly.

'Don't give up so easily, sir. If he has her—and I cannot leave until I know for sure—I promise you that I will get her back.' With that, he started off down

the path in to the wood. The remainder of Ross's vow
was unspoken, but recognised by both.

I will get her back. Or die in the attempt.

'We could do with Captain Rosevale's cool head for
this. And Sergeant Ramsey, too. With four of us, we'd
be sure of success.'

'We'll just have to do the best we can, Fraser. We
have two men, two horses, and four pistols. That
should suffice. After all, we are soldiers, and they are
only hirelings.'

Fraser looked sideways at his master and clamped
his mouth tight shut.

'Now, do you have everything we need?'

'Aye, sir.'

'Good. Then let us be off. Sir Angus says we should
catch the last of the ebb tide if we take the road to
Bowness at the gallop. We may catch them on this
side, if luck is with us. Our horses are fresh. Theirs
cannot be, surely?'

'No, sir.' Fraser swung himself up into the saddle
and was soon trotting off down the drive.

Ross ran a gloved hand down Hera's glossy neck.
'You've been much maligned of late, my beauty,' he
murmured. 'I promise to make it up to you. But, for
now, I need you to fly like the wind. Don't let me
down, Hera.'

The mare whinnied, as if she understood, and

danced around impatiently. It seemed that she could not wait to be off.

Ross mounted swiftly and gathered the reins. 'One beautiful lady after another,' he said aloud. It was almost a challenge to any fates who might be listening. 'And I swear that both shall recover their rightful place.'

Chapter Nineteen

Cassie bit and kicked and scratched and clawed. It was no use. James was so much bigger and stronger that he overcame her in the end. With help from the ever-present Tam. And from James's riding cloak which imprisoned her limbs and muffled her cries.

The two men hauled her through the woods to where they had left their horses. One of them was Lucifer! Cassie could hardly believe it.

'Get her mounted, Tam. But make sure you gag her. I'll no' have her shrieking like a wild thing.'

Tam produced a cleanish handkerchief to tie round Cassie's mouth. But he did not gag her at once. Nor did he tie her hands. Did that mean she might have a chance to escape?

'Your hands will be left free so you can control your horse, Cassie. The gag you may remove when we are well away from this damned estate. I'll tell you when. It will be well before we are likely to meet anyone who might remark on the state of you. Your reputation shall be preserved, even here in England.'

Cassie's eyes widened. Perhaps—?

'Be warned, my girl. If you try any tricks, you'll be bound hand and foot and thrown over my saddle bow. And I will shoot that vicious horse of yours.' A slow smile spread across his dark face. 'Yes, I would enjoy doing that.'

That smile sent a shiver through Cassie's heart. Given the slightest excuse, James would murder her beloved horse. She knew it was no idle threat. 'I will accompany you back to Langrigg,' she said quietly.

'Do I have your word on that?' he retorted with a sneer.

'I am surprised that you would take the word of a woman, James.'

'Ordinarily, I would not. But I do know you, Cassie. Do I have your word?'

'Yes.' What choice did she have? 'That being so, will you not dispense with the gag also?'

'You will promise not to cry out?'

'I will not make any attempt to escape and I will not seek help from anyone on the way back to Langrigg. You have my word.' She would keep it, too. As far as Langrigg. But she had made no promises about what would happen after that. If she could find a way to escape—with Lucifer—she surely would.

'Very well. Put away the gag, Tam. Give Miss Cassie her whip and help her to mount.'

They seemed to have thought of almost everything. With a whip, Cassie should be able to ride. She could manage without boots or gloves. She struggled to gain the saddle, but failed. The black dress was not fit for riding in. The skirt was not wide enough. That was one thing that James had overlooked.

'Damn women and their fancy clothing,' he spat. 'Don't know why you're wearing that hideous black affair, in any case. You used to have better taste.' He took a dirk from his boot and reached across to grab Cassie by the arm. Then he slit the skirt down the back. 'That will do. You'll be able to put your knee round the pommel now. But keep that cloak round you. You need to look decent if we should meet anyone.'

Cassie swung the cloak round her shoulders and allowed Tam to throw her up on to Lucifer's back. She settled herself as best she could, using the cloak to cover the petticoats that foamed out through her ruined skirts. With the strange summer weather, she was going to be very hot indeed under that stifling and rather smelly cloak. She resolved to ignore it. And to ignore her brother. She would think of something beautiful instead. She would think about that stately beech tree.

No! She would think about Ross.

* * *

'There they are!' Ross gestured with his riding whip. A small group of figures was just visible, far out across the firth. They were only a little way from the Scottish shore.

Ross set his heels to Hera's flanks and started out across the sand, paying precious little attention to the pools and eddies.

'Take care, sir!' Fraser yelled. He had quickly fallen behind, for his horse was no match for Hera. 'Remember the quicksands!'

The panic in Fraser's voice was just enough to register in Ross's brain and bring him back to a sense of where he was. He steered round a particularly dubious area of sand. James Elliott had lost his fine grey in the quicksands. And Ross would be no good at all to Cassie if he did likewise.

He leaned low over Hera's neck, trying to get as close as possible to the water so that he could better gauge the firmness of the sand ahead of him. He even slackened her pace. But only slightly.

Was he gaining on them? He thought perhaps he was. 'Good girl. We will catch them. We will.'

By the time he reached the Scottish shore, Elliott had disappeared and Fraser was lagging even further behind. Ross had a moment of doubt. Should he go on, alone, one man against two, and both of them armed? Or should he wait for Fraser, losing valuable time? The thought of Cassie in her brother's clutches decided him. Nothing was more important than her rescue. He spurred Hera on.

The Elliott party clattered through Annan at a fast trot. Cassie, in the middle of the trio, kept her head down, but she heard the comments as they passed. She knew she was blushing. The good burghers of Annan could see perfectly well who she was, and how improperly dressed. She had neither hat nor gloves. And why on earth would a lady be riding dressed in a black bombazine gown and a grey stuff cloak? The voices did not rise above low murmurs—the fierce frown on James's face was frightening enough to ensure that— but their unflattering nature was obvious enough. *Miss Elliott had been discovered doing something disreputable. She was being escorted home in disgrace.*

Cassie chewed her lip and fumed. Damn her brother. Damn appearances. And damn Ross Graham for failing her when she needed him! If he had followed her into the woods, if he had ignored her pleas to be left alone, none of this would have happened. She would still have been at Whitemoss. And safe!

The trio had just reached the first stones of the bridge when she heard a shout behind them. She was almost sure it was her name. She looked over her shoulder. Was that Ross? On his chestnut mare? Surely only Ross would call out her given name in that way?

She pulled on Lucifer's reins, preparing to turn and race back to him. He was going to save her, after all.

James, only a pace behind her, snarled, 'Your word, Cassie. Remember? Your given word.' Then, as if to reinforce the message, he slashed his riding whip across Lucifer's flank.

Lucifer bolted across the bridge.

There was nothing Cassie could do. Even if she could have controlled her horse, she could not break her word, even to James. She had given herself into his power until they reached Langrigg. But she must try to catch one more glimpse of Ross. Ignoring the dangers of her horse's headlong flight, she turned in her saddle. She must try to show him, somehow, that she needed him. And that she loved him still, even though she must seem to him to be in league with her kidnappers.

She gazed back at him, pleadingly. *Please understand, Ross! Please! I love you! Come to me at Langrigg. I will find a way. At Langrigg, I will find a way.*

A cruel hand grabbed her arm. James was still alongside her. 'Have a care, Cassie, or that damned horse will have you off. Lucifer may kill you if he likes, but that blackguard behind shall not have you alive.'

A laden cart lumbered out of an alley and started across the Annan bridge. Ross was not close enough to get ahead of it. He hauled on Hera's reins. She skittered to a halt, almost losing her footing on the damp cobbles.

Damn, damn, damn! He could barely see them now. They were disappearing, at the gallop, in the direction of the Langrigg estate. Ross closed his eyes, remembering Cassie's last look.

Why had she not stopped? Why had she not come to him? James Elliott could not have taken her by force in the middle of Annan High Street. She had had her chance of freedom. She had had the chance to come to him. And she had gone with her brother. Willingly.

He slumped in his saddle. He could not believe it. She had said she loved him. How could she, and yet go with her brother? He felt as if some sharp-fanged monster was gnawing his gut. He had lost her. He had lost the woman he loved.

He groaned aloud.

When he opened his eyes, he saw that the people around had recoiled from him, as if he were carrying some terrible disease.

And he was. For his disease was heartbreak.

He had known he cared for Cassie. But he had not been prepared to admit that he loved her, not even to himself. For to love was to take risks. And Ross Graham had long since ceased to be brave enough to take risks with his heart.

His heart had had other ideas. It was given—irrevocably—to Cassie Elliott. And the sight of her straight back, disappearing into the far distance, was enough to place a vice around it and tighten the screw. His whole body ached with longing for her, even though she was lost to him. It was only now—and much too late—that he recognised just how much he loved her. Oh, Cassie! Darling Cassie!

Yet that last strange look… What did it mean? She had galloped away with her brother, right enough, but that look… If she was glad to leave him, would she not have seemed triumphant? Proud? It had been so fleeting, so difficult to read. He closed his eyes for a moment, trying to picture her face.

Not triumph. Nor anger. It was…oh, God, he could not tell. It could have been rejection. For she had cause. He, by his own neglect, had lost her. She needed him and he had failed her. He was cursed.

In desperation, he tried to edge Hera forward across the bridge. He could not—would not—lose her like this. He had to tell her he loved her. Why was that confounded cart so slow? There was not room for even a single horse to pass it.

'Sir!' Fraser gasped, catching up at last. 'Where is she? Could you not stop them?'

Ross shook his head, still berating himself for his failure. He had lost her, perhaps for ever. He tried to master the searing pain that lanced through him. 'Elliott forced them through the town at the gallop,' he lied hoarsely. He would follow her. He had to know the truth. He had to—

'I can't see any sign of them, sir.'

That brought Ross back to earth. And to the need for plans before action. 'True,' he said harshly. 'By the time we get across this blasted bridge, Elliott will be well-nigh at Langrigg.' He made no attempt to hide his anger and exasperation. 'There is no point in galloping after them now. They are too well defended for a frontal attack. What we need now, Fraser, is guile.'

Cassie dared one more glance over her shoulder, just as they turned into the Langrigg estate. There was no sign of anyone following now. He had given up.

She wanted to scream with vexation.

James caught Lucifer's rein to slow him to a walk. 'No need to rush now, m'dear,' he said silkily. 'You are home now. And safe in the bosom of your family. Where you will stay.'

Cassie kept her eyes fixed on the road in front of her. She did not dare look at James. He might see, in her eyes, that she was still far from beaten.

'Until your wedding day,' James continued, totally ignoring her mutinous silence.

She stiffened.

'That got your attention. I thought it might.'

'I will not marry any man of your choosing, James Elliott.'

He sat back in his saddle and laughed harshly till the sound echoed round the valley. 'D'ye hear that, Tam? Your mistress thinks to defy me. A good joke, is it not?'

Tam managed a strangled cackle. 'Aye, maister.'

Cassie glowered at him. Tam would see out his days in a prison hulk if she had any say in the matter.

James looked through her. 'When we reach the house, you will lock Miss Cassie in her bedchamber and bring the key to me, Tam. There will be no risk of your escaping, Cassie. And since your faithful Morag is long gone, I can at last depend on the loyalty of the servants. You will stay in your chamber until your wedding day.'

'No! I will not be wed for you.'

'As you wish. Then you will remain in your chamber. For good.' He stroked his whip down his horse's neck. 'Unfortunately, as none of the servants will have a key, it will not be possible for you to be fed. Such a pity.'

Cassie felt her heart stop in her breast. He meant it. James truly would not care if she starved to death. She was not to be allowed to thwart his will. Whatever the price.

For a long time, she said nothing. But, by the time the house came into view, her common sense had overcome her simmering fury. She might never have another chance of placating him. 'Do I take it,' she said hoarsely, 'that you have already chosen a husband for me?'

'Oh, yes.'

'May I ask who?'

He turned to look her full in the face. 'How very polite you are, on a sudden, Cassie. To what do I owe this change of tone?'

She swallowed. 'I do not relish the alternative you offer me.' Her voice was so low and flat that it was almost inaudible.

He smiled, nodding. 'An acknowledgement, at last. By God, it has taken you long enough, lassie. By rights, I should keep you in suspense. But I am too kind-hearted for that. So I will tell you. Robert Munro, of Newton Douglas, is prepared to offer me five thousand pounds for you.'

Cassie blinked in astonishment. Only days ago, James had been demanding twenty thousand from Ross.

'Not the best price, I admit, but he is an old man. I doubt he will live long. And since he has no children, you will soon be a very wealthy widow.'

But, as a widow, she would be free!

'Oh, no, Cassie.' He had caught the gleam in her eye. 'Don't think you can escape me, even once you are wed. Munro has agreed that I am to be your trustee. Once our husband is safely planted, I shall control every penny of the Munro estate. It will be quite like old times, will it not? Indeed, if I am any judge, I'd say that Munro would be lucky to have strength enough to last the wedding night.'

'Morag! At last!'

The abigail bustled into the coffee room of Annan's best inn. 'Och, sir! Miss Cassie! Where is she? She—'

'Hush!' Ross put a finger to his lips and gave a tiny shake of his head. There were too many listening ears around them. He had made his decision. He needed Morag's help for his plans. 'Come outside, Morag. I need to talk to you. Fraser will take your things upstairs.' He took her by the elbow and hurried her out.

He did not allow her to say a word until they were beyond the edge of the town and walking along the open river bank where he could be sure that no one was within earshot. 'I need your help, Morag. I am going to rescue your mistress.'

'Aye, sir.'

'She is a prisoner at Langrigg House. Fraser has tried to buy the help of some of the servants there, but they are all too afraid of James Elliott.'

'Aye, sir. 'Twas always the way. He thrashed one wee lad till he was half-dead. And all but shot another. Nobody dares to cross him. Not any mair.'

'Not any more? Why? What has happened?'

'If he disna get the money from someplace soon, he'll lose Langrigg. That's what I was telt. Without

Langrigg, he'd have no power left. Selling Miss Cassie is all that he can do.'

'Have you heard something, Morag? These people will not talk to me. Or even to Fraser.'

'No, sir. Outrels.'

'What? Oh, outsiders.'

'At Gretna, when we had to bide a wee while for the horses, they telt me that Miss Cassie was to be wed. I didna believe it.'

Ross almost doubled up with pain. It was worse that being struck by a heavyweight prizefighter. He could not stifle a terrible groan.

Morag let out a strangled cry as the truth hit home. 'But ye'll save her, sir, won't ye? Ye must save Miss Cassie!'

He would try. By God, he would try. She could not have stopped loving him. He would not believe it. Not when he needed her…loved her so. Not when she needed him to take action to save her. Now.

'Tell me, Morag. Where will she be? He has her a prisoner. Where will he hold her?'

'In her chamber, at the top o' the house.'

'How can I tell which is her room? How do I reach her?'

'Ye canna do that, sir. There's split-new bars on the window. And ye canna climb the wall. Ye canna get her out by that way.'

'So I have to go in through the house?'

She nodded.

'Will there be many servants? Able-bodied men?'

'Aye, surely. The laird'll expect ye. He'll shoot ye. And there'll be nobody to cry "murther" when he does.'

Ross beat one clenched fist into the other palm. A suicide attack would not save Cassie. There had to be another way. 'Tell me about the wedding, Morag.'

'What d'ye mean, sir?'

'How will it go forward? I know nothing of the customs in this part of the world.'

'Well, a wedding hereabouts can be just a declaration, with witnesses. There disna even have to be a minister.'

'So he could force her, without even leaving Langrigg?'

'Aye, but he'll no' do that. A lady has to be wed in the kirk. Or before the minister, somewheres else. The gentles wouldna accept the marriage, without that.'

'I see.' Ross bit his lip. There must be something here he could hold on to. 'So…either she'll be wed in the church, or her brother will bring the minister to Langrigg House. Which church will it be? Which minister?'

'Annan kirk. 'Twould be unco strange to use another. Langrigg is in Annan parish.'

Ross put an arm round Morag's shoulder and gave her a quick squeeze. 'Time for us to go back to Annan, Morag. I think I need to have an interview with this minister of yours.'

* * *

The minister, Mr McLean, was a bald, cheery-looking man with a very florid complexion. He readily admitted that Miss Cassandra Elliott was soon to be married. He himself was to officiate.

Ross began to stride up and down in the neat sitting room of the manse. It was all he could do to keep his anger in check. 'I have to tell you, sir, that this is a forced marriage. Miss Elliott does not go willingly to the altar. You must prevent it.'

'I could not do that, my dear sir. I have the word of the lady herself that it is her wish.'

'I don't believe it!' The harsh words were out before he had time to stop them. And then he realised they were true. She would never have agreed. Never.

'I beg your pardon, sir?' The minister's red face had flushed an unbecoming purple at the implied insult.

Ross swallowed hard, fighting his emotions. What had happened to his vaunted self-control and his soldier's experience? He needed the minister on his side, but he had just called him a liar. Or as good as.

'Forgive me, Mr McLean. I did not mean to suggest… I had it on good authority that the lady was not willing in this match. Or so I thought. But I can see that I was much too hasty in what I just said. I ask you to accept my apology.'

The minister nodded. His colour subsided and his cheerful manner returned. 'No offence taken, young man. No offence taken. I can quite understand that Miss Elliott might not have favoured the match at first. The groom is…well…somewhat older than the lady, and already twice widowed. But he is a man of good standing in society. And with a fine estate over by Newtown Douglas. I imagine Miss Elliott became reconciled to the match when she learned of all its many advantages.'

Ross would not let himself reply. The minister seemed to think that Cassie Elliott would willingly marry some lecherous old man, just for his wealth and status. She would not. Not his Cassie. Not when she was already in love with Ross. She would not!

So why had she told the minister that she agreed?

'You saw Miss Elliott alone, did you, sir?'

'No. Why would I do that? There was no need. Her brother was by. 'Tis he who will lead her to the altar, after all.'

'Ah, yes. Of course. I had forgot. Will you be so good as to tell me, sir, when the wedding is to take place? I should very much like to be present.'

'Excellent. I like to see a good congregation for a wedding. All the Langrigg people will be there, of course, and some of the groom's people, too. But I am less sure about the gentlefolk hereabouts. They may not be aware…'

'When is it, sir?' Ross asked again, with quiet determination.

'Why, tomorrow morn.'

'So soon? My goodness. She must have changed her mind quite suddenly, sir.' Ross was trying to keep his tone light. 'It was only the other day that I learnt—from the lady's own lips—that she had set her face against the marriage.'

'Ah, well, sir. Women are fickle. Very fickle. Yesterday, I learned that the wedding was to go ahead with all speed.'

Ross's eyebrows rose. 'Indeed?'

'Aye. And with the ceremony due to her station, forbye. Her brother asked for just a quiet wedding, at Langrigg. But Miss Elliott was adamant that she had to be married in the kirk, or nowhere.'

Ah! The vice around Ross's heart slackened half a notch. Now he understood. His Cassie—and she *was* his—was risking everything on one mad throw of the dice. And on Ross's resolve being strong enough.

It would be.

Cassie's wedding day dawned grey and cold. She was perversely glad of it. She could not have borne to see sunshine, or a blue sky. This day would bring a new beginning. Or put a period to her existence.

She had to trust that Ross would come for her. And somehow rescue her. But, if he did not, she would take matters into her own hands. Even if it was a sin.

She smoothed the skirts of her fine muslin petticoat

and carefully unrolled the leather pouch that contained her sewing materials. She extracted her longest bodkin and tried it on her thumb. Aye, it was surely sharp enough. She wrapped it in a scrap of silk and stowed it carefully in her pocket.

But one weapon was not enough. What if someone noticed what she was concealing there? She needed to be sure she could carry out her plan. She scanned the bare chamber rapidly. There seemed to be nothing but the plain furniture and that cursed white gown that her brother had thrown across the bed an hour before.

In desperation, she pulled out the drawer of the night stand. Spills, wafers, a tinder box, some candle ends… Ah, the tiny little knife she had once used to pare her nails. She beamed in triumph. No one had thought to look there. She had forgotten it herself. The knife was small, but it was sharp. Sharp enough to stop a man in his tracks.

She dare not put it in her pocket. She must find a different hiding place for this. Where on earth…?

With a shudder, she remembered precisely when she was likely to need a weapon. A pocket was not the place to hide it. Very deliberately, she rolled the little knife in a muslin handkerchief and pushed it under the top of her silk stocking. Then, gritting her teeth, she donned her bridal gown and stood, facing the door, waiting for James to come for her.

'Ross,' she breathed, fingering the tiny bulge in her stocking through the layers of fine muslin and lace, 'I know you will come. I love you, Ross. I am yours. And I will be yours. Or no one's.'

Chapter Twenty

Fraser should be back by now. Where on earth was the confounded man? Unless perhaps he'd had problems with Morag? It was certainly true that she did not take well to horses, but in the hired gig…? There should have been no difficulty, surely? All Fraser had to do was deposit Morag, make a few arrangements and grease a few palms, and then return to Annan to collect his horse.

If he did not arrive soon, Ross would have to go ahead on his own. He stroked Hera's glossy neck. 'Easy, girl. You shall have your moment of glory soon enough. Just don't let me down when I put you to that great door.' Ross twisted the reins in his fingers, trying to remain calm. He knew it was utter madness. It would create an enormous scandal. There was no doubt of that. News of it might even reach London. And if it did not, it would certainly spread far enough around Dumfries to ensure that neither he nor Cassie would ever be able to return there. But what choice did he have?

Ross straightened his shoulders and shook his head, more at his own anxieties than anything else. He had gone through every possible avenue—some even more outrageous than this—but neither he, nor Fraser, had been able to arrive at a better solution. He would simply have to grit his teeth and carry out their plan. Cassie would understand, would she not? Yes. She was bound to. If the choice was between scandal and a forced marriage, she would understand. For she loved him. She did.

Hera was starting to fidget. They had been standing still too long. Perhaps the burghers of Annan were already beginning to wonder why an acknowledged wedding guest was still sitting on his horse at the other end of the street, rather than making his way on foot into the kirk. If Fraser did not appear in the next few minutes, Ross would have to make a move. Meanwhile, he sat quietly, trying to calm his mare and watching the various people entering the church. So far, almost all of them had seemed to belong to the lower classes: servants from Langrigg—some of whom he recognised—and probably servants from the groom's estate, too. One or two of the better dressed members of the congregation might be trades-men from Annan itself. If they were suppliers to Langrigg—even if they did not get paid—they would want to attend.

Ah, but that was no tradesman! A pair of fine horses

trotted down the High Street and halted by the church. The tall figure of Colonel Anstruther dismounted. The other rider, equally a gentleman though unknown to Ross, joined him and the pair entered the kirk. They were followed, a few minutes later, by three more gentlemen and two ladies. It did not matter that Ross had no idea who they were. The presence of gentlefolk would make a huge difference. No matter how many of his henchmen James Elliott had around him, he would have to behave like a gentlemen in the company of his peers.

It seemed the guests were now all assembled. For several minutes, no one else entered the church. Everyone was waiting for—

Ross found he was holding his breath, waiting too. At last, the moment came. The Elliott carriage drew up in front of the doorway. Ross strained in his saddle, but he could not see. His view of the entrance was obscured by the carriage.

She must have gone in. With her brother.

Ross must act quickly, before it was too late. But he needed Fraser. Where on earth was he?

At that very moment, Fraser rounded the corner and joined Ross.

'What kept you?'

'Morag,' Fraser groaned. 'Damned woman!'

'Never mind that. Is everything arranged?'

'Aye, sir. The King's Head at Springfield. The very

last village before the border. 'Twill be done the moment we arrive. And there's a secret room behind, for… Well, no need to discuss that. We need only ten or fifteen minutes' start on them and there will be no fear of your being interrupted.'

Ross nodded. 'I have changed part of the plan.'

Fraser's eyebrows rose. 'But you said yourself there was no other way. If you—'

'That was then, Fraser. I did not expect there to be anyone in the church to help me defend Cassie against her brother. But Colonel Anstruther, and several other gentlemen, have arrived. Some ladies, too.' He grinned and pulled at Hera's ear. 'I am sure this fine lady would have relished the challenge of prancing down the aisle of Annan kirk and helping me carry the bride off on my saddle bow, but she will not have the chance, now. I shall go in on foot. There will be a scandal. But nothing to compare with the one I would have caused by riding a horse up to the altar.'

Fraser nodded, clearly relieved. 'Thank God for that,' he breathed. 'If you had—'

'Now, Fraser. To business. We have little time. While I go in to rescue Miss Elliott, you must ensure that no one can follow us, at least for a while. The carriage there—' he pointed with his whip '—is Elliott's. You'd best cut the traces. As for the horses belonging to the other guests… Hmm. I don't want to offend Colonel Anstruther or any of the other gentlemen but, equally, I dare not leave any good horse that Elliott might borrow. No. You'd best untie them and take them off down to the river. They'll come to no harm. But it will buy us time.'

'Very good, sir.' Fraser grinned. It was exactly the sort of task at which he excelled.

Ross swung down from Hera's saddle. The heels of his boots rang on the cobbles. Throwing the reins to Fraser, he said, 'Wait until I am inside the church before you make a move. I should be a few minutes only, ten at most. Make sure you are waiting at the door with the horses.'

Fraser frowned a little, as if annoyed to be given orders that he already perfectly understood. Then he looked down into his master's face. Whatever he saw there made him smile reassuringly. 'You can rely on me, Captain. And I know you will bring the mistress off safely.'

'Thank you, Fraser.' Ross reached up his right hand. They shook, warmly. Not equals, perhaps, but friends and tried comrades.

By the time Ross reached the church door, it had been closed. He could hear noise from within, but it was impossible to make out precisely what was going on. He took off his hat and tossed it on to the step. He would retrieve it later. If there was time. Then he ran his hand through his hair, took a deep breath, pushed the heavy door open and stepped into the relative gloom beyond.

The congregation was clustered at the front of the church. No one appeared to have noticed Ross's entrance. Any noise he had made was covered by the loud, droning voice of the minister. Cassie was directly in front of the minister. Her brother was standing very close by her side and seemed to be whispering in her ear. Threats, probably. To ensure she could not cry off. On Cassie's other side was a small, pot-bellied old man, with a bent back and scrawny legs, displayed in black silk breeches and stockings with enormous clocks. The little man was just reaching for Cassie's hand.

Ross marched down the aisle, his boots ringing on the flags. Every head turned towards him. Including Cassie's. Her face lit up at the sight of him. He thought she breathed his name. His heart swelled with a surge of love. And longing. She did still love him.

Mindful of the dangers, Ross stopped a few yards from the minister so that he could keep Elliott and all his servants in view. 'Mr McLean,' he said in a voice worthy of the parade ground, 'this wedding may not go forward. Miss Cassandra Elliott is not free to marry this day. She is betrothed to me.'

Cassie's brother began to stutter a protest, looking round wildly. He reached into his coat, as if for a weapon, but of course he had none. There were certainly benefits to challenging him in a church.

'Captain Graham, this is outrageous!' The minister did not intend to be bested at his own altar. 'You know well enough—for I told you yesterday—that Miss Elliott herself had agreed to this match.'

'Under duress, sir. Under duress. If you do not believe me, ask the lady now.'

Cassie stepped away from her brother and her would-be suitor. She looked first at the minister and then at the gentlemen in the congregation. In a clear, strong voice, she said, 'My brother is trying to force me to wed Mr Robert Munro, who has paid him five thousand pounds for possession of my person.'

The congregation began to mutter.

'I repudiate this match, here in front of you all,' Cassie continued, looking straight at Ross, her eyes shining. He stretched out a hand to her. 'I am be-trothed to Captain Ross Graham. And as I am of full age, no one here—' she whipped round to stare at her brother '—*no one* has the right to prevent it.' With a fleeting smile towards the minister and a whispered word of apology for the deception that had been prac-tised on him, she placed her hand in Ross's and was drawn into the shelter of his arm.

'A moment, my dear,' Ross said. He had to ensure that the danger from James Elliott was removed, for ever. 'Mr McLean, gentlemen, let there be no doubt of what has gone forward here. This man—' he pointed at Cassie's brother, who recoiled from the fury in Ross's eyes '—this man has treated his own sister as if she were a chattel, a mere piece of goods to be sold so that he could pay for his drinking and gambling. And worse. You all know him. You must know I speak the truth. What is more, James Elliott kidnapped his sister from her godfather's home, on the other side of the Solway. And he forced her to agree to this sham of a marriage, by threats.'

He raised an eyebrow to Cassie, who nodded. 'He promised to leave me to starve to death in my prison if I did not agree,' she said quietly.

A collective gasp echoed round the church.

'So let no man here take Elliott's part. He is an out-and-out scoundrel. He is not fit to enter the company of gentlemen.'

Colonel Anstruther, who was looking exceedingly serious, nodded vigorously. He threw a withering look in Elliott's direction. No doubt the colonel would ensure that justice was done.

Ross squeezed Cassie's hand and, together, they turned from the altar and walked smartly toward the door.

Behind them Cassie's brother screamed, 'Ye'll no' take her! I'll kill ye first!'

Ross heard hurrying footsteps behind them as they reached the door. He did not turn. He simply put an arm round Cassie and ushered her through. Fraser was already in the saddle, waiting. 'Up with you, Cassie,'

Ross said, lifting her on to Hera's back and throwing himself into the saddle behind her.

He glanced round. The Elliott carriage and horses stood there. The riding horses were gone. 'Now, Hera.' He put his heels to her flanks. She raced forward down the street, making light of her double burden.

Fraser started after them, looking back over his shoulder every few moments to check if they were being followed. Suddenly he gave a great bellow of laughter.

Ross did not turn, but Cassie pushed herself up in his arms so that she could look over his shoulder. 'Oh, my!' she cried with a nervous laugh. 'James is trying to follow us. Was that your doing, Fraser?'

Fraser could not speak. He was laughing too much. But Ross nodded. 'Fraser cut the traces.'

'Jamie will have some fine bruises. And not only to his limbs,' she added with relish. 'The carriage horses have dragged him halfway along the street. And most of the townsfolk are doubled up with laughter at the sight.'

'Morag! Oh, Morag, I'm so glad you are here.'

'Wouldna have missed it for the world, Miss Cassie.'

'Best get a move on, sir, madam,' Fraser said. 'We can't be sure how much time we have in hand.'

'But is it really necessary? There was no sign that James was following us, was there? We could go on to Longtown, or to Carlisle. We'd be safe in England, would we not?'

'Are you having second thoughts, Cassie?'

'No. Of course not. But I should like to be wed in church.'

'And you shall be. But first, you shall be wed here in Springfield. I must have you safe, my sweet. Once we have been joined—even here—no one can part us. Ah, here is Mr Lang.'

'G'day t'ye, ma'am, surr.'

David Lang, nicknamed 'Bishop' Lang, was an enormous old man, with layers of jowls that made him look to have no neck at all. He was dressed from head to foot in rusty black. As if to emphasise his 'priestly' role, he carried a broad-brimmed hat to match his clerical garb. And he spoke in an accent so thick that Ross understood barely one word in four. However, Cassie and Morag were nodding eagerly at what seemed to be a speech of welcome and an explanation of what was about to happen.

Seeing Ross's puzzlement, Cassie translated with a grin. 'We have but to state who we are and that we are free to marry. Then it is simply a matter of making a declaration that we will wed each other.'

Mr Lang touched Cassie's arm impatiently. 'The beddin,' he urged, looking towards Ross. 'Ye'll no' be richt merrit wi'oot a beddin, surr.'

Cassie blushed to the roots of her hair. 'He says that we—'

Ross shook his head at her with a quick smile of

sympathy. 'No need, my dear. I followed the gist of what he said.'

Taking a deep breath, Ross squared his shoulders and looked at Mr Lang. 'Now, sir, let it be done. I, Captain Ross Graham, bachelor, presently residing in the parish of Annan, do hereby declare, before you and these witnesses, that I am free to marry.'

Ross held out his hand to Cassie. She laid her own in his and made her statement, in turn. Then, before David Lang, and before the two witnesses who had served them both so faithfully, Ross and Cassie declared themselves man and wife.

'And nane shall pit ye sunder,' 'Bishop' Lang intoned in his deep voice. Then he plucked at Ross's sleeve. 'Come by to the chaumber, surr. Ye'll need to be doing the beezness whiles I scrieve yer mairrage lines. 'Twill mak it all guid an' legal, ye see.' He pushed against a panel in the wall, which proved to be a door. Behind it, there was a hidden bedchamber and a bed with fresh sheets.

Morag made to follow her mistress. 'No, Morag,' Ross said firmly. 'Your mistress is my wife now. I will look to her.'

'Cassie.'

She went to his arms and nestled there, breathing in the wholesome scent of him, feeling at last that she was safe and where she belonged.

He held her close and stroked her hair. 'Cassie, forgive me, but Mr Lang is right. If our marriage is not…er…'

Cassie threw her arms round his neck and pulled his mouth down to hers. 'I have married an idiot,' she said with a wry grin. 'I may have been embarrassed by what Mr Lang said, but I do understand the importance of it. If our marriage is not consummated—that is the correct term, I believe?—James could try to have it put aside.'

Ross grimaced. 'We should take our time over this, our first lying together as man and wife. But if James is at our heels—'

'Oh, Ross,' she said, shaking her head. Could he not see how much she wanted him? She looked into his eyes. She saw concern, overlaid on tenderness. Where was the desire? Did he not feel it, as she did? 'Ross, I am no longer a shy virgin. Making love holds no terrors for me. Oh, my love, I have been praying for you, and for this moment, since the day James carried me off. When I looked back at you, by Annan bridge, I was trying to tell you so. Did you not understand? Do you not want me, too?'

It seemed that was all he needed, for he seized her mouth and kissed her as if she were the life-giving water for a man dying in the desert. The kiss went on and on. Cassie's heart was pounding in her breast. She could feel that familiar molten glow in her belly as her womb made ready to welcome his seed. She could not wait any longer.

She started to claw at his coat and his shirt. That made him laugh, even while he kissed her. He dragged his lips away for a second. 'You are a passionate woman, my little wife. Are you so very hot for me, then?'

She continued to struggle with his shirt buttons. The moment she saw bare skin, she put her lips to his chest and began to tease him with her tongue.

That was too much for Ross's self-control. He ripped off the rest of his clothes and threw Cassie on the bed, still fully dressed. 'If it's haste you want, my lady,' he groaned, pushing up her skirts and petticoats, 'then you shall have it.'

Cassie opened her body to him, welcoming his possession. Her need was urgent now.

Ross lay on top of her, kissing her mouth and stroking one breast through the layers of fine cloth. Cassie could feel her nipple peaking against his fingers. It was as if there was no barrier between her skin and his.

He readied himself, but hesitated.

Cassie could not wait. She bucked against him and he slid fully into her warmth with a long moan of desire and satisfaction. He had barely begun to move within her when her spasms started. 'Ross!' she cried. 'Oh, my love!' She clung to him as she spiralled higher. Her final cry of ecstasy contained no words. It was as old as woman herself.

* * *

It took Cassie a long time to come back to earth. When she did so, she saw that Ross was lying naked beside her, absently stroking her inner thigh with one finger. He was smiling into her eyes, a deep contented smile.

His wandering finger nudged against the bulge in her stocking. 'What, pray, madam wife, is this?' His dreamy smile had disappeared. For a moment, he looked startled.

Cassie's eyes widened. Heavens! She had completely forgotten. She might have injured Ross with that knife.

Slowly and deliberately, he extracted it from under her stocking and unwrapped it. He tested the edge with a finger. 'Ouch! That's sharp.' He glanced at Cassie's face, then back at the knife for a second, and then gazed at her face once more. Suddenly, he was grinning wickedly at her. 'Were you planning to cut off my manhood if I failed to satisfy you, Cassie?'

'No. Of course not.' She closed her eyes, thinking quickly. Was there any way of avoiding the truth? 'You know very well that you satisfy me in…er…every way.'

'I'm glad to hear it.' His grin had turned into a rather self-satisfied smirk. 'So why is it here, Cassie?'

Oh dear. There was no way out. 'I…I…I could not have let him touch me, Ross. I belong to you. Only you. If you had not rescued me, I was going to use it on Robert Munro.'

'But that would have been mur—'

'And afterwards on myself.'

'Oh, God. Cassie!' He hurled the little knife to the floor and pulled her into a fierce embrace. 'Cassie!' His strong, proud body was trembling against hers. Probably thinking how close they had come to losing each other for ever.

She held him tight against her until his trembling stopped. It would have been better if he had not known at all, but… At least he could now be in no doubt of just how much she would have sacrificed for him, and just how much she loved him.

She touched a hand to his chest and allowed her fingernail to graze his nipple. He groaned. She smiled towards the ceiling. Very satisfactory.

'Cassie, I have said before that you are a witch. Your very touch makes my whole body burn with desire. I love you, wife of mine.' His voice sank even lower. 'I love you to the depths of my soul.'

Cassie's breath caught and her heart began to race. Had he really said he loved her? Had she imagined the words? She had so longed to hear them.

He was starting to stroke her hair once more, and letting her curls wind themselves around his fingers. 'Ah, my love, my darling wife, I think I have wanted to do this since the first time I set eyes on you, with your mane of wet and tangled hair hanging down your back and Lucifer's reins wrapped tight around your hand.'

A great calm surrounded Cassie, like a velvet cloak, soft and rich, settling on her skin. It *was* true. He did love her. It made everything complete at last. She lay completely still, not daring to move lest she break the spell of his mesmerising touch. His loving touch.

He dropped a kiss on her lips. It surprised her. It was not a kiss of passion, but of love and commitment. As if to seal their bargain. Their love. 'Mmm. You taste divine, Cassie. Exactly as a wife should taste. Nectar and rose petals.'

She sighed deeply and relaxed into the soft mattress. She had nothing more to wish for. She would like to stay here for ever, sharing this intimate feeling of fulfilment alongside the man to whom she had given her heart. And who had given her his.

At last, very gently, Ross pushed down Cassie's skirts. Dropping a final kiss on her brow, he said, 'I should like to lie here for ever, Cassie, my love, but it may not be. Beyond that door, they are waiting for us.'

Cassie gasped. In the heat of passion, she had forgotten the others. What had they heard through the panel?

Chapter Twenty-One

Ross leaned back in the wing chair in their private parlour in the Graham Arms at Longtown. Its name no longer intrigued him; he had discovered more than he needed to know about the history of his appalling family. He intended to forget them, if he could. And he would never use his father's name. Never. That was certain.

He smiled across at Cassie. 'We'll be off as soon as Fraser arrives. It is a long way to London, I'm afraid, and liable to be very uncomfortable for you, even in a post-chaise.'

'I'm sure it cannot be more uncomfortable than my journeys to school in Edinburgh,' Cassie replied equably. 'My father insisted I attended the best possible seminary—he would not allow any child that carried his name to associate with the lower classes—but he did not see a need to pay a groat more than necessary to get me there.'

'Well, this time, we shall travel in as much comfort as I can contrive. You understand, I hope, my love—' he attempted a leer, but she only laughed '—that post-chaises are not made to accommodate three persons. Morag will have to travel separately. You are going to travel with me.' He grinned. 'Alone.'

She beamed at him. 'There will be post-boys, however, will there not?'

'Sadly, yes. But if they dare to look round to gaze on their betters, they will lose all chance of seeing my extra guineas. And so I shall tell them.' Cassie was blushing again, just a little. Delightful. He dropped a kiss on the end of her pink nose.

'Ross! What if someone should come in?'

He shrugged. 'You are my wife. Or rather—' He looked suddenly very serious. 'Cassie, you told me, at Springfield, that you wanted to be married in church. And I promised that you would be. I intend to keep my promise.'

She smiled up at him. 'Thank you. A church wedding would make everything…feel right. Everything was so quick, at Springfield, and—' She stopped dead, blushing fierily. Everything had indeed been quick. And she had been the one responsible.

Ross patted her hand. 'When we reach London, I will arrange for a special licence so that we can be married at once. Would St George's, Hanover Square, suit you, ma'am?'

'I don't know. I have never been to London. I'm sure that any church you choose would be splendid.'

'Good. That's settled. One thing more, Cassie.' He took her hand. 'Until we are properly wed, in church, we will sleep apart.'

'No!'

'Yes, Cassie. As you yourself said, we need a church wedding to make us feel truly married. What happened…er…at Springfield… It was necessary then, but it will not be repeated. Not until we have been joined in church.'

Cassie did not like the sound of that at all. Yes, she wanted their union to be blessed by the church. But they *were* married. And married couples should share a bed. She did not want to sleep alone. 'Ross, I—' she began tentatively but, before she could start to argue, the door opened.

It was Fraser, looking remarkably grimy from his long ride. He grinned at them. 'Afternoon, ma'am. Sir.' He put his whip on the table and began to strip off his gloves. 'I've brought Lucifer for ye, ma'am,' he said with quiet satisfaction.

Cassie jumped to her feet. She almost wanted to kiss him. Instead, she seized his hands and danced round the room with him.

'Miss Cassie! Mrs Graham, ma'am! Stop!'

Cassie did not stop until she was almost out of

breath. Then Ross caught her round the waist and pulled her to a seat beside him.

Fraser stood in the middle of the floor, straightening his stock and trying not to look flustered.

'Did you have any difficulty in bringing Lucifer away?'

'No, sir. None. Langrigg is all at sixes and sevens. No one appears to be in charge.'

'My brother—?'

'Your brother, ma'am…well, he…'

'He is not dead?' Cassie had gone pale.

Fraser hastened to reassure her. 'No, ma'am. Not dead. He…he rushed back to Langrigg, right after you left Annan. They say he went to get the money from his strongbox and to make off with it. It was five thousand pounds and more, so they said.'

Cassie and Ross exchanged glances.

'But he was not quick enough. Mr Munro was furious that he had not got himself a bride in return for all that money. He insisted that the gentlemen should go straight back to Langrigg with him and demand the return of his cash. When they arrived there, your brother was still in the house. As soon as he heard their horses, he barricaded the door against them. He was at the window with his pistols.'

'Did he fire on them?'

'No, sir. He…he seemed to have some kind of seizure, they said. One minute he was ready to shoot them, the next he was screaming like an injured animal, according to one of the manservants. And he appeared to recognise no one, not even his own henchmen. When the steward saw how the land lay, he opened the door and let the gentlemen in. Mr Munro just took his money and left. It was Colonel Anstruther who took charge of the household. He…he had your brother restrained. And then the doctor said he had to be taken to the Bedlam. For his own safety. I'm sorry, ma'am.'

Cassie took a deep breath and closed her eyes for a second. 'God have mercy on him. But it may be for the best,' she whispered at last. 'I had begun to wonder, some months ago, if James might be going slowly mad. His tempers were becoming ever more violent. As were his threats, to me, and to others. And the risks he was taking… I shall write to Colonel Anstruther and ask him to ensure that James is well cared for. Then I—' She stopped and looked up at Ross. 'Forgive me. I should have consulted you first. Do you think that—?'

'I think that you are doing exactly right, my love,' Ross said gently. 'He may be a wicked man, but if he is stark mad—and I can well believe it, given some of the things I have seen and heard about him—he needs to be restrained, and to be cared for. Do you write to Colonel Anstruther as you suggest. I will ensure that there is money enough at Langrigg to pay for your brother's care.'

'Thank you,' she said quietly. 'After what he tried to do to you, that is more than generous.'

'I do it for you, my love, and for your peace of mind. Not for him.'

Two post-chaises, each with four horses, stood in Longtown High Street outside the Graham Arms. The three riding horses were tied on behind the second of them.

Cassie gazed thoughtfully down at the scene from the parlour window. Her husband was certainly sparing no expense to ensure that their trip to London was as speedy and comfortable as possible. But the horses…? Surely that was strange?

Fraser came back at that moment to fetch the last of their travelling valises. He was to collect the rest of Ross's baggage in Carlisle.

'Are you not riding, Fraser? I thought my husband—' she stumbled a little over the unfamiliar word '—I thought the captain had said that you were bringing the horses to London by easy stages?'

Fraser could not quite meet her eye. 'Er…Morag… she…um…she suggested that we might share the chaise for a stage or two, ma'am. Just to be companionable, like. 'Tis only as far as Penrith, ma'am. I'll be bringing the horses on from there.'

'Oh. I see.' Cassie had to bite her lip to stop herself

from grinning with delight. Goodness, what a surprise! Fraser and Morag?

She was almost certain Fraser was blushing as he hurried out of the room. The moment the door closed, Cassie began to dance round the furniture, humming a reel. Fraser and Morag! Nothing could be more wonderful.

A moment later, her husband caught her round the waist and lifted her into his arms.

'Where did you come from? I—'

He whirled her round. 'I slipped in when you were not looking. You were so busy dancing and singing that a man-eating lion could have crept up on you. Grrr!' He bared his teeth at her.

'Humph! You make a very poor lion, sir!' She freed one hand from his embrace and ran her fingers through his thick red hair. 'Not much of a mane, I'd say. And quite the wrong colour, too!'

'Indeed? What impertinence! I'll teach you to say such things to your husband, Mrs Graham. Just you wait.' He whirled her round and round until she was so dizzy she had to cling to him. Then, at last, he fell on to the sofa with her still in his arms. 'Have you learned your lesson now, ma'am?' He pulled her close. 'Or must I play the dominie again?' He grinned wickedly at her.

Cassie knew exactly how to deal with that. She wrapped her arms round his neck and touched her lips to his. In a heartbeat, passion had flared between them. He was no longer grinning, but groaning.

She, too, was rapidly losing control. She felt a desperate urge to rip off his clothes. Again.

'No, Cassie,' he moaned, tearing his lips from hers. 'Oh, my darling witch, we must not. Especially not here. Not now.' He sat up and set her on her feet in front of him, though his hands lingered on her waist. 'There will be plenty of time for loving, once we are properly wed.'

A voice in Cassie's head protested. They were already properly wed. But there was no point in telling him so. Later, she would find a way. Later.

'It is time for us to leave. And we shall travel to London with the utmost propriety, like any other married couple.' He raised his eyebrows warningly and shook his head at her. 'No tricks, mind, Mrs Graham.'

Cassie adopted as demure an expression as she could.

'Remember that post-boys have eyes. And ears.'

She nodded slowly. 'I hope that Fraser and Morag are aware of that.'

'What do you mean?'

Cassie took Ross's hand and pulled him over to the window. 'See?' She pointed at the riding horses. 'Fraser will be riding in the chaise. With Morag. As far as Penrith, he says.'

Ross did not look in the least surprised. And he was smiling down at her in a very superior way.

'You knew!'

'Of course I did. I am only surprised that you did not, Cassie. I can see that I shall have to revise my opinion of you. I had thought you were such a downy one.'

'Oh, you wretch! I had…er…other things on my mind. As you know very well. I—'

The door opened again to admit Fraser. He seemed to have recovered his composure for he said, in his normal voice, 'The baggage is stowed and the chaises are waiting, sir.'

Ross and Cassie exchanged knowing glances. Fraser ignored them.

With a smile, Ross offered Cassie his arm. 'If you are ready, Mrs Graham?'

Cassie took it without a word and allowed him to lead her down the stairs and out to the waiting chaise.

Fraser followed, carrying a heavy rug and the case containing Ross's pistols. He was humming as he arranged the rug over Cassie's knees.

At first, Cassie did not recognise the tune. Then, as Fraser went round to check the fastenings of the luggage, the humming got louder. She fancied that Morag, standing by the second chaise, was humming, too. Why, it was—! Cassie clapped a hand over her mouth to stop herself from laughing out loud.

'Cassie? What is it?' Ross was looking puzzled. Then he shook his head. 'Strange, very strange. In all the years Fraser has been with me, I don't think I have ever heard him singing. I can't imagine what's come over him. Do you think he has found himself a secret store of whisky while we've been in Scotland?'

Cassie pressed her lips tight together. She didn't dare say a word. But behind her, the humming was getting louder. She felt an overwhelming desire to join in. She shouldn't.

But, in the end, she could not resist. Soon, three voices were humming loudly.

'Cassie? Is the world going mad? Confound it! What on earth is going on?' He started to climb down from the chaise.

At that moment, Fraser, and then Morag, began to sing properly. With words.

Cassie collapsed in whoops of laughter.

And Ross, standing beside the chaise, understood at last. For the ballad that his faithful valet was singing— and that his helplessly laughing wife had encouraged—was Sir Walter Scott's *Young Lochinvar*.

'*So light to the croupe the fair lady he swung,*' Fraser carolled, his voice getting ever louder. '*So light to the saddle before her he sprung! She is won! We are gone, over—*'

'Fraser,' Ross said ominously, 'would you prefer to walk to Penrith?'

Too late. Fraser grinned impudently and continued to sing to the last verse. '*So daring in love, and so dauntless in war, Have ye e'er heard of gallant like young Lochinvar?'*

Ross turned over yet again in his solitary bed. After such a day, his body should be exhausted. So why could he not sleep?

Stupid question. Was it not obvious? This morning he had married the most amazing woman in the world, a woman he would adore until his very last breath, and yet—for honour's sake—he had insisted she sleep alone. They were legally man and wife, but he knew that Cassie would never feel in her heart that they were truly wed until they had been joined in church. So he had no choice. In spite of what had happened between them, in that mist-shrouded barn, and again this morning, he had no choice.

But it was damnably difficult when she was lying in a chamber only yards away!

He groaned aloud at the thought of her delectable body, warm and fuzzy with sleep, with only a wisp of silk between her tender skin and the fine linen sheets. If only… He reached out a hand, stroking the cool linen where she would have lain, if only she had been here. Beside him.

It was not difficult! It was impossible!

He threw back the bedclothes, strode across to the window and flung it open. The cool night area flooded in, chilling his naked body. But it did nothing to cool the desire that was burning in him. Was he to suffer like this every night of this journey? If so, he would be a sorry excuse for a man by the time they reached London, for he would have had no sleep at all.

He put his elbows on the window sill and leant out, craning his neck to look up at the stars. Perhaps he should count them? Perhaps, like sheep, they would help him to sleep? Or at least to take his mind off Cassie. He tried to concentrate on identifying the constellations. He had done it often enough in Spain, after all. The plough, for example. That was always easy to spot. It should be—

Somewhere close by a floorboard squeaked.

'Who's there?' Ross quickly ducked his head back into the room and turned to face the door. Had he not locked it? He was almost sure he had. Perhaps the noise had come from outside, in the corridor?

Perhaps, in his frustration, he was imagining things? He stood absolutely still for a long time, straining his eyes and ears. Nothing.

Eventually, he decided that he was still alone. He should go back to bed. He must at least try to sleep. 'Oh, Cassie,' he sighed. 'If only you knew what you are doing to me.'

'I do know,' whispered a voice from the direction of the bed. 'And I feel it too.'

'Cassie!' He flung himself at the bed and found himself struggling in the dark with a tangle of sheets and coverlets. 'Cassie!' His questing hand found an edge of lace. He clung on and pulled. 'Now I have you.'

But he did not. For she rolled away from him. There was a sound of tearing, loud in the darkness, and he was left with only a fistful of silk and lace.

'Cassie, where are you?' He reached out blindly across the bed. Nothing.

Then, in the darkness, a low laugh. She was no longer on the bed. She was somewhere on the far side of the room. She was truly here. With him.

He padded swiftly to the door. This time, he made absolutely sure it was locked. She was here. His Cassie. And she was going to stay.

Grinning broadly into the darkness, he made his way back to the bed and smoothed the torn silk across it. Then he lay down beside it. And waited.

He could hear her rapid breathing.

'I fear 'tis still not the best velvet,' he said softly. 'Only silk. Would it please you lie on it again, my lady?'

With something between a gasp and a sob, she was beside him. 'Ross! Oh, my darling, please do not send me away. I need you so much. I—'

'Hush,' he said, pulling her close. Somehow, he was not surprised that she was as naked as he. He ran a hand down her flank. 'You are chilled, my love. Come, let me warm you again.'

With a low murmur, she fitted her body against his, sighing deeply when he lifted the coverlet over them both. 'I love you, Ross,' she whispered, raising her lips to his.

'My love,' he groaned. 'My life.'

They traded kiss for kiss and touch for touch, giving and receiving pleasure, stoking the fire that burned between them until there was no knowing where was woman and where was man. Until they were one joyous flesh, joined together in lasting love.

HISTORICAL ROMANCE™

LARGE PRINT

A DESIRABLE HUSBAND
Mary Nichols

Lady Esme Vernley's unconventional first meeting with a handsome gentleman in Hyde Park has damned him in the eyes of her family. Felix, Lord Pendlebury, is taken with this debutante's mischievous smile. But his secret mission for the Duke of Wellington in France could jeopardise any relationship between them…

HIS CINDERELLA BRIDE
Annie Burrows

Lord Lensborough was a man well used to getting exactly what he wanted – and he wanted Hester! Convinced that this badly dressed, redheaded waif was a poor relation, the noble lord was about to receive the shock of his life…from a lady who would break all his very proper rules!

TAMED BY THE BARBARIAN
June Francis

Cicely Milburn has no intention of marrying anyone, let alone a Scottish barbarian! But when Lord Rory Mackillin rescues her from a treacherous attack she reluctantly accepts his help – even though his kisses trouble her dreams. The Border Reiver is determined to guard his charge on their journey. Yet he cannot shield his own heart from Cicely's beauty and bravery…

MILLS & BOON®

HIST0108 LP

HISTORICAL ROMANCE

LARGE PRINT

MASQUERADING MISTRESS
Sophia James

War-scarred Thornton Lindsay, Duke of Penborne, can hardly believe the news when a beautiful stranger comes to London proclaiming to be his lover. Caroline Anstretton is on the run and desperate. Courtesan or charlatan, Thorn is intrigued by both sides of this mysterious, sensual woman. Could she be the one to mend a life he'd thought damaged beyond repair?

MARRIED BY CHRISTMAS
Anne Herries

Josephine Horne ignores convention. She never intends to marry, so why should she be hedged about with rules? When loyalty to a friend demands Jo risk her own reputation, she doesn't hesitate. Then she meets handsome Harry Beverley…and her ideas about marriage begin to change…

TAKEN BY THE VIKING
Michelle Styles

They claimed they came in peace, but soon Lindisfarne was aflame. Annis of Birdoswald fled in fear, but she could not escape the Norse warriors. One man protected her – Haakon Haroldson. The dark, arrogant Viking swept Annis back to his homeland, taking her away from all she held dear. Now Annis must choose between the lowly work that befits a captive, or a life of sinful pleasure in the Viking's arms!

MILLS & BOON®

HIST0208

iⁿS